Kade's Dark Embrace

Immortals of New Orleans, Book 1

Kym Grosso

MT Carvin Publishing, LLC
West Chester, Pennsylvania

Editing: Julie Roberts
Formatting: Polgaris Studios
Cover Design: CT Cover Creations
Photography: Wander Aguiar Photography
Model: Tristan Elgart

ACKNOWLEDGMENTS

I am very thankful to those who helped me create this book:

~ My husband, for encouraging me to write and supporting me in everything I do.

~ Julie Roberts, for proofreading and editing.

~ My beta readers, Barb & Sandra, for volunteering to read my first novel and provide me with valuable feedback.

~ Polgarus Studio, for formatting Kade's Dark Embrace.

~ Gayle Latreille, my admin, who is one of my biggest supporters and helps to run my street team. I'm so thankful for all of your help!

~ My awesome street team, for helping spread the word about the Immortals of New Orleans series. I appreciate your support more than you could know! You guys rock!

Chapter One

The sultry, summer night bustled with mortals seeking entertainment in the heart of the city. Listening to the sounds in the distance, Kade recognized a familiar jazz song being played by street performers. After the long flight to Philadelphia, he needed to stretch and gather his thoughts. Unable to resist the lure of the waterfront, he leaned against the cool railing, watching the lights of the boats passing by and flickering in the rushing water. Sensing great evil on the horizon, he breathed deeply, letting the sight of the water soothe him.

His cell phone buzzed; glancing at the text, he swore. A dead body had been found near the airport. *Goddammit.* He was too late. Kade waved to the waiting limo driver, gesturing that he needed to leave. Pivoting, he noticed an attractive woman sitting alone at the end of the dock, far away from the crowd. She appeared confident yet alone, as she sat in the darkness, her long blonde hair shimmering in the moonlight. *What the hell is a woman doing down on the docks alone this time at night?*

Glancing at the enchanting stranger, Kade struggled to push sex from his thoughts. It had been far too long since he'd felt the touch of a woman. Aroused by the possibility of an encounter with her, he swore once again. *Not now.* He needed to concentrate on the real reason he was here in the city. Tristan, an old friend and Alpha of the regional wolf pack, had called him in New Orleans nearly a week before, requesting his assistance. He had planned on seeing Tristan later that night at his club; there he'd find a donor willing to play. Right now, this woman was just a lovely, human distraction. One who was naive to be sitting alone in the dark by the waterfront. Yet he could not seem to tear his eyes off of her. The thought crossed his mind that maybe he should just have a sip of her sweet, young blood before work. Her delicious scent registered in his brain, and his fangs began to elongate.

Over the centuries, he'd been with plenty of women, but none held his heart. As for his thirst, there were many willing women who offered themselves to vampires these days. What was it about this alluring stranger that he found so intriguing? Perhaps it was the chase? Like a fox spotting a rabbit in the woods, he could not resist the temptation of the hunt. Slowly approaching her, he admired her long curly blonde hair, wishing he could run his fingers through it. She was of average height, around five-four, if he had to guess, with a strong, athletic build. As she stretched her toned arms up over her head, he admired her full breasts which strained against her tight white t-shirt. Her black spandex miniskirt accentuated her lithe tanned legs. He watched with curiosity as she glanced at her watch and folded her arms impatiently. *Is she waiting for someone? A date?*

She lifted her gaze, scanning the docks. Kade darted into the shadows and attempted to cloak his presence, yet she stared straight at him. *Bloody hell. Can she see me? Interesting…is she supernatural as well?* His cell phone went off again, reminding him that he needed to get to the site. With a parting glance, he memorized her face, hoping he'd see her again. Silently he returned to the car, reluctant to leave the woman, but anxious to wrap up this case and mete out justice to the murderer.

Down by the river, Sydney waited for her friend. God, it was a beautiful night in the city. She always enjoyed coming down to the waterfront. She worked such long hours; she rarely had evenings available for pleasure. She loved her job as a cop, busting criminals in one of the toughest cities in America. Even on a good day, working in Philly could be rough, but she enjoyed the city's history and rich culture. Tonight, though, instead of cracking heads, she'd made plans to meet a girlfriend. All work and no play made Syd a dull girl, and she was looking forward to playing hard tonight. She needed a stiff drink and good conversation. *Where the hell is Ada?* That girl was always late. They had reservations at Vincent's at nine, and she didn't intend to miss out on dinner. She hoped like hell Adalee hadn't got called back into the office.

A cold breeze came off the water, sending a chill up her spine. She truly wished it was the sudden rush of air that put her on alert, but she'd been around the block long enough to recognize danger when she felt it. Inspecting her surroundings, she spotted an innocent pair of lovers strolling past the tall ships. Still, she felt eyes on her. In the distance, Sydney spotted a large, very male silhouette in the shadows. *Criminal? No, someone else, something else, a supernatural?* Human or otherwise, someone was out there. It wasn't that she was naive about supernaturals, it was just that she generally didn't arrest them. *Damn. I so don't need this tonight.*

Reaching up under her skirt, Sydney checked the silver knife holstered to her thigh; it was secure. She nonchalantly slid her hand into her purse, unlocking the safety on her trusty Sig Sauer. Then she casually pulled out and applied her favorite pink lip gloss and pretended not to see him. Her body tensed ready to spring into action. She smiled and tossed it back into her bag. *A girl has always got to look her best when she kills.* She glanced away for a second to the couple on the dock, who remained infatuated with each other. Within a split second, her eyes darted back to the shadow in the night. He was gone. *Where the hell did he just go?*

As the sounds of the jazz band filled the air, she willed herself to relax. *Maybe he was a lost tourist?* Whatever, he was gone, just another predator in the city. The music in the distance reminded her of the last time she was in New Orleans. Damn if she didn't love everything about that town, from its delicious beignets to its unique architecture. Sydney shook her head, disappointed that she didn't have a vacation planned this summer. *Shit, I am so stuck in Philly,* she thought as she took note of another wasted loser being cuffed by the local beat. Okay, sure, there were drunks in New Orleans, but this was Philly. Inebriated fools here wouldn't think twice about booing Santa. They got in more trouble than a dog with an Easter basket, and like the dog, they usually ended up either sick or dead. Ah yes, another lovely eve in the big city.

"What now? I'm supposed to be having fun tonight," she snapped as her cell phone went off. *The Freaks Come Out at Night* blared from her purse. She could tell from the ring tone that Tony, her partner, was calling.

"Hey, Tone, what's up?"

"Gotta floater out of the Delaware down near the airport. Captain said it looks messy, and I was kinda hoping you could join me for the party."

"Okay, but you owe me. I'm at Penn's Landing right now waiting for Ada. Guess our girls' night isn't happening."

"Uh, Syd...One more tiny detail..."

"Seriously?"

"P-CAP is meeting us there."

"Hell no, I don't feel like dealing with their shit tonight." P-CAP: Paranormal City Alternative Police. Sydney wasn't a fan of working paranormal cases. For the most part, she stuck to the cut and dry, run-of-the-mill human murders. She didn't have to work with supes, nor did she want to. She wasn't exactly prejudiced without reason. Two years before, when working a supposedly simple hit and run, an unknown were-bitch had shifted into tiger mode and killed two cops. It turned out the perp was related to the hit and run driver, and the tiger had thought she could fix the problem by killing the humans. Too bad for her, Sydney always carried a silver knife. Sure, she came out with a few scratches, and almost died in the I.C.U., but Sydney came out of the skirmish alive. The tiger didn't.

Sydney sighed. "Okay, Tony, but I swear if there are any kitty cats workin' this case I'll be taking them directly to the vet to be fixed and declawed. I'm not dealing with shifters tonight."

"Yeah, yeah, one close call with a pussy cat and now you're allergic to all of P-CAP?" he jokingly asked.

"It's all fun and games until their claws come out, and the next thing you know the knives are flying. Good thing I've been practicing my aim. See you in ten." Okay, so it was probably more like twenty, given the city traffic on a Friday night, but at least she was going. She was annoyed that her one night off was screwed thanks to a floater. It was probably just another fool who had thought it would be a great idea to take a swim in the Delaware on a muggy August night.

By the time Sydney showed up on the scene, there must have been at least ten black and whites, not to mention the crowd of spectators who had decided to show up to see if they could catch a glimpse of a dead body. *What the hell is wrong with people?* She knew damn well the answer to that question was 'everything'. It wasn't as if she hated the general population, but she tended to see the worst in people, human or not: drug users, rapists, murderers, and perhaps the worst of the bunch, child abusers and pedophiles. The sick bastards never ceased to amaze her. She shuddered, thinking about what might be waiting for her beyond the yellow tape tonight.

Walking down the gravel sidewalk, she ended up in trampled, soggy weeds that formed a makeshift path. The scene teemed with CSI and fellow officers. She felt a chill in her bones and swiveled her head around, searching for its source. It was ninety degrees outside. Something was off, really off. Unable to find an immediate cause, she continued to make her way to the body. She tried to remain steady on her feet as she gently eased down the slope of the slippery grass.

"Sydney! Over here!" she heard Tony call.

As she approached the body, the smell hit her first.

"Oh God, what the fuck is that smell? Dead body mixed with algae? Shit, that is just terrible," she complained.

"Nice mouth, Syd. Soon you're going to have to carry that cuss jar around with you in the car," Tony teased.

"Yeah, well, fucking sue me. I've given up on the damn cuss jar. I'll just write your favorite charity a check. That should cover me for the year." She winked.

"Okay then, I'll be waiting on it. Yeah, I know the smell is pretty bad, huh? I guess I failed to mention that the gal who discovered the body passed out from it. Buck up, Syd. I'll buy you roses afterward," he chuckled.

Tony thought he was so damn funny. He was a tough cop, born and raised in South Philly. Six-three, Italian goodness wrapped in a hot, witty package, he had no difficulty getting dates. He had dark olive skin and cropped raven hair. Muscular, he looked like he could bench press a bus. To top it off, he knew the city like the back of his hand, and there was no one Sydney would rather trust to have at her back.

She loved him…as well as she could love anyone. He was a good friend. Sometimes she thought of him as a very good friend and was often tempted to turn things into a 'more than friends' arrangement, but she had worked hard to get where she was in the department. Sydney would be damned if she gave in to her primal urges to screw her partner and then end up an office joke as the 'cop who liked to be on top'. Still, she couldn't help but admire his physique, which reminded her that she needed to get out tonight and find someone to play with. A meaningless quickie would give her the release she desired, one she very much needed to prevent her from breaking her own 'no-dating-on-the-job' rule.

Thoughts of sex were pushed to the back of her mind as the body came into view. It was that of a young woman. Her skin was nearly translucent after being in the water for so long. She was dressed in a long white gown, which shimmered in the harsh lights. She resembled the porcelain dolls Sydney's mother used to collect, beautiful to look at but no touching allowed. Yes, this girl looked innocent, fragile. How old could she have been? Maybe twenty-one?

Sydney blew out a breath. "What a fucking sicko. What the hell? What is that stuff on her eyes, her face?"

As she leaned in for a closer look, Tony tapped notes into his cell phone. "I know, Syd. We definitely have a demented one on this case. It's almost as if the perp wanted her to look a certain way, cared about her appearance...well, except for the whole 'sew her eyelids shut and dress her up like a doll' shit...and of course, we still need to find the cause of death. The coroner is on her way. Take a look at her face."

The girl's eyelids were sewn shut in the shape of an 'X', and she still had what looked like makeup on her face. She'd been in the water for at least a day or two. Maybe it was something else besides makeup? Tattooing? Sydney had a friend who tattooed eye makeup on women so they looked fresh as a daisy, day or night, no muss, no fuss. Well, except there was plenty of muss here. The waterlogged loose skin looked like you could pull it right off the girl, as if it were a translucent glove. Sydney might be a cop, but the unusual way murderers killed their victims never ceased to disgust her.

"Tony, her skin looks so pale. Paler than what I would expect from your average floater. It's almost as if..." Sydney's skin pricked in awareness. It was like the feeling she'd had on the docks. The guy who'd been watching her earlier, had he freaking followed her? What the hell?

"It almost looks as if her blood was drained from her body, and indeed, it was. Allow me to introduce myself. I am Kade Issacson from P-CAP, and I am now officially in charge of this case. You're welcome to stay on and assist." Kade stepped into the spotlights, dominating her space and finishing her words. He spoke confidently, concealing his excitement. He could not believe the woman at the docks was here at his scene. What was she? Her sweet scent called to him, arousing all his senses. He struggled to remain professional, determined to find out who she was, while controlling the situation.

Sydney tsked. She could not believe the sheer audacity of this guy. As she spun on her heels to address him, her eyes locked on the source of her chills. The heat began to rise to her face as she realized this guy was a serious supernatural being...dangerous. Added to that, he was drop dead gorgeous. She could barely bring words to her lips to argue with him. Desire pooled in her belly. She quickly focused her thoughts back on the body, letting her anger rise to the surface.

"Name's Willows, Detective Sydney Willows." She was infuriated that P-CAP thought they could come in here and boss the little human woman around. *Nice try.* "Seriously? You guys finally decide to show up and you're all like, 'It's our case now.' Well, here's a newsflash. This girl's a human. According to the regs, 'human vic, human cops'. So you can move along, friend, or watch. Whatever you're into. Just stay out of my way." Damn if she was going to let some hot, supernatural guy tell her what to do at her scene.

Kade smiled. "Ms. Willows, while you are indeed correct that the vic is human, she was murdered in a very supernatural way. Therefore, according to the regs, this is officially a P-CAP case that requires your mandatory cooperation," he lied.

Sydney rolled her eyes and blew out a breath. *Well good and fuck.* She was having a fine evening up until now, day off and all. And now this. She had no idea what the hell he even was. "Mister?" she spat out.

"Please, call me Kade." He spoke with just the slightest hint of a British accent.

"Kade, our police department would *love* to cooperate with P-CAP just as soon as we get the coroner's exam completed," she said, her voice dripping with sarcasm.

"That would be lovely, Ms. Willows. Now, may I please continue with my work?" he asked.

"Yes," she curtly replied, moving out of his way so he could get past her. Sydney could not believe her day. She reasoned that maybe she could work with Kade, as long as he didn't bite her, or claw her or bespell her, or whatever other supernatural shit he did. Even if she didn't know what his deal was, she was convinced that he was capable of doing things that she would not like. She crossed her arms, irritated with the entire night. She knew one thing for sure; working closely with Kade was going to add exponentially to her overall sexual frustration.

She glanced over at him as he conversed with Tony. Kade's sexy frame towered over her. He was well over six-five, with dark blond hair that reached his collar. The strikingly handsome, hard planes of his face accentuated his piercing, ice-blue eyes. Sydney could tell he was athletic and muscular, and wished she could see what was hidden beneath his navy linen sport jacket. He defied her notions of how she imagined most supernaturals dressed; she would have expected him to be clad in black leather and chains. Instead, he struck her as classic, masterly, sensual. Sydney smiled to herself, thinking that Kade looked like he had just stepped out of a freaking Ralph Lauren ad. His cream linen pants hung loosely on his tapered hips, revealing just a glimpse of what supernatural 'assets' he had under them. *Shit, Sydney, are you really looking at the man's crotch at a crime scene? You so need to get laid.*

As she looked up, he caught her eyes and smiled. *Oh, God...please don't let him have seen me looking there.* She quickly glanced at Tony, who chuckled.

"Hey, Syd, whatcha lookin' at? There really is a lot to observe at the scene, huh?"

"Shut it, Tony. Need I remind you that I was supposed to be off tonight?" she retorted.

"Off or getting off?" he quipped.

"Ha, ha. Tony. You boys keep talking. I'm actually going to work. I'll be with Ada, finding out what she's got." Her face flushed red in embarrassment. Sydney was eager to put some space between herself and Kade. She needed to get her hormones under control and concentrate. Why cover the body with tattoos? Why all the presentation? Obviously the perp must get off on some kind of ritual during the actual killing. Some killers liked to take their time, play with the victim.

The coroner made her way down the hill toward the body. Dr. Adalee Billings had been on the job as long as Sydney could remember. With not many women on the force, Adalee was the closest female friend Sydney had. She was a beautiful, African-American woman with dark cocoa skin. At five-eight, she could have easily been mistaken for a model. Her ebony shoulder-length hair was usually pulled back in a scrub hat. But because she was supposed to be out having dinner with Sydney tonight, her hair was fashionably coiffed into a French twist. Quick-witted and insanely intelligent, Adalee could go toe-to-toe with any person in the department, so the men just didn't mess with her. Sydney loved having a smart girlfriend on the force, given she usually worked in a sea of men.

As Adalee leaned in to examine the body and set down her evidence kit, Sydney sidled up next to her, anxious to get her first impressions. The scent of the body was overwhelming. Death, animal or human; it was a smell that permeated the lining of your nostrils and could get into your clothing. Damn if she hadn't just dry cleaned this blouse.

"So, what ya got, Ada?" Sydney inquired.

"Hard to tell without being in the lab, but the tattooing is interesting. Maybe some kind of ritual? Magical protection?" Adalee stared narrowly at the girl's face and hands.

"Yeah, I was thinking ritual. The perp took his time on the girl; the dress, the makeup. Sick fuck. What makes you think magical protection?" Sydney asked.

"Early tattooing was thought to have mystical protection, to be a talisman of sorts worn on the skin. We'll take pictures of the tats and get them to research. Damn, if this city isn't getting freaky tonight. Is P-CAP down here? Honestly, Syd, my take is that this might be their case, but if you want us to run the body, I'm on it."

"Yes and yes. P-CAP may end up taking on the case, but all the same, I'd like you to run the body first. So if you could put a rush on it, I would appreciate it. This could be a human copycat playing with magic, trying to make it look paranormal, or it could be something that needs to go over to the wild side." She glanced toward Kade. "And if that happens, they can have it. Personally, I wouldn't mind turning it over to what's-his-name…Kade over there, so I can get him out of my hair."

Adalee looked at Kade and smiled.

"You mean that whole lot of sexy goodness over there talking to Tony? I would love to work with him, or just work him, period. Whatever, you send him down to the lab, and I'll be happy to review the results in detail with him. I bet he'd give a girl some sugar."

"Yeah sure, if you'd like a bite with your sugar, I'm sure he'd be happy to oblige you. Not sure if he's got fangs or claws, but something's going on there."

"Girl, you sound like you doth protest a little too much. Why not just look at it as a perk of the job? Lord knows there aren't many. Or maybe that hot partner of yours could spice up your coffee?" She laughed.

"Yeah, you're right about that. There's a whole lot of sweetness there, but tasting his candy wouldn't be good for my career. Ada, I just need to get out and satisfy my needs with someone safe. Unfortunately, that's gonna have to wait. Can you tell that I'm a little distracted tonight?"

"Well, girl, you have about five hours to satisfy your needs, and then you need to get your ass down to the lab. I'll bag her up, start the autopsy, snap the pics, and get the trace out. Now, look at this thread." Adalee held up a tiny, brown, stringy substance in her tweezers. "Maybe something unusual about that, too? Could be regular sewing thread, or something else?"

"Okay, run it. We gotta move quickly. This girl was tortured, and I have a feeling she isn't going to be the perp's last play toy. It's like the killer enjoyed this…took his time. He's sharing his work with us. Wanting us to see what he did to this girl. God, it makes me sick."

"I know. We've got a predator here. Not sure if there's anything to the tats or the thread, but I'll start right away." Adalee shook her head in disgust. "Now why don't you get back to your night off? Well, at least for a few hours until I gather some evidence. Kade over there looks awful lonely. He certainly looks like he could take care of all your needs."

"No way, Ada…not him. I'm outta here for now. See ya down at the lab." She gave Adalee a wave and turned to leave, determined to get at least a few hours to herself. As Sydney readied herself to go, she felt eyes on her back. She glanced at Kade, to find him staring at her. She nodded and turned around quickly so he wouldn't think she was interested in him.

Something about him bothered her despite the supernatural, hotter-than-hell vibe he had going on. He had told her he worked with P-CAP, but his story didn't jive with her instincts. Sydney read people well, and there was something about him that said he wasn't a cop. Or even a supernatural cop. He looked like he belonged at a country club. Maybe he was a lawyer, or a businessman? Taking in one last glance, she memorized his clothing and shoes. The suit wasn't right. So not the inexpensive cop wear she was used to seeing at the station. Boss? Calvali? And the shoes, he was wearing Salvatore Ferragamo. Something wasn't adding up. He looked too perfect to be working a detective beat, even for someone not human.

She hurried to catch up with Tony, who was heading towards his car. "There's something not right about him," she said, glancing back toward Kade. "I want to see his credentials."

"Already checked them. He's good. And the boss says he's got full access to the scene," Tony confirmed.

Sydney wondered what kind of supernatural he was. *Wolf?* No, he didn't strike her as the rugged, outdoorsy type. Kade was refined, sleek, and uber-sexy. Primal and dangerous. *Vampire?* Yes, she'd bet he was a vampire. Damn curiosity was getting the best of her as she surreptitiously hoped she'd see him again. Kade might be keeping a few secrets, and Sydney was going to find out exactly what he was up to…as soon as she engaged in a few secrets of her own.

Chapter Two

Sydney wasn't looking for love; her current career didn't afford her that luxury. When she wasn't working, she was still thinking about work, but that wasn't the only thing that kept her from getting seriously involved with someone. She was acutely aware of the very real danger she faced every day on the streets. In her profession, the odds were higher than average that she might not go home after a shift. Why bother with a husband and family when they would need to live with the constant worry that she could be killed on the job? Given that she was only twenty-eight, she didn't feel the need to have kids at the moment. She loved kids, but she didn't want them to grow up motherless because something had happened to her. Maybe someday, when she moved into management and found someone she loved completely, she'd consider having kids, but not now.

As she walked into Eden, the pounding music and glaring lights hit her hard. The smell of cigarette smoke and sweat from the dancers permeated the room. There was a faint hint of bleach; the place was clean even if the activities were down and dirty. Eden was an upscale club that catered to singles and couples who were looking to watch or be watched, serving both humans and supernaturals.

The multicolored lights bounced off the mirrored ceilings. The bluish walls appeared to move as the lights danced. A large, wall-sized water fountain ran along the entire length of the club opposite from the bar. If you stood next to it, you could faintly hear the hiss of the water and feel the spray on your face. Behind the bar, a fifteen-foot yellow boa constrictor named Eve, slithered behind the glass of a vivarium. Inside, Eve moved about the large space, wrapping herself around a tree. In the club, a large, winding staircase led upstairs to the private rooms where clients could go to talk, or engage in sexual activities in private or public, depending on what they wanted.

Sydney knew that she could comfortably lose herself in here for a few hours before going back to death; death always waited for her. It was patient, but never kind. Quickly scanning the room, she darted into the ladies' room. She changed into her tiger-striped, spandex minidress with matching fuck-me heels; she was ready to hunt. Her tanned skin shone beneath the plunging cowl neckline exposing her ample cleavage. A black lacy thong was all she wore under the dress. She shoved her clothes into her tote bag and the custom locker Eden provided its guests. Pulling her hair free of the ponytail holder, she let her blonde curls slide down her back. With a quick spritz of hair spray, she was ready. Sydney had officially transformed from cop to chick, and looked every bit the bait she intended herself to be.

"Hey, Tristan. Perrier with lemon, please." She waved to the bartender.

"No champagne? What's up, mon chaton?" Tristan shouted over to Sydney. He liked calling her 'my kitty'. Tonight the nickname fit, given that she appeared to be a cat on the prowl.

"No alcohol for me tonight, mon loup. I've only got a few hours for dancing and fun. Then I'm outta here." She certainly had every intention of making him her wolf. She took the glass from Tristan, sipped the effervescent water and then made her way into the crowd.

Sydney could feel people watching her as she danced, swaying her hips as she felt the music. There was a reason she came to Eden; music, sex, all of it for the taking, confidential without judgment. It was everything she needed this very moment. As she danced on the floor, she slowly opened her eyes to see Tristan coming straight at her. She yearned to release her sexuality, to relax, to forget, and he could take her there.

Sydney's Alpha wolf was sex on a stick. His rugged, earthy, dominating presence commanded attention when he walked into the room. He was good-looking but not exactly handsome. With captivating amber eyes and wavy platinum-blonde hair, he looked as if he could have been a California surfer. And even though his tan skin gave off a radiant glow, his hard eyes served as a warning to others that he, indeed, was a predator. Tonight he was dressed in light blue jeans and a white linen shirt that he wore untucked. Casual, but not messy, serious, but cool. He entertained the guests with his adventure stories, and was able to deflect the interest of ladies in a way that made them still feel special.

As Sydney danced, she felt strong hands clasp her waist. She leaned into his embrace, recognizing the feel of the muscular chest up against her back. She loved the woodsy, clean scent of Tristan, and felt his arousal as they moved to the music.

"Hey, Syd." Tristan pulled her around so he could see her face.

"Yes," she whispered, glancing from his chest into his intense, golden eyes.

"Tell me, how do you want it, mon chaton?" He gave her a wicked smile.

"Tris, I don't have a lot of time." She shivered at the thought of him taking her quickly. He was dominating, pushing her to tell him her fantasy.

"No games tonight. How do you want it?" he pressed.

"Fast, hard, private," she teased.

"Let's finish our dance, shall we? Your wolf has everything you need."

Sydney smiled and let the arousal overcome her, feeling the warmth grow in her womb. She wanted this…no, she *needed* this tonight. Both the stress of the grisly murder, and then Kade showing up at her scene trying to run the show, had put her on edge. She wanted to forget, and Tristan could give that to her. He understood her the way no one else did, a lover who didn't judge her. She laid her head back on his chest, enjoying the warmth of his arms.

The crime scene disturbed Kade. Killing and violence was part of his world, but the torture of an innocent was unacceptable. As the leader of vampires in New Orleans, he suspected that he knew who had committed the crime, but he would have to investigate further to be sure. Kade had convinced the head of P-CAP to let him on the scene, because he did not trust the local authorities to handle the case. It wasn't his job to investigate the murders like a detective, but being the leader he was, he planned to find the rogue and mete out justice.

He worked out of a brownstone graciously loaned to him by Tristan, the local Alpha. They were good friends from times long ago. Tristan was the one who had phoned him to tell him there was talk of a possible rogue vampire in his region who was practicing black magic. There were rumors of rituals, but nothing solid to go on. Finally, the evil had shown itself, and Kade had jetted out of NOLA on his private plane as soon as he got the go ahead from his inside source at P-CAP. As much as he wanted to leave it up to P-CAP to find the perpetrator, he felt compelled to come to Philadelphia, suspecting the magic was being drawn from his territory.

What he hadn't expected was the confrontation with the spirited Miss Willows. What an interesting, sexy distraction she was. She smelled of lilies, and he could practically taste her sweetness in the air. *What would it be like to taste her?* He had to stifle his arousal in front of her. Had she been a paranormal creature, he wouldn't have lied to her. Given that she was human, however, it had been necessary to do so for her own protection. Despite what she may have thought, guns were no match for dark magic or vampires.

But damn, if he didn't enjoy a little sparring with the blonde detective. She was altogether alluring with a sharp mind to match. The scent of her arousal at the scene had driven him wild with desire. He craved her. He admonished himself for his lustful thoughts, knowing he wasn't there to get involved with women. Kade figured he was a little agitated from all the stress of flying up to Philadelphia in such a hurry. He needed blood, maybe sex, not necessarily in that order. What this vampire didn't need were complications.

"Luca, let's swing by Tristan's place. I could use some refreshment. I told him I would fill him in on what I've learned." He signaled to his second.

Luca barked out an order to the limo driver and turned to Kade.

"We'll be there in ten minutes. Do you wish for me to find a private room… procure a donor?"

"Yes. Thanks," Kade replied as he stared out the window, his thirst gnawing at him. He was growing irritable; he needed blood soon.

On the dance floor, Tristan grabbed the nape of Sydney's neck and pushed his long fingers through her hair. She leaned back, giving him full access to her throat and chest. The wolf in him howled at her submission, and the man in him was left breathless at the sight of her smooth skin and the rise of her breasts. He continued to pull her head back, and kissed her throat near her ear. Looking down, he could see the rosy edge of her hardened nipples. She wasn't wearing a bra. God, this woman was killing him.

"Tristan, please..." Sydney gasped as Tristan slid a hand up her belly and cupped her breast. She moaned in response.

He leaned and whispered in her ear, "Like that, mon chaton, do you? Come on now, tell me what you want."

"Tristan, you and me upstairs...now. I am done playing." Sydney had had enough with the games. She could barely speak as she licked her lips. Dancing and pulling him close, she ground against his hard arousal.

"Ah fuck," Tristan grunted, noticing that Kade had just walked into the bar. "Sorry, Sydney, but an old friend just came into the club. You have no idea how I hate interrupting our fun, but I have to talk with him...important business. It'll only take a few minutes, though. Do you want to go up to my room and wait for me? I'll meet you upstairs in ten minutes." He was irritated with the interruption, but this was important.

As Sydney contemplated her answer, she felt a chill similar to the one she'd felt down at the docks. The hair on the back of her neck stood up. *He's here.* Rapidly scanning the room, she saw Kade sitting at the bar staring at her. She wasn't imagining things. Kade was actually in the bar, and for some reason he didn't look happy. What in the hell was he doing at Tristan's club? Did he follow her from the crime scene?

Unable to control her curiosity, Sydney took off across the dance floor toward Kade. She glanced back to Tristan whose face told her that he'd suspected her intention. Irritated that the vampire had followed her, she struggled to control her anger.

"What the fuck are you doing here? Are you following me?"

"Miss me, did you?"

"Perhaps we need to get a few things straight if we're going to work together." Her heart began to race in his presence, and she suspected it wasn't caused by fear. As her eyes caught his, she was drawn to him. Her arousal flared and she found herself even angrier that her traitorous body was responding to his presence.

Before Kade had a chance to answer, Tristan held out his arms to his friend.

"Hey, Kade! Welcome! I've missed you, brother."

The men exchanged hugs and then both stared back at Sydney, as if waiting for her reaction. He wasn't sure how, but so far this didn't look good. Immediately, Tristan recognized that Sydney had switched into work mode, and that meant things could get ugly.

Confusion swept over Sydney as she watched the two sexy men hug and talk as if they were good friends. *Tristan and Kade know each other? Friends? Shit. Seriously? Can my night get any worse?* She had been trying so hard to relax, trying not to think about the murder or how Kade had completely thrown her at the scene and tried to steal her case, or how he turned her on beyond belief. Now here he was, watching her while she danced and practically had sex on the dance floor. *Just freaking great.* Worse, he was looking at her seductively, noticing her clothing…or lack thereof. She guessed her air of professionalism was shot to hell. Whatever, he wasn't supposed to be here anyway, screwing up her entire night.

As she was about to bolt, Tristan grabbed her possessively around the waist, and turned to Kade. "So, you two know each other? Care to share?" he asked.

Sydney wanted to shove Tristan's hand away, but she didn't want Kade to suspect she desired him. The thought crossed her mind to let Kade think she belonged to Tristan. What would it hurt? Tristan knew the truth. Didn't he? He was holding her as tight as a dog held onto his bone, so she decided to go along with the charade.

"Yes, we do." Sydney sighed. She shot Kade an annoyed look. "As much as I despise discussing work while

I'm at play, and I was so about to get into some play, Kade and I met today on a case. Would you like to enlighten me as to how you know Kade?"

Tristan smiled, knowing she wasn't telling him everything.

"Well, Kade and I go way back, good friends from the bayou."

She raised an eyebrow. "Bayou? Really? Okay then, well, you two have fun, talk about old times and all. Sorry, Tris, can't wait around tonight. Gotta get back to work. Until next time, mon loup." She placed a chaste kiss to Tristan's lips as Kade watched with jealous eyes. Narrowing her eyes at Kade she quipped, "And you, mister P-CAP, not sure if or when I'll see you again, but later."

Kade reached out to grasp Sydney's hand at the same time Tristan released her waist. He gazed intensely into her eyes and spoke firmly. "Yes, my dearest Sydney, when we meet again, and we will meet again, it will be a pleasure. I promise."

Sydney stared at him for a moment, almost unable to break their gaze. Unsettled by her reaction to him, she thought it must be some strange kind of a paranormal, chemical reaction. His smooth voice wrapped around her like silk, and she imagined how it'd sound while he embraced her in his arms. The disturbing thought jolted her back into the moment, and she tore her palm from his grasp. She had to get out of there before she lost control.

Taking a deep breath, Sydney turned on her heels and walked away, not looking back.

She practically ran to the ladies' room, her mind racing with confusion. She'd wanted to have sex with Tristan when she'd first arrived. Leaving, the only man she could think of was Kade. As she began to change her clothes, questions spun in her head. *How well does Tristan know Kade? What the hell is happening to me? I know that Kade is lying, but he's freaking hot. Down, girl, get a grip.* Short on answers, she decided to get back to the lab as soon as possible. Since sex was out, work was officially back on the schedule.

Tristan laughed out loud, shaking his head. He wasn't exactly sure what was going on with Sydney, but he loved watching her dress down another guy, even if it was a friend. Sydney was a great girl, but she did get her feathers easily ruffled when her 'needs' weren't met.

As much as he hated being interrupted, he knew exactly why Kade was here, and he didn't want to wait to get the details. He also wasn't ready to share information with Sydney. That was why he'd told her to go upstairs. But the stubborn woman didn't ever listen. He expected nothing less from Sydney though; she was a detective, after all. But he still didn't want her involved in the paranormal business that he needed to discuss with Kade. Sure, Sydney was a tough as nails cop, but she was still human, and he was determined to protect her from whatever evil had just set up shop in his city.

"So, what's the deal?" Tristan inquired. "I'm glad I called you. I knew that shit was going to go down soon. Just glad you were here and could go to the scene."

"Definitely black magic, but it was a vampire; the girl was drained. I'm not sure of the ritual, but if I had to guess, I'd say someone is trying to build power. I'll be encouraging P-CAP to recommend full takeover of the case in the morning once the coroner has run an autopsy," Kade disclosed.

"I want you to know that I'm very appreciative of your offer to come and help." Tristan's face hardened. "It's bad news that a rogue vamp is targeting women. I want to assure my pack that P-CAP and the vampire community are taking care of it. Even though the vamp went after a human this time, the next victim could be a wolf. I can't have it."

"Tris, I'll take care of this asshole. I'm sure it's a vampire, but there may be more than one person involved. Whoever is responsible will be dealt with. You can trust me on that."

Tristan blew out a breath, and sat next to Kade. He spun his stool around to face the dance floor.

"So, what else is up? Seems you have been a busy boy since you've been in town. Getting in trouble already, huh?" he joked.

"Who, me? I can't possibly know what you're talking about," Kade said.

"Yes, you. What the hell's up with you and Sydney? You know, the hot woman I was about to have sex with until you arrived and so kindly interrupted us. My girl was really pissed at you. You haven't even been in town twenty-four hours. What did you do to her?"

"First of all, I did nothing to her. I simply informed her that she was not leading the case, and I think you'd agree with me on that point. She may be a cop, but she's human. I might let her consult after the coroner is finished, but she will not lead this case. And secondly, from what I can tell, my friend Miss Willows is not *yours*. You may have thought you were getting sex, but it didn't take much to interrupt you. She flew off like a little bird. So she must be just a friend, and I've been around long enough to know that she certainly does not belong to you." Kade was dead serious as he challenged Tristan. The tension was palpable, thanks to the words that had just left his lips. *What the fuck is getting into me that I would challenge a friend, let alone an Alpha, for a human woman on foreign territory?*

"My brother. You challenge me in my own club?" Tristan raised an eyebrow and reached over to put his hand on Kade's shoulder, asserting his dominance while diffusing a potential argument. "I realize you've had a long day of travel, so I'll overlook the way you just expressed yourself. As for Sydney…let's just say that she is, shall we say, a close friend, a very close friend. A friend who occasionally shares and experiences her most intimate desires with me. However, as you so eloquently just pointed out, she remains uncommitted. And while I would love for her to figure out why she builds emotional walls around herself, I am a businessman, not a psychologist. Most days, Sydney is a bad, ass-kicking, ask-questions-later cop, but she does walk on the wild side here in my club. I may join her or even watch her at times. But make no mistake about it; even though we are not committed, Sydney is under my protection and the protection of my pack. She will not be hurt if I have anything to say about it. And from where I'm sitting as Alpha, I have everything to say about it." He sighed heavily and paused for a second to judge Kade's reaction and then continued, "Kade, you and I have known each other for a long time, so I can tell by the look in your eyes that something is stirring in you. You want her. I can't tell you not to pursue her, but I am warning you; do not hurt her, emotionally or otherwise, and if at all possible keep her away from this killer."

"She'll be safe," Kade promised, refusing to address the rest of Tristan's observations.

He blew out a breath, frustrated with his attraction toward the blonde. He shouldn't give a shit what the wolf did with the cop, but he did care. He tried to shuck that pang of jealousy that stuck in his gut. What was he thinking? Frustrated with himself and his feelings toward the human woman, he struggled to focus on why he was even here in Philadelphia. He was supposed to find a killer and then get back to business in New Orleans, nothing more, nothing less. He needed to put Miss Willows out of his mind if he was going to get anything done.

"Are you going to offer a vampire a drink or what?" Kade asked with a smile. "I just need some blood. I'm not looking for extras tonight."

"You just traveled a long way. We have plenty of anonymous donors available tonight. If you want to grab the first private room on the right, I'll send up a few donors for you and Luca. Is it just the two of you tonight?" Since when did his friend not want extra, as in extra-sexual activities? Tristan was growing tired of trying to figure out what was going on in Kade's head.

"Yeah, just Luca and me tonight. Thanks, Tris. I appreciate your hospitality. It's been a long day." Kade nodded to Luca. "Let's go, Luca."

Tristan notified his manager to send two donors upstairs immediately. Now that weres and vampires were out in the open, there were plenty of humans who were willing to come to the club. Either they were interested in sex and the orgasmic bite of the vampires, or they just enjoyed the bite sans the sex.

Management kept a list of volunteer donors as they entered the club, and they were given a buzzer that was worn around their neck or clipped onto their clothing. If it buzzed, the donor would approach the hostess and be directed to a private room. Everything was consensual and safe. Vampires who wanted a donor were vetted out so Eden could ensure the safety of its guests. Draining until death was strictly forbidden. Tristan could not afford for there to be mistakes, so security monitored the rooms to make sure there were no issues upstairs, and donors could opt out at any time.

While vampires were sexual in nature, not all vampires were looking for sex when they ate. Many who came into the club were committed to another person and were only looking for fresh blood. Vampires did not need to feed every day, nor did they require large amounts of blood to sustain their strength. There were humans who sought excitement, who were looking for the vampire experience any day of the week. Eden capitalized on the synergistic relationship between donors and vampires. Instead of going for just a coffee, humans could get a coffee and a bite. Orgasm and coffee to go…what more could one ask for?

As Kade relaxed on the sofa, he let his thoughts drift to Sydney. While he'd initially felt angry seeing her on the dance floor with another man, he could not deny his arousal as he'd watched Tristan touch her breasts, wishing it was he who was touching her. His cock had been rock hard when Sydney had approached him earlier. He'd tried to hide his arousal by acting pissed. Maybe Sydney hadn't noticed, but he was quite sure that Tristan had.

An attractive, bleached-blonde twenty-something, walked into the room and knelt down next to Kade. She lifted her eyes.

"No extras tonight, sir? I promise to make it good for you," she purred as she rubbed her hand across his thigh and over his hard bulge.

On another night, he would have sucked and fucked blondie high and hard, but not tonight. He was growing tired of meaningless sex with his food. Kade sighed.

"No thanks. Just a drink and then I'm out of here." It had been a long day. Yes, he did want extras, but he wanted them with a certain fiery detective. This donor would quench his thirst for blood, but would do nothing for the erection pressing against his zipper.

Looking disappointed, she laid her bare arm against his chest. He could smell her young aromatic blood. He put his fingers around the woman's wrist and held it to his nose. She moaned in delight when he licked the inside of her arm. His fangs elongated and he bit into her soft, pale flesh. He closed his eyes as he drank the essence of the strange woman. Kade fantasized that he was biting Sydney, pretending she was the woman before him writhing in ecstasy on the floor. When he was sated, he licked the wounds so they healed, then he strained to stand up. Shit. He was harder than ever. *Why am I so attracted to that damn woman?*

He glanced over to Luca who had just finished fucking his donor up against the wall. As Luca released the girl, his eyes met Kade's. Luca raised a questioning eyebrow at his boss, clearly wondering what was up with him, but Kade just silently watched. They were out of town, and it was customary for them to blow off some steam. Drinking blood and having sex were acceptable within the vampire community, especially when neither of them was committed.

Luca was Kade's right hand man in charge of security operations in New Orleans. Although raised in Australia, Luca had returned to his father's British homeland as an adult, and had subsequently found himself in New Orleans fighting in the War of 1812, where he was severely wounded during battle. Kade found Luca dying in a field and offered him the choice to be turned into a vampire. Once Luca agreed, Kade drained him of his blood to the point of death, and then he fed Luca his own lifeblood.

After the transformation, Luca had sworn allegiance to Kade. He worked for Kade, but they were also best friends, comrades in life. He was loyal and forever grateful to his savior. When they traveled, they often fed and fucked, casually enjoying the women donors.

"Hey, I'm almost done here," Luca said. "You okay?"

"Yeah, I'm fine. Finish up. I'm eager to get back to the brownstone. I have some calls to make. I'll meet you downstairs." Kade had to get the fuck out of there. The club smelled of blood, sex, and sweat, but none of it was Sydney's. He had to see her soon and find out exactly what the little detective had found out at the autopsy.

Chapter Three

After Sydney left the club, she drove directly to the station. She was used to working night shift, so even though it was midnight, she had plenty of time to get organized before she met with Adalee to get the initial findings from the autopsy. She was lost in thought when Tony slammed a wrapped cheesesteak on the desk. "Hey, Syd, thought you could use some food."

"Oh, you do know exactly what a girl wants." Sydney licked her lips and ripped the wrapping away. She bit into the sandwich, letting the onions fall down her chin. "Thanks so, so much! Mmm....messy, but soooo good."

Tony shook his head, laughing. She looked like she was coming, not that he knew about that. He would love to have her just once, but he knew that was a line that he probably should not cross. Ever since he'd met Sydney Willows, he'd fought the urge to kiss her senseless and slam his cock into her, but he was pretty sure she didn't date guys that often, and he was one hundred percent sure she didn't date fellow cops. No use thinking about what he couldn't have. Dragging his thoughts back to the case, he pulled out the file on the girl.

"Glad you like the sandwich, Syd, but you gotta eat quickly. Billings called an hour ago. She said she's ready for us to review her initial findings and is expecting us in thirty minutes. Eat up. I gotta stop in and see the captain, then I'll wait for you over by the elevator, so we can go down together."

"Sounds good to me. And Tony…thanks for the steak sandwich. You're a lifesaver. Not sure what I would do without you." Sydney was miffed after the incident at the club and couldn't stop thinking about Kade. She was about to get her freak on with Tristan when that damn vampire came in and interrupted things. If he was a detective, she was the Queen of England. There was no way on Earth that guy was a rank-and-file detective. He was lying to her, and he was cocky. And shit, he was hotter than hell. *Fuck. I have to get my shit together, get the vamp off the case, get some sleep, and then solve this murder.* It was turning into the longest night she'd had in weeks.

After inhaling her food, she and Tony rode the elevator in silence, ready to get some clues from the coroner. As the doors opened on the basement floor, Sydney and Tony walked down the long, gray corridor that led to the morgue. The overhead lights flickered, providing a dim path to their destination. She had walked this hallway more times than she cared to count, but every time she did, the gray walls reminded her that she was there to face death. No amount of fresh paint could make it seem like just another hallway in the building.

She pushed ahead of Tony through the black double doors that led into the autopsy room. The smell of death hit her as the air wafted into her nose. It was something she never got used to, but it reminded her of why she became a cop. Someone's life had been stolen. The girl was dead, and she would catch the bastard who did it.

"Hey there, Ada. So, what ya got?" Glancing around for a mask and gloves, she leaned over the body, inspecting the girl's wrists.

"It's a damn shame. This city is filled with some sick fucking bastards, but this one…he just…well, come see." Adalee looked up through her plastic mask. She gestured down to the girl's torso.

"She was tortured." Sydney peered over the now naked body. The translucent skin seemed to float over the young woman's muscles. Her body was littered with small cuts and marks, but none appeared to be deep. Sydney gritted her teeth and took a deep breath.

"That would be a yes." Adalee took samples from the body as she spoke. "Not sure what made all the cuts, but it looks like she was whipped with something. Also cut with a small knife of some sort. And these," she pointed to the girl's wrists, "Looks like she was bound with rope. I found some fibers embedded in her skin, still waiting on trace. As for the cause of death, we're looking at exsanguination. How she lost the blood? Not sure yet, but there's no blood left in this poor girl's body."

"So we have a tortured girl who is drained of all her blood? Sounds like a vampire, which would mean we have to turn this case over to P-CAP. But there are no bite marks on her, so that means it could still be ours. What's the deal with the tattoos on her body, on her face?" Tony scribbled a few notes and glanced at Sydney.

"Well, it looks like he not only tattooed her face, but also something here." Adalee pointed to the girl's breasts. "This poor girl suffered before she died. I'm estimating that she's been dead for a day or so but the water sped up decomp."

Sydney pointed to the tattoo on the girl's breast. "The tat…it looks like a sun, but the face, it's strange. It's possible she got the tattoos on her own."

"Maybe, hard to tell with the decomp. There's something going on here that makes my skin crawl. What if the tats are ritualistic?" Tony suggested.

Sydney was about to comment when she felt him around her. Kade. *What the hell is going on? It's him, and how do I know it's him?* She spun around to find Kade's ice-blue eyes staring at her.

"Very observant. The tattoo is the sun god Huitzilopochtli. He symbolizes a belief in the afterlife. Could be a ritual, or could be nothing." Kade took note of the body and started walking toward them.

Sydney looked over at Adalee, seeking her input, but she shrugged in response. "So, I take it you've been down here already?"

"Indeed."

"Then you know that this is our case, not yours."

Kade smiled at her, turning her insides to jelly. Everything in her past had told her to stay away from vampires, yet there was something about the way he spoke to her. She needed to establish her dominance before he took over not just her case but her resolve not to date vampires.

"It was great meeting you, Detective Issacson, or whoever you really are, but we've got this." She cleared her throat, attempting to compose herself. "We have a lot of work to do. Really, you can go now."

"Well as much as I would like to make you happy, and trust me, Miss Willows, I would, I have already talked to your superior, and it looks like you and I will be working together from now on. As you well know, when there is even the slightest chance of paranormal activity on a case, P-CAP has a right to request a co-investigation. I requested. Your department agreed."

Sydney's face reddened. She took a deep breath and exhaled.

"Okay then. But this is my city and my ass on the line. I expect honesty from the people I work with, and they expect the same from me. I'm telling you right now that I'm not putting up with your P-CAP secret shit. If you know something, you share it, and vice versa." She wasn't going to bring up the fact that he was lying to her, or question him about how he really knew Tristan.

"By all means, detective. Now, how about we get out of here and walk through the case? For the record, I know there are no bite marks, but I still suspect the perp is a vampire. We certainly prefer to bite our donors to satisfy our nutritional needs and our sexual appetites, but there are other ways to drain a body to get the blood. I intend to ask my vampire contacts to see if there has been any strange activity in town."

Sexual appetite? Sydney's face grew hot, and she cursed her reddening cheeks. She thought for a moment about what it would be like to have Kade's lips on her neck, his teeth grazing her tanned skin, biting her, drinking as he thrust into her. She felt warmth pooling downward, desire flowing through her blood. She shook her head, trying to think of something else, wanting to shake the lust she was feeling.

"Well, we better get going." Sydney forced herself to look away from Kade and glanced back to the girl on the table, a cold reminder of the task at hand. She caught sight of a pile of photos on Adalee's desk. Snatching one off the top, she sighed. "Well, you may know some vampires, but I've also got some sources in this city. I think we ought to take a trip to a tat shop I know. If this girl got work done here in the city, we'll find out who did it. And maybe even get an ID on her."

"I'll let you know as soon as I find anything else," Adalee commented, snapping off her gloves.

"Sounds good. Thanks for the update."

Sydney started to walk out the door. As she brushed by Kade, a chill ran up her arm. There was something about this man, this vampire. She didn't know why he was making her so crazy but she'd have to get it together if she was going to work with him.

Kade smiled to himself, smelling her arousal. She might not like him but she lusted for him. He would take that for now. In the meantime, he would play nice so she didn't end up staking him first.

Chapter Four

Sydney drove her convertible down South Street, enjoying the feel of the warm wind on her face. Owning a new car wasn't an option, but she'd splurged on the used Mercedes. It gave her the feel of luxury without the worry of how she'd replace it were it to be vandalized or stolen. By the time she arrived at the tattoo parlor she felt slightly more relaxed than she had in the morgue. The captain had put Tony on another murder case just as they left. Her new partner, Kade, would be with her. She didn't trust him, but the captain was crystal clear that she was to work with him on the Death Doll case…that was what the press was calling it.

Sydney had grown frustrated with the political games involved with her job. She was a good cop, but not exactly the most tactful person. Diplomacy wasn't her strength. Despite her reservations, she had come to terms with the fact she'd be working with Kade to solve the case. Once it was all over, he'd go back to New Orleans to bite necks and suck blood, or whatever else vampires did with their time.

On her way out of the station, she'd told Kade she'd meet him at Pink's Ink Tattoo shop. As she waited outside the storefront, a black limo pulled up and beeped at her. *Kade. A limo? Detective, my fucking ass.* A door opened and a large, good-looking man with long, dark hair got out of the car. She recognized him as the man who had been with Kade at Tristan's club.

He walked around the car and opened the door. Kade exited with grace, as if he was going to a movie premiere. He was almost beautiful, if one could use that word to describe a man, but there was no mistaking the predator he was. Dangerous, no one would mess with this guy…even on the cold streets of Philly. Sydney caught her breath, noticing how handsome he was in khaki pants and a blue linen shirt with rolled up sleeves that accentuated his broad, muscled chest. He smiled at her as he caught up with his vamp friend.

"Hope you weren't waiting long. Sydney, meet Luca. Luca, this is Sydney."

As Sydney extended her hand to Luca, he gently took it and kissed the top. She was captivated by his green eyes that seemed to draw her in. With an Aussie accent, Luca whispered, "Nice to meet you, Sydney. So, it is you who has Kade out of sorts." He let her hand go and chuckled to himself.

"I'm sorry, but I'm just not used to the hand kissing." Sydney laughed as Luca released her hand. "In my business, I usually have guys either running away from me as I'm trying to cuff 'em or trying to grab my ass. I know I should appreciate the chivalry, but it took me by surprise. Nice to meet you, Luca, you coming in with us?"

"Luca, you stay out here and keep watch. Let's go, Sydney." Kade shot a look over to his friend and stepped between them.

For the first time since he'd met her, Kade saw Sydney smile. He felt a stir of jealousy knowing it was Luca who'd brought it to her lips…so soft and full. He couldn't help but wonder how it would feel to have those lips on his cock. Her scent was like breathing in the aroma of a fine wine, delicious. He wanted a taste. He couldn't wait much longer. Damn, he almost forgot why the hell he was even here. What was it about her that seemed to distract him from any rational thought?

Kade held the door for Sydney. She'd walked past him, pretending not to notice that he had effectively blocked Luca from touching her any further. The shop was filled with teenagers and young adults whose eyes were fixed upon the pictures on the wall. They were searching for the perfect artwork, discussing where they'd paint it on the canvas of their young bodies. Holding up her badge, Sydney pushed through the patrons as if she was parting the Red Sea. It was crowded, so Kade was forced to stand up behind her, against her. She could feel the hardness of his chest on her back as they stood waiting at the counter. The contact between them distracted her, but there was no room for him to move back. Attempting to concentrate,

Sydney scanned the room looking for her source. Her eyes lit up when she located her.

"Pinky! Hey Pinky! Over here," she yelled over the rumble of voices.

Pinky was the owner of Pink's Ink. She was a petite girl whose black, cropped pixie hair had just a wisp of hot pink flowing through her bangs. Her bright pink halter-top showed off her back, which was adorned with two large butterfly wings in various shades of pink and indigo. Pinky was well known as one who ran her shop with an iron fist in a velvet glove, and lived up to her reputation as she turned around to yell at a potential customer who was peeling a drawing off the wall.

"Get the hell off the art or get the hell out! Hey, girl, what ya doin' down here? Finally come to let me put on that tat we talked about? And who is mister tall, dark and lickable behind you? Yummy." When she turned to face Sydney, her large voluptuous breasts almost spilled out of the tiny top, which complemented her short black latex skirt. She turned up a corner of her mouth and ran her tongue across her lips, eyeing the large hunk of man standing behind Sydney.

While Sydney was used to Pinky and her flair for the English language, she could not help but feel slightly embarrassed. She could feel the hard heat of Kade up against her back and found it difficult to speak. For a second, she found herself wishing they were alone, naked, Kade thrusting up into her and...*Get back in the game, girl! Focus!*

"Hey Pink, this is Kade. Listen, I need a favor." Sydney coughed, trying to act nonchalant. She held out the photo of the girl's sun tattoo. "Before you ask, don't. It's a case I'm working." She looked over her shoulder at Kade. "Ugh, a case *we* are working. All you need to do is ID this tat, okay? Is there anything about it that looks familiar? Do you recognize the artist's work? Maybe a customer who got a tat like this recently?"

Pinky stared at the photo and turned white. She peered over her shoulder to make sure no one was listening. "This...the lines, points and turns...it looks like the work of a guy who used to work in here. I fired him six months ago. I caught him wanking off in the alley. Just no. Seriously, who can't keep it in their pants at work?"

"So, what did he say when you eighty-sixed him?" Sydney glanced at Kade and quickly focused her attention back on Pinky.

"Well, that's the thing. He just looked up at me and kind of just...well, he just kept going, ya know? He finished. I told him that if I ever saw him near here again, I was calling the cops."

"And you never thought to mention this to me over drinks?"

"Come on. You know how it is. This city is filled with sickos. No offense, Syd, but I can't call the cops every time some asshole is out there waxing the bishop. I know it isn't pretty but look around here. Cops got murders to solve. They don't have time to arrest assholes who worship their dicks."

"Point taken. So what's his name? You got an address?"

Pinky began flipping through a candy-red, glittered address box on the counter, and pulled out a dingy index card.

"His name was Jennings, Drew Jennings. This address might be old, but here you are…it's on the card. Looks like he was staying in North Philly…a few blocks off Broad Street. Syd, I know you're a cop, but watch your ass. You and I both know it isn't the greatest area."

"Thanks. Okay, we're out of here." Sydney turned to Kade, brushing her thigh against his. "We can take my car. Your limo's going to look a tad out of place up there, and I'd like to try not to get shot at before we even get out of the car."

"Listen, Sydney, if we do this, we do it my way," Kade stated decisively. "I get this is your city, but I will not allow you to put yourself in danger. I see that you are strong, but you're not strong enough to go against a vampire."

"You may be a bad-ass vamp and all, but I know what I'm doing, this is my job. I am going. There will be no more discussion. If you need to enlighten me about the various ways you folks suck the lifeblood out of others, I'll be happy to listen on the way up Broad Street. But let's get this straight; it's not my first time at the rodeo. I have studied supernaturals and even sparred a few times with a werewolf. I know how to kill a vampire as well as I know how to kill a human, so let's go. We're taking my car. If Luca wants to follow in the limo, that's his funeral, but

I'm outta here." She stood with her hands on her hips, tilting her head in defiance. All thoughts of how sexy he was rushed out of her mind and were quickly replaced by anger. *Does he see me as some kind of damsel in distress? I'm a cop; what doesn't he get about that?*

"You don't seem to understand what I told you down in the morgue. I lead this case, and you bloody well do not. You will go with me, because I allow it to be so. Do not make the mistake of thinking otherwise, Ms. Willows." Kade shot her a look of irritation.

"Yeah, yeah, vampire. Keep talking but I'm the one who got us this address, and I'm the one driving. So sit your butt down in the car and let's go." She jumped in the car and started it, watching as he silently sat down next to her, looking as if he was about to explode. Working this case with him was going to be a lot of fun, just a laugh riot, she thought. She rolled her eyes and started off toward north Philly.

Chapter Five

As the wind whipped Sydney's hair forward, she pushed it behind her ears. She loved her car, especially when she drove along the open highway. Philly was finally starting to quiet down. Aside from a few transients sleeping on the sidewalk, and the police, not many people were on the streets.

She glanced at Kade, who stared at her. She couldn't help wondering what he thought of this place. She knew that vampires could be very old, and suspected Kade was an elder of some kind. Aside from his arrogant presence, he seemed well-spoken, well-traveled, and knowledgeable. She could only imagine how many things he knew about women; how to please them, make them scream. She wanted him to make her scream, but she knew getting involved with him would not be a good idea. But no matter how hard she tried, Sydney couldn't deny her attraction to him. He was dangerous, hot, and sexy. And he would probably shatter her heart in a thousand pieces if she let him get close.

And then there was the little fact about his lying. Kade was not a run-of-the mill detective. He was not telling the truth, and she damn well knew it. They were about to go into a fucked-up situation that could get her ass killed, and she had a right to know what the hell was going on with him. *Enough of the games.*

"So, what's your deal? I can tell by your pretty shoes and overall style that you are *so* not a P-CAP detective. We're about to go into some shit, and I want to know what the hell's really going on," she yelled over the rush of wind,

"Ah, you're quick, Detective Willows," Kade replied. "You are correct that I'm not a detective, but I am in a position of authority in my world. So for the sake of argument, let's just say that I'm a third party who is very interested in seeing this case come to an end expediently. As you know, Tristan is a close friend, and we have mutual interests. He requested my assistance, and I'm here to put a rest to this situation."

"Okay, so you're telling me I'm about to go into a potentially deadly situation with an amateur?" *Just fucking great.*

"My dearest Sydney. I may be many things, but an amateur is not one of them. I have lived many centuries, fought many wars. I will protect you with my life," Kade replied. "You must know that while I respect your desire to apprehend the perpetrators of this girl's death, I have every reason to believe a vampire is responsible, and I will bring him to justice. That is all you need to know for now; this is the truth."

Truth? Yeah right, mister sexy vampire. Whatever. Sydney shook her head, unsure of what to believe. Maybe he was telling the truth, maybe not. At this point, she had already made the decision to find Jennings.

As they neared the location, she noticed the street was deserted. Several of the row homes lining the block had been boarded up and covered in graffiti. Sydney pulled her car into a parking space, which was not hard to find. She took a deep breath and cased the street. "See the house over there with the boarded up windows and red door? That's it. Here's the deal. I'm going to go around the front. How about you hit the back…keep the exit covered."

"There is no way you're going into that house alone."

"We need an element of surprise. I'll go in the front and you can come in from behind, scope out the house while I distract him. As you keep saying, I'm a human, so Jennings will perhaps think I'm alone. He'll be surprised as long as he only sees me, not you."

Kade raised a questioning eyebrow at Sydney. "What if Jennings doesn't answer? What if a vampire answers? What then?"

"You vampires have some kind of preternatural senses, right? I promise I'll yell for you if I get even a hint that something's wrong. And then you can take him by surprise."

"Do you have weapons? Human or vampire, you need to be ready to defend yourself." Kade looked at the house and then back to Sydney.

"I'm good. I've got silver in this gun here, so at the very least, I can slow a vamp down." Sydney quickly checked her ankle holster where she kept her secondary Sig Sauer. Before she left the station, she'd loaded it with wooden bullets in case she needed it for vamps. Her primary Sig Sauer in her shoulder holster was loaded with silver. If you shot a human or were with a silver bullet, the perp was going down either way. She also kept a silver knife in a secret compartment in her sleeve and another one in the tip of her right boot.

"Look at me, Sydney." Kade reached for the door handle. Pinning her with a hard stare, his eyes narrowed and his mouth tightened. "If you sense anything off, call for me immediately. I'll go around back and sneak in quietly so he doesn't hear me, and search the back of the house while you distract him. I still don't like this, but we'll do it your way. If there is a vampire, stay out of the way and let me handle it. Do you understand?"

Sydney nodded. "Let's roll."

Before she had a chance to open the car door, Kade was gone. *Damn vamp speed.* She shook it off and approached the front door and knocked once.

"Police. We're just here to talk." Met with silence, she lifted the rusted metal knocker and slammed it down several times. "Police! Open up!"

Sydney sucked a breath and kicked the door open, with her gun drawn and pointed. *Fuck me. Here we go.* The house looked empty, but she knew that things weren't always as they seemed. As she entered the building, the smell of urine and vomit hit her. *What the fuck?*

"Who's there?" she yelled into the darkness. "This is the police, just here to ask questions. Come out with your hands up and we'll talk. Let's do this nice."

While Sydney heard nothing, she sensed she wasn't alone. She reached into her vest and pulled out her flashlight, flicking it on. She steadied her gun and proceeded into the darkness. As her eyes adjusted to the lack of light, she noticed movement across the room. A shadow lurked in the distance. Slowly she crept across the floor. When she approached the area where she'd seen it originate, she shone the light on the floor; blood. Adrenaline rushed through her veins as she attempted to see who was in the room. A small creaking drew her attention. But as she swiveled to locate it, a rush of pain seized her upper back. Sydney fell hard against the wooden planks, struggling to breathe as her face hit the bloodstained floor.

"What are you doing here? You're desecrating the ritual area, bitch! He'll like you, though. Yes, he'll enjoy hearing you scream as he whips your flesh."

Sydney pushed onto her side and caught sight of a dirty, apparently human, man. He was holding a fourteen-inch wooden baton, which she recognized as a martial arts tonfa. The man was overweight and bald, and could not be more than five-eight, she estimated. His eyes were empty and cold as he poised to strike her again with the weapon. Sydney took a breath, gritted her teeth, and turned all the way over so she was sitting on her bottom. Facing him straight on, she scooted backward into the corner, using her hands and feet. She wanted to stand up and run, but her muscles spasmed, bringing tears to her eyes. She scanned the room, looking for her gun that was lying lost in the darkness. She considered her options, aware that she had another gun. A surprise. *Just keep him talking.*

"Jennings, is it?" He loomed above her, refusing to reply. "Yeah, okay, don't bother answering. Listen, I'm not going to hurt you. I just need to sit up."

"You're going to suffer more than you ever thought possible. I don't even care why you're here. Let's just call it a fortunate circumstance. I will give you to my master. He'll be happy with my gift. He'll take everything from you while you bleed," He laughed.

"Jennings, I hurt my ankle." She feigned injury, wrapping both her hands around her leg until she was able to finger the grip of the pistol. *Almost there.* "I think I might have broken it in the fall. It hurts so badly."

"Listen, this will go easier if you just put out your hands." He pulled out a roll of duct tape from his jacket. "If you can't do it, I have no problem bashing your head in until you give up the fight. What's it gonna be?"

Sydney's pulse raced as her assailant leaned forward to grab her. As she drew the Sig Sauer and fired, a blur jetted across her vision. She coughed as dust scattered throughout the air. As the cloud settled, Sydney could make out a dead body slumped against the wall. A scream tore from her lips, realizing the blur had been Kade.

"Sydney, look at me. Are you okay? Are you hurt? Let me see." Kade rushed to Sydney's side and carefully lowered her arm, taking the gun from her hand. While he had been out back staking a rogue vamp, he'd heard a loud noise, and immediately regretted his decision to allow her to go in alone. He should have been with her. Whoever was behind this would easily be able to kill humans, and he knew it.

Flying into the room, Kade had grabbed Jennings by the shoulders and thrust him hard against the brick wall. In an instant, Sydney had fired off a round, the shot landing in Jennings' chest. Kade heard his last heartbeat. And even though he was disappointed that he hadn't had a chance to interrogate him, Sydney was okay. Bleeding yes, but she was alive.

"Don't touch me. It's just a little blood. I'll be fine," Sydney protested, shaking. She stared at her bloodied hands, red streaks dripping down her fingertips. Furiously, she rubbed them onto her pants as if she was afraid he'd be enticed by the scent of it. "Please, let's just call this into the station so they can scrub the site for trace."

"You're hurt, love. Please let me help you." Sensing she was in shock, he moved slowly toward her as if approaching an injured animal. This time instead of recoiling, she fell into his arms, allowing him to comfort her. "Just because I can smell your blood, that does not mean I am going to bite you. You're safe with me. Let's get you home."

As he took her into his embrace, the sweet lily fragrance in her hair filled his senses. Kade was angry with himself for leaving her side. She was his responsibility. He wanted to take her to her home and tie her to the bed so she would stay the hell away from the vampire who was killing these girls. He didn't care that she was a cop. She was human nonetheless.

"I'll be okay. I just need to rest a minute. I'm fine. I'll probably have a huge bruise on my back though." She winced as she tried to move in his arms. Forcing herself to relax, Sydney let her head fall onto Kade's shoulder. For a moment she let herself enjoy the hardness of his chest and the spicy scent of his skin. She knew she should push him off and walk away, but what could it hurt to pretend someone cared?

Without letting Sydney slip from his arms, Kade managed to pull out his cell phone with one hand and place a call. "Luca, call the station and give them the address. Yeah, Jennings is dead. They need to scrub it. I want you here with them. You get anything, call me, got it? Okay. Bye."

Kade's conversation jarred her from her brief respite, reminding her that she was on this case. Sydney pulled away from Kade, breaking their embrace.

"Let's check the rest of the building and make sure no one else is here. Jennings got me with the baton before I ever made it upstairs. Did you find anyone out back?" Her cool demeanor returned, as she resurrected her emotional walls.

"I had myself a dance with a rogue vamp in the yard." Kade noticed the change in her demeanor and played along, respecting her independence. He might not like that she put herself in danger, but that was part of her job. And he needed to try to worry a little less about his detective. Soon he would stake the offending vampire and catch his jet back to NOLA. As much as he wanted Sydney, he knew the reality of the situation. He would have to let her go. "They must have seen us coming. If you want to check the rest of the place, let's do it together this time."

Thirty minutes later, Kade and Sydney had searched every square inch of the row home. Soon after backup arrived and with no clues to be found, Sydney did something she had never let any man do; she let him drive her baby, her convertible. She'd been hesitant about turning over the keys, but she was nursing a major headache and the lump on her upper back was throbbing. The bleeding on her hands had stopped, but she was pretty sure she was going to be black and blue.

As they pulled up to her building, Kade carefully parked the car. He got out, handed her the keys, and opened her car door. Sydney groaned as she shoved herself up onto her feet.

"Thanks for driving. You sure you don't want to take my car back to the station? I can have Tony pick me up later."

"I'm quite all right. No need to inconvenience you."

"Um…you wanna come up for coffee?" She felt stupid even asking. Did a freakin' vampire even drink coffee?

"You tempt me with your offer. While I do enjoy a spot of tea, I am afraid that my tastes require more than you are willing to give," Kade said, his voice cold. He didn't want to tell Sydney yet, but there were rumors back home that someone was working black magic to gain power, but at the moment it was just talk. There was always some asshole looking for more supernatural power. Once you were a vampire, there was no democracy. You reported to the head vampire in the area; comply or die. Most accepted their new life, some didn't. Luca would have a full update on possible suspects for him when he arrived. "I have to make some calls."

"You've got my cell number. If I don't hear from you, I'll be in touch tomorrow afternoon and we can plan the next steps. It's been a hell of a night, and I need to get a shower."

"Sydney."

"Yes?"

Kade reached for her hand, turned her palm upward, and kissed it.

"I will call you with any news. Please do the same. Please forgive me…ah, my car is here." The limo pulled up to the curb.

As Sydney entered the code for the building, Kade caught her stealing a glance back at him. In that moment, he considered his attraction to her. But almost as soon as the thought came, he shoved it to the back of his mind. Any distraction whatsoever could cause him to make deadly mistakes. And Miss Sydney Willows, while beautiful, was a distraction he could not afford.

Chapter Six

After taking three Advil, Sydney showered and dressed in her favorite red sundress that accentuated the swell of her tan breasts. Unfortunately, it also showed off her upper back that had started to turn bluish. She didn't bother to dry her hair; her blonde locks looked wild and curly. It was late at night, no use blowing it out.

She had considered going to bed. It was nearly two in the morning; she knew she should get into her pajamas, read a book and get some rest, but accustomed to working nights, she was wide awake and her nerves were on fire. Nearly dying can do that to a girl, but it wasn't what was making her jumpy. It was Kade. She wanted, she needed, needed something, someone, him. But she wasn't going to have *him.* Like a wanton slut, she'd asked him to come in with her 'for coffee' a.k.a. 'sex', and he seemed uninterested. She had thought there was a sexual tension there, but maybe she was wrong. He had lied about being a detective. He seemed to have plenty of other secrets.

What else is he lying about? Maybe he has a girlfriend. Or worse, maybe he's married.

Sydney longed to forget her lustful thoughts of Kade. She didn't believe in love at first sight anyway; lust maybe, but lust could be controlled…or redirected. Determined to get him out of her system, Sydney decided Tristan was just what she needed. She knew he cared about her, desired her. He'd always been there for her, the one stable man in her life besides Tony. Life was too short to sit around moping. After her attack, she didn't want to be alone tonight, and Tristan would help her forget.

As Sydney strolled through Eden's doors, she spied Tristan leaning against the bar, talking to a redhead who was flirting with him and flipping her hair. Setting her sights on him, she strode across the dance floor, ignoring the stares from all the other men. They meant nothing to her; this was a club, a place to come and be noticed. Dancing, drinking, sweat, blood, sex, it was all here, and she was going to sate herself until she felt better. Stepping in front of Tristan, she flashed a badge at the girl.

"Get lost. I've got business here," she ordered. Her face held no smile. Her competition promptly rushed away, not wanting to be involved with the police.

As she'd expected, Tristan was not going to be bossed in his own house. He instantly grabbed her arms, dominating the situation. He pulled her flush against his firm body.

"What gives, Syd? My girl looks a little tense. You need something tonight?" he whispered in her ear, his cheek brushing against hers.

"I need you," she responded.

She quivered in his arms, his erection pressing into her belly. There would be no stopping him tonight. It had been weeks since they'd been together. Even though there was no commitment between them, tonight she was his. She allowed him to take control, leading her up the stairs.

Tristan led her into his private office. Soundproofed and secure, its royal-blue walls were decorated with modern art. A cherry desk sat center, complete with matching chairs. He flicked a switch and flames flared to life in a gas fireplace.

Sydney stood still, unable to make the first move. Even though she'd felt an instant attraction to Kade, she told herself that he was nothing more than a mysterious stranger, one who was uninterested in pursuing a relationship. She needed to be with someone who cared about her; she needed Tristan. He'd always been there for her, and she for him.

"Tristan, I…." she stammered.

"Shh…you don't need to say anything. I missed you." He brushed the back of his hand across her cheek, and she leaned into him and kissed his hand.

"Tris, this case. It was a rough night. I just need to relax. I just need you."

Tristan raised an eyebrow at her. "You sure, baby? You seem, I don't know, a little different tonight. Distracted. You okay?"

"I'm fine, Tris, really. I got hurt earlier tonight out with Kade, but I'm okay." Sydney didn't want to tell Tristan that she'd asked Kade to come up to her apartment or how she'd almost got killed tonight. She was reluctant to tell him the truth, but knew that he'd discover her bruises.

"Dammit, Syd. What happened? Let me see you." He pulled her closer to the fireplace and circled around her, inspecting her skin. When he caught sight of her back, he sucked a breath and ground his back teeth. "You're hurt. Mon chaton, did you go to the doctor? Where was Kade when this happened?"

"I'm okay," she whispered, a tear escaping her eye.

Tristan leaned over and kissed her gently on the shoulder, rubbing her neck. Sydney moaned in response, relaxing into his touch. Allowing him better access to her throat, she submitted to his wolf's need to dominate. Usually, she had to be in control. But here, she could let down her walls…only with Tristan. He knew what she wanted in life, sexually. She would never let him fully into her heart. Wolves never mated with humans. Long ago, they'd both accepted that this would have to be good enough. But within Tristan's arms, she would purge the thoughts of Kade from her mind. She'd get her release, go home, sleep and be back on the job tomorrow with a smile on her face.

A sigh escaped her lips as Tristan slid his fingers over her skin, pushing down the strings of her sundress. The fabric fell to her feet, her bared back exposed to him. He reached around her belly and cupped her breasts. His hands were full as he took her nipples between his forefinger and thumb and squeezed. She moaned again as heat rushed to her sex. Tristan gently turned her around and pressed his lips to hers.

"Tristan," she gasped, "I need you now."

"I've got you," he replied.

Reaching down, he cupped her ass. With his other hand, he grazed over her breast and stomach, sliding his fingers underneath her silk thong. His entire hand covered her mound, his fingers exploring her folds, gently building a rhythm.

"More, Tristan. In me. Please." She rocked into his hand.

He loved it when she begged. His wolf was aching to fuck her but he wanted to make her come first. He knew how to please a woman, especially his Syd.

"That's it, mon chaton. Feel me."

"Don't stop," she pleaded as she dug her fingers into his shoulders as if she was holding on for dear life.

Tristan slowly inserted a finger inside her, circling her clit with his thumb. As she trembled, he knew she wouldn't last long. Intent on pushing her over the edge, he slowly added another finger, increasing the pace.

"That's it, baby. Just let go."

Her chest heaved for breath. Trembling, she came by his hand. Clutching his shoulders, she rested against his chest.

Tristan eased up his hold, and Sydney knelt down in front of him. She wanted to taste him, make him feel good too. Tristan groaned as she reached up and grabbed the outside of his pants, cupping his groin. She quickly unbuttoned his jeans and let his erect length jut out. She grabbed the base of his sex, slowly stroking him, and looked up into his eyes. Taking him into her mouth, she pleasured him until he came.

After his release, they fell gently to the floor, relaxing on the rug in front of the fire. Even as she lay in Tristan's embrace, her thoughts drifted to Kade. She wished she could understand why she wanted him so badly. He was both good looking and charming, but she'd just met him. It was as if the sexual tension between them escalated exponentially every time they exchanged a glance. She closed her eyes and prayed that whatever she felt for Kade would go away when he left town. Kade hadn't wanted her when she offered, so why shouldn't she enjoy a little fun with Tristan? Despite her rationalization, knowing she'd done nothing wrong, she felt a twinge of guilt, having made love to Tristan.

"What's going on in that pretty little head of yours?" Tristan asked, as if reading her thoughts. "Listen, I know something's got you upset."

"What are you talking about? I'm fine," she denied.

"Come on, Syd. I can feel it. Remember, Alpha magic and all? I know you're just off today…even if you did just blow my mind." He laughed. "You're so alone all the time. It's not good for you. Maybe you should think about being here more often…with me. I can protect you. And before you get all riled up, I get that you are a super cop and all, but face it, you're a little beat up tonight…albeit a beautiful shade of blue. You need someone to care for you. You know you mean a lot to me. I don't want you getting hurt while you're working this case. Why don't you think of spending the rest of the night here with me? No pressure. Just spend the night and we'll see how it goes tomorrow."

"Tristan, I really appreciate the offer. But nothing's wrong," she lied. Sydney kissed him gently, rose off the floor, and started to get dressed. "I just have a lot on my mind. I swear I'll be fine."

"Okay, but I'm here for you if you need me. And Kade will protect you too. He and I have been friends for a long time. He's a tough son of a bitch and has sworn to me that he'll protect you with his life, if needed."

"Don't worry. I'll be okay, Kade or no Kade." Sydney sighed. Kade was her problem. "Thanks for everything tonight. I really gotta get going. You were exactly what I needed."

Tristan quickly shrugged on his clothes, and opened the door. Sydney kissed him as she brushed by him. As they walked down the winding stairway, the pounding music reminded her she was in a club, not someone's house. Halfway down, she felt his presence and looked across the crowded dance floor. *Again? Really?* She could not get away from that damn vampire. Sydney looked over to Tristan and saw him wave at Kade. She glanced back to Kade and found him glaring at her. *He knew.*

Sydney momentarily wondered how the two men had become friends, given their different personalities. Even though she'd been intent on going home and getting a good night's rest, seeing Kade ignited the flame of desire in her that had only slightly dimmed during her little tryst with Tristan. She'd known it would be temporary but she'd been hoping to at least get through five minutes without thinking about Kade. *Damn.*

As she descended the rest of the stairs, she fought the guilt that rose in her throat. She silently told herself that she had nothing to be ashamed of, she was single after all. She had no ties to anyone. Sydney turned to Tristan, whispering goodbye and placing a kiss to his cheek. She kept her gaze toward the door, attempting to ignore Kade as she pushed through the dance floor.

Kade spotted her on the stairs with Tristan. He fought the instinct to run up the stairs and rip into his friend. What the fuck was he thinking? He held no claims to Sydney yet and could not challenge his friend here in his territory. In fact, a few hours ago he'd refused her invitation. He damn well knew she wanted more than coffee the instant she offered. But he'd chosen to meet Luca instead, so he could continue working the case without her.

After Luca picked him up, Kade's deepest suspicion was confirmed. He'd found a Voodoo bracelet with a vampire's scent on it. A vampire who Kade knew well. There was no denying her scent; this vampire had come for him, and was somehow using the humans, perhaps a mage, to assist her. He did not intend to tell Sydney about Luca's findings tonight. She was mortal and too vulnerable. Kade planned to oust his determined detective from the case, keeping her safe and off the radar.

As his eyes met hers, he could not deny the intense feelings that were growing inside of him. He almost lost it, watching her kiss his friend. As she attempted to reach the door, her scent grew stronger and he could smell Tristan as well. The thought that she'd been intimate with the wolf bore a hole in his belly. Jealousy flared as he rushed over to stop her from leaving. Certain he'd made a mistake earlier, refusing to come up to her apartment, he grew intent on letting her know in no uncertain terms to whom she would belong someday. She was his. He wasn't sure how or when, but she would belong to him.

In an instant, Kade slipped behind her. He softly placed his hands on her shoulders, frowning at the now deep black and blue marks on her upper back.

"And what do you think you are doing out here? Your bruises...you must be in pain."

"I've been through worse," Sydney said, her voice calm as if she were all business. She turned to face him, pushing out from under his hands. "Did you talk to Luca? What did he say?"

"A dance, love? Indulge me." He slid a hand around her waist and drew her into him, sniffing her neck. "I can see you have been busy."

"One dance," Sydney agreed. Slowly, she reached up and put her hands around his neck, leaning her face against his chest. "Just tell me....did Luca find anything we can use?"

"He found a bracelet. It is a Voodoo bracelet, possibly charmed. I have contacts in New Orleans I will consult."

"Ada called me. She's running the hair. By tomorrow, we should have something else to go on. I'll meet you at the station tomorrow night around six."

Kade felt her stiffen in his arms, as if she was struggling to fight what he knew was happening between them. He held her closer, refusing to let her go just yet as they continued to slow dance. "I know you're a cop, but this danger...you cannot fight it. You must trust me when I say that there are evil, supernatural forces that await us...you will need me to keep you safe." He leaned in and kissed the top of her head.

"Evil is a reality of this city. This is what I do."

Kade stopped dancing. He reached over and cupped her face gently with both his hands, his eyes pinned on hers.

"We will do this together, love, but know that it will be done my way. I will keep you safe, and after this evil is extinguished, you will be mine and no one else's."

Sydney felt the blood rush to her face. She wasn't sure whether to yell at him or fuck him right there in the middle of the dance floor. Somehow she knew his words were true…she would be his.

Determined not to let him see that he had just gotten to her, she pulled away, turned and looked back at him over her shoulder, and smiled. "Kade, love, you should know here and now that I belong to no one but myself."

With that, she walked out the door. She knew it wasn't true. Something about him drew her in and threatened to change her entire life. He made her want to belong to him. She wanted to love someone and have him love her back…she wanted Kade.

Chapter Seven

After sleeping a good ten hours, Sydney got dressed. She sped off to grab a latte at her favorite coffee shop then stopped by the sporting goods and craft stores to pick up a few things for the kids at the children's center where she volunteered. She loved seeing their faces as she brought in her weekly presents. New markers meant more pictures, more happy faces, and more creativity. Sydney knew how great it felt to create: inspiring, fulfilling, accomplished. These kids felt it too. Their creations were evidence they had a future, not one on the streets, but a future perhaps in art school or college. These kids had a dream to get out from under the poverty and violence of the streets, and Sydney was determined to help them.

Even though she had a busy life, mostly filled with work, the truth was that she had only a few trusted friends and no family to speak of. Her mother had been tragically killed by a drunk driver several years ago, and the grief from her death had brought Sydney to her knees. She just wasn't the same after losing her mom and neither was her dad. Sydney's father fell into a deep depression, moved to Arizona and died a few years later.

Death was a merciless teacher. It taught Sydney to steel her emotions, build a wall big enough so she would not have to feel the grief. Having her mom die only confirmed her decision that she would not get married, because she couldn't stand the heartbreak of losing someone else. She'd had several boyfriends over the years, even a few she thought she could have loved, but she never really could commit to any of them, because of her job. In addition, she had watched the men she worked with get married and then divorced more times than she cared to. The hours and the stress of the job did not make a marriage easy. In her mind, it didn't make you available enough to be a good parent either. It was easier deciding to be happy with the life she did have: a good job, a few good friends, a boyfriend here or there who was willing to just be a boyfriend and nothing more.

Although Sydney loved kids, she'd convinced herself that she would never have any of her own. So she devoted much of her spare time and money to a local after-school center. Every week she would spend a few hours at the center, talking with the kids, playing games, and doing crafts. She wasn't the only one who was alone; these kids needed her. The fact was that many of the city's kids were raising themselves. Their parents never made it to the PTO meetings or teacher conferences. Whether they were too busy working or missing entirely, it didn't matter. The result was the same; kids alone on the street after school.

The center gave them something constructive to do. Through play, they learned.

Sydney knew she was lucky to have been raised by loving parents in a middle class home where chocolate chip cookies and encouragement were plentiful. She might not ever have kids of her own, but she had the knowhow to help other kids. She knew how to teach a group of girls to bake a cake, do their algebra homework, learn about science, sing a song, or paint a picture. Her mom had been an artist so creativity was valued in her house. Sydney wanted these kids to have every experience she'd been allowed to have, even if at the end of the day the cold streets awaited them. They deserved to know about the wonderful activities that could fill their young lives instead of gang banging, prostitution, and drugs. Despite the bitter poverty, the center helped girls and boys to grow up educated, strong, and empowered.

Sydney knew she wasn't a saint, but she still gave as much of herself as she could. At the end of the day, the kids filled her soul with hope and love, two things that she very much needed.

After spending a few hours with the kids, Sydney hurried back to the station, to Kade. It was still light outside. She wondered where he was sleeping. Did he even sleep? Did he go out during the day? She knew much more about werewolves, both the good and the bad, than she knew about vampires. She got the fact they drank blood, but other than that, she tried not to hang out with them to find out the details of their habits. She did have a sense of self-preservation.

As she buckled up, her cell phone buzzed with a text from the station. *Shit.* Another dead girl had been found. She hated the evil that lurked within humans and paranormals. Why did they kill? Power, hate, passion, mental illness? There were many reasons, none of them good. Sydney didn't even care anymore. She was growing tired of the death. Sure, she would try to understand motive to the extent that it would help her find the perpetrators and lock them away forever, but aside from self-defense, there was never a justified murder.

The dead girl had been found in Olde City at Elfreth's Alley. America's founding fathers had come together in this very place, creating documents that would give birth to a country. Benjamin Franklin had once walked these streets. Its cobblestone alley was lined with renovated row homes that proudly displayed the preserved eighteenth century, working class homes that remained. The country's past, and sadly, now the present lay across the stones, marring the historic site.

Sydney ducked under the crime scene tape and approached the body. She knew she should have called Kade, but she figured someone on his team would let him know. After last night, she was afraid of her body's response to him. Eventually she would have to see him, she knew, to hear his voice, and breathe in his delicious masculine scent. He would be pissed that she hadn't waited for him. But Sydney figured she'd take action and apologize later.

She leaned in to get a better look at the body, another "Death Doll." The girl was a brunette this time, but had the same almost pure white, porcelain skin. She was not damaged by water like the other victim had been. Instead, it looked as if she had been gently laid on the street only hours ago. She appeared as if she were simply sleeping. She was as young as the other girl, in her twenties, but was dressed differently this time, in a long evergreen velvet dress, sans shoes. Again, her eyelids had been sewn shut with thread. Someone had taken care to put makeup on her face. She looked like a collectible doll you would buy on home shopping television. The scoop neckline dress was fitted tightly around the front of her body. Sydney snapped on a latex glove and reached over to lift the neckline slightly.

The tattoo was small enough that it adorned the top of the girl's breast. It looked almost like a cross, but with a round, large protuberance on the head.

"Jennings is dead, so either he did this before he died or there's someone new doing the tattoos, and what is this?

It isn't exactly a cross. I know I've seen this somewhere." Sydney stood up straight and spoke aloud to herself. She shook her head at the needless loss of life.

"It's an Ankh. Ancient Egyptian symbol of eternal life."

Sydney spun around, startled by the velvet caress of Kade's voice. But his tone was not warm. No, he was angry with her, presumably for not calling him. *Great, here we go.*

"Forget something, Sydney? You know, I'm not above punishing you for your blatant disregard of my orders."

After Sydney had left the club the previous night, Kade talked to Tristan about what Luca had found; a ribbon with *her* scent on it. *She* was back, *Simone.* Kade had first met Simone in New Orleans in 1822. He found her beaten and starving in an alley. Newly turned, she was a lost fledgling. Not wanting to watch her kill or be killed, he took her under his wing and taught her how to feed on humans without killing them. Along with several other young vampires, including Luca, Simone lived with him in his safe compound that he had created within the city. Despite the apparent abuse she had suffered over the years, she came to trust Kade.

Simone had told him that a man named John Palmer had sent for her from England and brought her to Jamaica. She was given as a gift to his new wife, Annie

Palmer. She worked as an indentured servant, a handmaiden. It was in Jamaica where she had learned Voodoo from Annie, who was a dangerous and abusive mistress known as the White Witch. Annie regularly tortured Simone and the other workers and slaves on the plantation. Simone had been beaten or whipped nearly every day she'd been there. Nothing ever made the mistress happy except when she practiced her dark arts. During these sessions, Simone was expected to assist the mistress, but she was not happy to merely assist. She kept her eyes lowered but secretly copied Annie's notes and memorized whatever spells Annie cast.

One night during one of the many extravagant parties they held on the plantation, a guest had expressed interest in Simone and Annie had offered her handmaiden as a gift to him to use as he wished. Simone reluctantly took the stranger's hand out of fear of a whipping. The stranger had led her out into the fields, where he raped and turned her.

She was not aware that she had left Jamaica until she awoke in a dirty hotel room in New Orleans. Her new master sat on a chair next to her and explained she'd been turned into a vampire; she'd be his new slave. While she shook in bed, trying to come to terms with what he was saying, the door burst open, and a man shot a wooden arrow into his chest. The vampire disintegrated on the spot. Assuming Simone was an innocent human, the killer said nothing as he turned and left the building. Simone scrambled out onto the street, but realized she was weak.

She had stumbled into the muck and had lain helpless until Kade found her.

During the next few years, Simone had adjusted to life in New Orleans and transformed into a beautiful woman. Her pale skin highlighted her lush, ebony hair. It wasn't long before Kade and Simone became intimate. He wasn't in love with her, but he'd been lonely and she was available. He couldn't risk being involved with a human during those times, so another vampire offered him the companionship he needed. What Kade hadn't realized was that Simone never gave up practicing Voodoo and had started secretly practicing the dark arts when he was out of town. She knew Annie's secrets and wanted the power she knew could be hers. It wasn't until a werewolf, named Tristan, approached him and told him about his missing sister, that Kade found out Simone had evil intentions. Tristan had come for Kade's help, and an agreement. Tristan would offer peace with the local wolves. In exchange, Kade would get his sister back from Simone.

Kade was horrified to find Simone in the barn that day. She had captured at least ten girls, including Tristan's sister, and was holding them hostage. The girls were barely alive, cuffed with silver, beaten and naked, hanging on the walls. Infuriated, he commanded Simone to him and shoved her to her knees. While he initially wanted to kill Simone for her crimes, she begged for her life. Granting her mercy, Kade banished her forever from the United States. Forced to leave, Simone went with only a ticket for passage overseas and the clothes on her back. He destroyed her ritualistic objects, her spell books, and all that remained was a burned field where the barn used to stand.

He had nearly forgotten about Simone until Luca told him he had scented her at the Jennings' scene. If Simone was involved, he knew she would kill Sydney without a second thought. If she was able to capture and torture strong werewolves, like Tristan's sister, she could easily kill a human. He didn't know what he could do to convince Sydney of the danger that she faced. He knew he couldn't stop her from continuing the investigation, but damn if she was going to go out on the streets without him. He had to be serious with her and make her understand that she had to obey his orders in order to work with him. He needed to tell her about Simone.

Sydney tensed at Kade's remark that he'd punish her. She'd never seen him this angry. Yet his outrage only served to put her on the defensive.

"Newsflash, vampire, I'm not your daughter, nor are you my boss. So, let me make myself clear. I don't take orders from you. We may be partners for now, but this is my city. I apologize for not calling you, but I figured you'd be…I don't know…sleeping or whatever it is that vampires do during the day. I figured your office would call you." She knew she was wrong, but that was the best apology she could cough up at the moment. She was not going to let some guy tell her what to do. There was a murderer killing women on the street. They'd catch the guy and then, next year, it would be a different perp out killing people; that was life in the big city. She was here to catch bad guys, and was not a little girl playing cops and robbers. "How about we just move on? You're here now, so let's get to work."

Kade stared down at her and moved closer. God, he was sexy, but dangerous. Sydney could see his muscles bulging out of his tight black t-shirt. For a minute, she thought about what it would feel like to slip her hands under his shirt and skim her fingertips along the hard ridges of his stomach.

"Sydney, love, I know you know these streets like the back of your hand, but we need to learn to trust each other. There are things you don't know about. I promise I will tell you everything when we get time, but right now, I need you to give me a little trust. Do not go on calls by yourself. It isn't good practice anyway, and you know it. Even though we are technically sharing this case, I could easily get you pulled off it if you don't listen to me. There is a vampire involved in these killings, and possibly another creature with supernatural abilities. I don't want to push you off the case, but I will if you don't start cooperating, and that means that I lead the investigation, not you. Most importantly, you go nowhere alone, am I clear?"

"Crystal," Sydney responded, refusing to look him in the eye.

Sydney focused on the body. Arguing with Kade wasn't going to solve the case. *What other similarities are there to the first girl?* She pulled another glove on and reached for the girl's wrist. The dress had long sleeves that fell past her fingers. Sydney gently pulled up the material to see if the girl had marks on her. Sure enough, she had bruises on her wrists, indicating that she'd been bound and then perhaps cut loose after she died. Sydney scanned the site for evidence of cuffs or ropes, anything that may have been discarded in the rush to dump the body.

"Check out her wrists. She was bound, too…just like the other vic. We need to scour every inch of this alley to see if anything else was dumped with the body. Killers are careful, but these guys always make mistakes. We just need to find them."

As she turned around, Sydney saw the coroner's van pull up. She waved to Adalee, who walked toward her with kit in tow. "Hey Syd, another vic, I see?"

"Yeah, I can't be sure but it looks like she's been drained. The site looks clean, no blood or urine around the body."

Adalee blew out a breath while she stared down at the dead girl. She glanced at Kade, who was coming over to see her, and then back again at Sydney.

"So listen, trace came in on the wrist fibers from girl one. Get this, looks like the hair was human, also hemp mixed in. So, whatever rope or binding this is, it's got human hair in it."

"Do we know who the hair belonged to?" Sydney asked.

"No. But I can tell you that it doesn't match the vic's." Adalee bent down and started working on the body, but kept talking. "And there was something else. We found residue on the body, some kind of oil. Trace came back showing mostly lemongrass. A few other small things, but it definitely was some kind of lemon oil. This case keeps getting weirder and weirder."

"Lemongrass? Maybe it was just some kind of skin cream or lotion? We don't know it has anything to do with the perp."

"Well, all I can tell you is that it was only on her forehead, nowhere else on the body." Adalee spoke to Sydney as she pulled out the body thermometer. "The only time I've seen that kind of thing is in the church. You know, like Catholics do with the healing masses."

"What is it, Kade? You're awfully quiet over there." Sydney waited for Kade to weigh in on Adalee's assessment.

"I told you, Sydney. There are forces here that you are not used to fighting." Kade knelt down to inspect the girl's face. With a gloved hand, he reached over and carefully pushed a stray hair off her face. He sighed. "Lemongrass oil. Voodoo, Hoodoo. These are all practices which use oil and herbs. Sometimes practitioners create a hybrid of Voodoo, Hoodoo, witchcraft, and black magic. Not all are pure of heart. Some seek power or money, even love."

"Seems like a sick way to find love." Sydney shook her head. "Honestly, Kade, this just sounds like a bunch of mumbo jumbo to me, but I've seen people kill for all kinds of reasons…even for a pair of damn sneakers."

"In Hoodoo, there is a substance called Van Van oil." Kade stood up, his face tightened. "Lemongrass is used to make it. I will need to contact my sources to find out the purposes of the oil, but I assure you the folks who use these tools are serious in their desires. The perp may be anointing the victims."

"Even if they aren't purposefully placing the oil there, there could have been some kind of cross contamination. I agree that we need more information on why someone uses the oil in the first place. It could help with determining a motive. What about the hemp and human hair? Why the hell go through all the trouble of making a rope with human hair when you can just go to Home Depot and get a synthetic rope?"

"Human hair and hemp have uses in witchcraft. My guess is some kind of cord magic, possibly intended to make death more painful. My understanding is that cord magic is not usually used as an actual rope to tie someone. I have heard of it being placed under a victim's bed, or such. The witch or mage could have used it as part of a ritual while they were binding the girl."

Witches? Mages? Vampires? Sydney suddenly felt like a fish out of water. This was exactly why she hated to deal with the supernatural. She was not part of that world. But a killer was a killer no matter how they did it or who they were. She had learned long ago that evil was not exclusively a supernatural phenomenon. Sydney contemplated turning the entire case over to Kade. She'd be done and could resume fighting normal, everyday human crime. But already the faces of these poor girls were ingrained in her mind, and she felt a duty to find their killers so they could be at peace. Besides, Sydney was too far into this case to simply turn it over to Kade. What she wouldn't admit was that she was too far into Kade to let him go.

"Ada, Kade, I don't see any tattoos on this girl's face. The other vic had them. You think maybe Jennings didn't get a chance to finish his work on her?"

"Maybe Jennings did the tattoo on her breast? And did the other tattoos post mortem? He could have been a human slave to whomever is killing these girls, but he wasn't the mage, and there definitely is magic here. I can feel it…there are remnants of it all around. But even though there are signs of magic, I am certain a vampire is behind these killings."

"Kade, Sydney…what the hell is this?" Both Kade and Sydney snapped their heads around to see what Adalee was talking about. They both knelt down and watched Adalee cradle the girl's chin in her left hand, while with her right she took out a long pair of tweezers. "There is something in here. Syd, flashlight please."

Sydney grabbed her flashlight, flipped it on and shined the light down the girl's throat. Kade reached around to lift the girl's head and helped to keep the mouth open so

Adalee could work. Slowly she reached in and pulled the tweezers back out. "It looks like maybe a small scroll or a piece of paper?"

Kade held out his gloved hand and took it from her. The object was a red paper, folded into a five-sided star, a pentagram. He carefully unfolded it.

"Looks like someone's been practicing witchy origami. There's writing on it. Let me see." Sydney leaned in close to Kade, attempting to get a better view of the object. As her shoulder brushed his chest, the heat of his body enveloped her. Her nipples tightened in response. She needed to get this case finished soon before she lost her mind from lust. *Hello? Crime scene. Dead body.* Sydney pulled her thoughts back into focus and read the note.

Written in black ink, there were only four words. '*You will be mine*'. As she leaned toward the note, she smelled the faintest hint of cinnamon. She turned her head, her eyes locked on Kade's.

"You will be mine? What kind of note is that? Kade, do you smell that?" She knew he had super vamp senses. She wasn't sure if it was her imagination.

"Cinnamon? Yes, I smell it. It's a common ingredient in witchcraft, probably infused into the ink." Kade tried to keep a poker face as Sydney read the words. *Simone.* He had banished her from the country and from his bed. He would never be hers no matter whom she killed. Kade's protective nature urged him to take Sydney right then and there and lock her up to protect her from this evil woman. He knew that he had to tell Sydney. He needed to find a way to share with her what was happening so he could get her off the case without completely pissing her off. If he could get her alone, he could tell her everything. "I have to consult with a few people about what we found. I have a witch on retainer back home. Let's get the scene cleaned and then we can go back to my place and make some calls, together."

"All right, let's get the scene wrapped up," she agreed. "The faster we get this done, the sooner we can call this witch of yours."

Kade felt an enormous relief as she acquiesced. She was finally beginning to trust him, and they were starting to work as a team. He was acutely aware of the intense sexual connection growing between them, one that he wanted to explore as soon as he knew she was safe from Simone. Sydney was turning him inside out, and he suspected she was destined to be his, and not just for a night. Kade wanted to make love to her until she screamed his name in ecstasy. He wanted her to know that with every cell of her being, she was his.

For now, he needed to keep his feelings hidden. It was hard enough keeping his hands off of her every time he saw her, let alone torturing himself with thoughts of what would happen in the future. If Simone was indeed after him, she would see Sydney as competition to be eliminated. He would not let her be harmed, even if that meant taking her off the case. Better she hate him than end up dead.

Several hours passed before everyone had left the scene. Sydney continued inspecting the area as Kade called Luca. She carefully paced the perimeter of the alley, hoping she'd find something the killer left. A cold breeze swept across her neck, causing her to shiver. She looked back at Kade, who seemed unfazed, as if he hadn't felt it. She didn't think they were expecting rain tonight, but it was common to get thunderstorms in the summer.

As she moved further away from Kade, she heard laughing. A conversation? She couldn't be certain, but it sounded like a woman's voice. Sydney waved over to Kade, getting his attention and pointed down the small covered tunnel that ran between two of the row homes.

Sydney covered her nose as the stench of trickling, stagnant water hit her. The odor was overpowering; urine, rotted food, feces. Struggling to see where she was walking in the darkness, she dug in her vest to find her flashlight. Her fingers touched its metal casing and flipped the switch. A woman's laughter cackled in the distance. As if she was frozen, Sydney watched in awe as a small orb of light appeared about twenty feet away from her, floating in the air like a tuft of feathers. It flashed, instantly replaced by an apparition.

A ghostly woman with a beautiful face and long flowing black hair hovered in the cramped, dank alley. Sydney could hardly believe what she was seeing. While the woman seemed to have the outline of a body, there were no feet, only a long, red dress that stopped a foot off the ground. The woman began to laugh maniacally as she glared at Sydney. The laugh died into deadly silence as the woman's lips straightened into a tight line.

Sydney had dealt with enough women to know that this one was aggressive; there was no mistaking a bitch on wheels. Ghost or no ghost, she had no intention of letting any woman frighten her off the street. Sydney quickly reached for her gun. She had no idea what killed ghosts but she wasn't going down without a fight.

"Kade! Could use a little help down here!"

"He! Is! Mine!" the ghost shrieked.

In a flash, the spectral woman flew toward Sydney, and she fired off a round. Dodging the apparition, she fell into the gritty, wet alleyway and everything went black. She fumbled for her broken flashlight, her heart racing. She felt Kade pick her up off the ground and promptly wrapped her arms around his neck, allowing him to carry her out of the tunnel.

"I'm good. Really, you can put me down. I just fell, that's all. She's gone," she said, aware that she was enjoying him picking her up a little too much. She blew out a breath as Kade gently let go of her legs, placed her upright and pulled out of the embrace.

"Sydney, are you sure you're okay? I heard you scream for me. And then I heard a shot. What happened down there? I sensed no one. No humans. No supernaturals. Wait, who do you mean, *she*?"

"Yeah, I'm fine." *Really? A floating ghost woman and my vampire sees nothing?* Doubt crept into her mind. "I have to tell you…it's going to sound crazy. I heard voices, a woman. She was laughing. In the tunnel, there was just this small light and then it turned into this ghost She was beautiful, with long black hair, and then she seemed like she wanted to attack me. That's when I called for you…and then she screamed, 'He is mine,' and rushed me, and that's when I got off a shot. Do bullets even kill ghosts? All I know is she missed me and then I fell down. And shit!" Sydney looked down at her clothes. She was covered in slimy, malodorous water. "Look at me! Ewwww. This is so gross…I gotta get home and take a shower. What the hell was that thing back there, anyway?"

"Wait, Sydney. Let me see you and make sure you are okay," Kade said, checking her for injuries. There was no blood and she appeared uninjured as she claimed.

"I'm fine. Really, I just fell when that…that 'woman' flew at me. I'm telling you, Kade, I didn't really believe in ghosts before tonight. But that was no person. I don't know what the hell it was." Sydney shook her head in frustration.

While Sydney may have been surprised by her spectral experience, Kade was shocked at her description. It was Simone. But how had she transported herself as an apparition? Magic? Someone or something was helping her. He had to get Sydney home and away from this place.

On the ride back to Kade's brownstone, they told Luca what had happened in the alley. Kade knew that though he didn't mention Simone by name, Luca would know from Sydney's description exactly who had visited them in the alley.

"I want you to locate Ilsbeth," Kade told Luca. Ilsbeth was a local witch from the French Quarter. She was cagey at times and not always easy to deal with, but she and Kade had been allies for several years. He could not claim they were close friends, but she could be trusted.

"You got it. I'll call her on my way over to Eden. I was planning to go there to feed and see Tristan. Do you want me to update him on today's events?"

"Thank you, yes. Please let him know what happened, but do tell him up in his private office. We cannot afford to be overheard. Tell Tristan that Sydney and I will be at the brownstone for the rest of the night."

Sydney shot him a look of surprise, but didn't voice her concern. *I'm going to be there all night? Working the case? Or working Kade?* They did need to go over the details and work through the facts of the case. She suspected Kade wasn't being completely honest with her. She hadn't pressed him back at the crime scene, but she would damn sure find out after she got a shower and some food.

When they arrived, the garage door opened to let the limo in under the house. As they entered Kade's home,

Sydney took in the sight of the mahogany walled rooms. Its décor was both rich and masculine, suiting Kade.

"Nice place. I love the woodwork. Dark, but beautiful," she commented.

"Thanks. It's a rental that belongs to Tristan. As much as I like visiting, I have no plans on living here. As soon as the case is over, I need to get back to New Orleans."

Sydney wasn't sure why she felt sick hearing him say that he was going to leave. She'd known he wasn't going to stay here forever. A small part of her had hoped that maybe he'd visit longer if he found something, or someone important enough. His statement spurred her to build up that emotional wall she'd learned to do to protect her heart. She didn't want to have feelings for him, but she was having a hard time denying her emerging desire for the mysterious vampire. She needed to get back to business…talk about the case, in an attempt to shift her focus.

"Kade, can you show me to the bathroom? I've got to clean up."

"Yes, sorry. This way." Kade would love to show her his shower…with her naked and him thrusting into her against the tiled walls, he thought. Silently they walked up the stairway and down a long hallway. He opened a door and gestured for her to enter. "Here you go. I can have your clothes laundered while we work. Just put them in the laundry chute. I will call for the maid to take care of them. There are towels inside the closet, and there is a black robe hanging on the back of the door that you can wear until your clothes are finished being cleaned. Just come down when you are done. I'll have some Chinese food delivered while you're bathing."

As they stood alone in the quiet hallway, Kade's eyes fell to her lips. He took her hand in his, trailing his thumb over her palm. His gaze moved to meet hers, and he fought the urge to kiss her.

"Sydney..." he began.

"I just want you to know that I was glad you were there today," she interrupted, her voice trembling. "Um...I mean...I know I wasn't hurt, but it felt good to have someone at my back. I don't know what the hell that thing was tonight in the alley, but I'd be lying if I said it didn't shake me up a little. So anyway, thanks."

Before Kade had a chance to respond, she tugged her hand out of his, entered the bathroom and quickly shut the door.

Sydney leaned against the back of the bathroom door and sighed. She had almost kissed him. What was she doing? *Get your head out of your ass. He just told you that he's not staying. He's leaving and going back to New Orleans.* Frustrated, she reached over and turned on the hot water, stripped out of her rank clothes and tossed them down the chute. A maid was going to *launder* her clothes? *Must be*

nice, she thought. She stepped underneath the hot spray of the water and let the tension run down the drain.

As she washed her hair with shampoo, she noticed that it smelled of strawberries. *A vampire with strawberry shampoo?* She smiled, thinking of Kade. As she washed her body with soap, she let her hands run over her breasts. What would it feel like to have Kade's strong hands massage her breasts? To have him suck her nipples? Sydney closed her eyes and moaned, letting her hand wander down over her bare, waxed mound. She slipped a finger into her folds, finding her core. Gently circling her most sensitive area, she imagined that it was Kade touching her. She groaned as the tingle built in her womb, shaking as she came. Sydney let her forehead rest against the dark blue tile, afraid to face him.

Kade nearly died when he heard Sydney moan and smelled her arousal. He wanted to charge up the stairs, break down the door and fuck her senseless. Didn't she know that vampires had enhanced senses? Or maybe she knew exactly what she was doing? As he listened to her pleasuring herself upstairs, he couldn't hold back. He sat back in the large leather chair and unzipped his pants, pulling out his rock-hard cock. Was she thinking of him as she touched herself? He stroked his shaft, faster and faster. He could not believe he was doing this in the den, but shit, she made a man lose his mind. Another moan from upstairs. He could sense she was close. He glided his palm up and down his length, bringing himself closer to climax.

She was coming. He was coming. Kade cursed as his seed went flying onto his pants.

"Ah…fuck. What a fucking mess. What are you doing?" *What am I doing? Great, now I'm talking aloud to myself, just fucking great.* He was going to need to see a therapist after this little incident. He grabbed a wad of tissues, jumped up, and stomped up the stairs to his bedroom. He needed to get changed before she saw him.

Kade jumped in the shower, washed, and quickly dressed in a pair of worn jeans and a black cotton t-shirt. He heard her in the shower. If he hurried, he could get downstairs first. He was just about down the flight of stairs when the doorbell rang; the Chinese food. He quickly paid the driver and set off to get things ready in the kitchen.

Sydney padded into the kitchen wearing just his robe, and sat at the granite counter bar. Relaxed from her shower, she smiled at him.

"So, Kade, not to be rude or anything, but vampires and Chinese food? What gives? Thought you guys only had blood on the menu. Unless you got that delivered too?"

Kade laughed. "Ah, you do have quite a bit to learn about us, and I would love to be the one to teach you." He winked at her, causing her to blush. "Vampires do need blood to survive, but we only need to feed a couple of times a week. We can eat food, and it tastes great, but it will not keep us alive; only blood does that. My favorite food is Peking duck, but I also got Szechuan shrimp, dumplings, moo shu chicken, and garlic broccoli. I wasn't sure what you liked."

"So, are we having company?" Sydney laughed.

Kade shook his head, no.

"Well, it smells wonderful. I'm so hungry. And just so you know, I love everything you ordered...it's as if you knew what I'd like."

"You are very welcome. And I do believe I know what you would like," he teased, desire in his eyes.

Looking down into her shrimp, she tried to hide her embarrassment. He knew she wanted him. Then it occurred to her that he might have known what she was doing in the shower. *Shit.* She was hoping that he wouldn't hear or smell anything, with the shower going and that delicious strawberry shampoo. Guess she was wrong.

"So, you like it spicy? I must confess that I love it that way as well. I just can't seem to get mine hot enough."

Oh yeah, she loved it hot all right. Sydney gazed into his sexy blue eyes and smiled. She would have loved to have had some pithy response but her mouth was full of duck and she enjoyed his play on words.

After they finished, Kade poured her a glass of brandy. He lit a fire, and they sat on twin leather recliners that faced the fireplace. "So, what's the deal with the note?" Sydney wanted to sit back and relax, but knew it was time to get down to business. The man had secrets, and she was going to find out what the hell was going on. "I know you're keeping something from me. We're partners. It's time to talk." She stared at the crackling fire, hoping it would make it easier for him to tell her if she wasn't looking at him.

"You know, we live a very long time. There is a specific vampire I suspect is involved in these murders. Luca found her scent at the Jennings' scene. I wasn't sure, but today, after the note, the apparition you saw…it's her."

Sydney knew she wasn't going to like whatever he had to say. But she needed the truth.

"Whatever this is, whoever this is, you can tell me. Evil is evil. Supernatural or human, all races can be touched by it."

Kade was aware that she was trying to make him feel better, but there was nothing that could do that when it came to Simone and what she had done to those girls. He stood, getting closer to the fireplace, with his back to Sydney.

"Simone, Simone Barret. She was turned in the 1800s. I found her on the streets and took her in. I was lonely, we…we were lovers."

Sydney cringed. Okay, so this was it. She pulled her knees up to her chest and kept still. What had she thought? That he was a virgin? Of course not. The man had lovers. He was a hot, sexy vampire. Logic told her that he'd probably had hundreds of lovers over the years. So why did she feel jealous all of a sudden?

"I have not had as many lovers as you would think." Kade turned around and gazed directly into Sydney's eyes as if he could read her thoughts. "Sure, I am a vampire, and it is no secret that we often have sex during feeding, but that is all it is, sex. Lovers have been few, a person to share my home and life with…but there has been no one I have ever been in love with. Simone, she was vulnerable and I…I was lonely. We helped each other. She had been trained in magic, Voodoo, and she betrayed me. When I found out she had captured and tortured several young women, I banished her. I should have killed her on the spot, but times were different back then. I thought if I banished her, that would be punishment enough, but it appears that I was wrong."

Sydney could not believe what she was hearing. He had a lover, an evil lover, who killed and tortured girls and now was coming back to kill more girls? *What the hell?* She wanted to get up and leave right then, but decided to hear him out. She knew that things were not always how they seemed. She stood up and walked over to Kade.

"So, what? Are you in love with her? Why is she here? To get you back? Why kill the girls? She's in this city?" She heard her voice getting louder and louder; so much for staying calm.

"I am over two hundred years old. You must understand that while I loved her, I am not nor was I ever *in love* with her; there is a difference. Why is she back? Revenge, I suspect. I banished her and maybe even broke her heart, if she had one. But if you could have seen what she did to those girls…I should have killed her." Kade blew out a breath. "And why here? My guess is Tristan."

"Tristan?"

"Yes, Tristan's sister, Katarina, was one of the tortured girls. He came to me seeking my help. He knew it was Simone who took the girls. He offered pack protection in exchange for finding his sister. It was how we met and later became friends. But Simone, she knew it was Tristan who told me. She may have come here seeking to stir up trouble in his territory. She would have known I would come to his aid eventually. What she didn't count on was that Tristan would be smart enough to recognize right away that a vampire was stirring up problems in his community, even before the first death occurred. He contacted me right away."

Sydney's thoughts were spinning. Simone was here in Philadelphia? How did she know where they were? Why did she come as a ghost?

"Okay, so lover girl has an ax to grind. She comes up here instead of New Orleans to get at Tristan? And to get back at you? Not buying that. I get that she's mad at Tristan for ratting her out to you. But she isn't from this area. You said she left the country. And what the hell is with the ghost? Why not just show up in person?"

"My best guess is that she is not here physically. She may have a mage or witch helping her. Possibly vampire or human minions, maybe both. Jennings belonged to her, there could be others."

"Nice trick, huh?" There was a reason Sydney didn't get involved with the supernatural, and this was it: human slaves, witchcraft, Voodoo. She felt she had heard enough for tonight. As much as she wanted to be with Kade, she had an overwhelming need to get home.

Kade approached Sydney, taking her hands in his. "Sydney, I have given this some thought, and I believe Simone is somewhere in New Orleans. Somehow…maybe through magic…she is projecting herself here. I need to go search for her there. I know you want to work this case, but things are going to get more dangerous. I need to keep you safe. I am going to talk with Tristan and leave tomorrow night."

She had felt the electric desire running up her arms and throughout her body, but at his words, she snatched her hands away from him. Who the hell was he to tell her that she had to get off the case? And he was leaving?

"Listen, Kade, if you want to jump a plane back to the bayou, be my guest, but I'm not getting off this case just because you think there could be danger. Danger is part of my job; I'm a big girl. A girl who happens to own a lot of guns and knows how to use them. There is no way I am just giving up this case while you go off chasing an old girlfriend, *so* not happening." She paused and glanced away. She couldn't just stand around and let innocent women be killed in her city, she had to help find the perpetrator. "Listen, I appreciate you telling me everything. I need to think on this…get some sleep. Ada may have run more trace, and I want to get down to the station tomorrow to talk it through with her. Where are my clothes?"

"Upstairs bathroom," he said, gesturing to the stairs. "I asked Sara to put your clean clothes in there when she finished with them."

"Thanks." Sydney set her glass on the table, avoiding eye contact as she went upstairs to get dressed. As she worked through the details of what Kade had told her, it wasn't making sense. She found it hard to believe this was as simple as a lover scorned. Why all the drama with the girls? The ritual? The tattoos? Something wasn't right. Maybe Simone did want revenge, but there was something else. Sydney wasn't sure what the missing puzzle piece was, but she certainly wasn't going to let Kade push her off the case.

Kade refrained from chasing after Sydney despite his desire to do so. Knowing that she was so close to his bedroom made him crazy. He wanted to kiss her full lips, taste her and make her his. Although doing so at this point would only draw attention to her, and that was not something he would do. She was already in enough danger. Tomorrow he would request that she be taken off the case. She'd be angry with him, but at least she'd be safe.

He had to get back to New Orleans and find Simone. He planned on questioning Ilsbeth to find out what Simone might be trying to accomplish with the oils and the girls. She was up to something, and he was going to find out what it was. This time she would not go unpunished.

While he was gone, he'd ask Tristan to keep an eye on Sydney, even though he hated that she might go to Tristan for more than friendship. It was killing him to know that Sydney and Tristan had been sexually involved, so asking the Alpha was not something he wanted to do, but he needed to try to keep her safe and he could trust Tristan to do that.

They rode in silence on the way back to Sydney's condo. She stared out the window, willing herself not to look at Kade. She struggled with her emotions, still aroused by their earlier encounter. Even though she knew it was irrational, a twinge of jealousy ate at her, as she thought about Simone. As the limo pulled up to her building, doubt crept into Sydney's mind. She sat still, unsure about leaving Kade. Her hesitation gave Kade the opportunity to move closer to her. She reached for the door handle, and Kade placed his hand on hers.

"Sydney love, after I take care of Simone, I will be back for you. We have unfinished business."

"Kade…I…" Her words trailed off as Kade pressed his lips to hers. Sydney kissed him back, slowly allowing him access. Kade reached around and held her by the nape of her neck, deepening the kiss. It was passionate, yet tender. Sydney knew she had to go. She shouldn't let herself get distracted by a man, but he tasted so good, and she wanted him here and now, inside her. She wanted more, but he was leaving. Coming to her senses, she reluctantly retreated from him, averting her gaze to the floor.

"Um...yeah...goodnight, Kade." Her hands shook as she pushed open the door. Flustered as she was, she still had enough wits about her to get up and out of the car on two feet. *Just keep on walking, girl.*

Chapter Eight

Sydney woke to the sounds of the city: beeping horns, trucks, yelling, and laughter. It didn't bother her, though; she was used to the constant buzz of urban, background noise. The cacophony meant Sydney was alive, and so was the city. Like the swashing hum of the ocean, it was soothing to her ears.

It was late afternoon when she heard her door buzzer go off. She doubted it would be Kade. While he had told her that he was old enough to go outside during the day, it weakened him. And besides, why would he come by her condo when he was returning to New Orleans? She wondered if he was packing and when he was leaving. She kept thinking of the kiss: hot, passionate, erotic. She'd fantasized about melting into his arms, making love to him right there in the back of the limo. It had taken every bit of self-control to pull away and go home without him. She had to force herself to remember she was irritated with him because he wanted her off the case, and that he was about to go chasing after a psycho ex.

She felt frustrated, wishing she could order him to stay, but then that was part of what attracted her to him. He was strong, authoritative, domineering. She laughed. What was wrong with her? She swore she would not pine over a guy, especially some bossy vamp. She had plenty of men on her dance card. *Whatever, Syd. Get over it. He's leaving anyway.*

Checking her security camera, she saw a man in a uniform holding what appeared to be a vase. He held up a name tag, indicating he was from Belle's Petals, a local flower shop. She clicked on the security panel, answering the call.

"Hello. Can I help you?"

"Yeah, I'm looking for Condo 225 B. Miss Willows."

"Okay, come on up," she said, buzzing him in.

There was a knock at the door. Sydney peered through the safety hole in her door and all she could see was red.

"Delivery for Miss Sydney Willows," he announced.

Sydney slowly opened the door, gasping at the sight. There were more roses than she had ever seen in her life.

"Oh my God, they're beautiful! Here, put them on the dining room table," she instructed.

As soon as she ushered the deliveryman into the hallway and locked her door, she ran over to inspect her gift. She was astonished at the five dozen long-stemmed red roses tastefully arranged in an enormous Tiffany crystal vase. She leaned into the flowers to sniff one of the buds, which smelled heavenly. Attached to a plastic holder was a small, red envelope. There was a single name written in calligraphy on it; *'Sydney'*. She gingerly opened the envelope, not wanting to accidentally tear the card. She pulled out the card and read it. 'Dearest Sydney, Your kiss is still on my mind. Be good while I'm gone love. I will return soon so we can finish what we started. Yours, Kade.'

Her first thought was that he'd mentioned the kiss. The hot, steamy kiss. He had not forgotten that. But 'be good'? Did the man seriously think a bunch of flowers, albeit an incredibly gorgeous and very expensive bunch of flowers, was going to convince her to leave the case willingly? She knew he wanted her safe, but it was her job to solve cases. She laughed at the irony. He infuriated her and aroused her all at once, and no matter how hard she'd tried, she couldn't stop thinking about him.

Sydney glanced at the time on her cell phone. Damn, it was almost six o'clock and she was late. Sydney had promised Adalee earlier in the day that she'd meet her at the station. She considered what Kade had told her about the danger they faced. She padded down the hallway to her guest bedroom. In the far corner, an antique cedar trunk sat against the wall. She flipped open the top, pulling out several blankets. Reaching inside, she retrieved two metallic cases. She laid them on the carpet and unzipped one.

Tristan had given her these as a birthday gift, having known that she loved weapons of all kinds. A dozen silver knives of different sizes lay sparkling, encased in foam liners. Sydney grinned as she ran her fingers across the flat side of the sharp blades. "Thank you, Tris. The gift that keeps on giving."

She moved to the second case, which held a small crossbow with a strap that could be slung over the shoulder, several wooden darts, and five large, wooden stakes. Sydney was well trained in how to use weapons to kill both humans and supernaturals, but she'd never imagined using them before now. Usually her Sig Sauer was more than enough to bring down a human, but whoever was killing these girls clearly was not in that category.

Sydney gathered the weapons she intended to use and put them next to her jeans and t-shirt. She planned to arm up before going on duty tonight. She tested the feel of the stake in her hand as she walked toward the bathroom, slashing it through the air. She would have no problem turning a vamp into ash, if needed. She shoved the stake in the pocket of her robe, hung it up on a hook, and went to turn the shower on. It was getting late, and she wanted to get going.

Sydney reveled in the hot spray of the shower. Feeling relaxed, she yearned to stay a little bit longer, but didn't have the time. As she shut off the water, she heard a hiss coming from outside her door. Grabbing a towel, she haphazardly dried herself, and threw on her robe. Someone was in the living room.

Did Kade stop by before leaving? No, Kade would never break into my condo. Who's here and how the fuck did they get in? Thinking quickly, she reached into the vanity cabinet, where she kept a spare gun for emergencies, and peeked out the door. Nothing. Maybe she was just being paranoid. She looked both ways down the hallway and saw no one. Quietly, she tiptoed down the hallway into the living room. Before she had a chance to look around the room, something rammed into her, sending her and her gun flying across the room.

She lost her bearings for a second, stunned from the hit. As pain tore through her body, it brought her back to focus, making her remember where she was. *What the hell was that?*

A huge man stood across the room. He had to be at least three hundred pounds, and was bald with a scar across his face.

"Hey, chica, you think you can kill me with that gun of yours? I got news for you, we vamps don't die easily. My Mistress is not pleased with you. She doesn't like that you have been sniffing around her mate."

Kade?

"Yes, that's right. My Mistress says you are a distraction, but maybe I will have you for myself before I kill you. You like big men? Oh yeah. I might break you in half, but man, it will be sweet." Did this sick vampire think he was going to rape her? Good fucking luck with that. Too bad, she had other plans for her attacker. *Keep him talking.*

"You always take orders from a girl?" She scrambled to cover herself, keeping her eyes on him as she used her peripheral vision to search for the gun.

"I only obey my Mistress. And you…you have angered the Mistress." He stalked toward her. "She wants you taken care of, but I didn't expect it was going to be so much fun. Your blood smells so sweet. I'm gonna have a nice little taste. How 'bout we play a game before you die?"

Sydney slowly scooted backward on her buttocks and hands, inching toward the kitchen. *Where's the damn gun?* She spied it over near the refrigerator. Then she remembered the stake in her pocket, but in order to use it, she would need him close to her. She pretended to move toward the gun, hoping he would think she was going for it.

"You are a bad little girl, aren't you? You think you gonna reach that gun? Stupid concha. You really think you can run from me? Maybe I will fuck you so hard that you can't walk before I drain you. I am gonna make you bleed. Oh yeah…you'll scream for me. I love to hear a girl scream," he snarled.

Sydney would die before she let him rape her. There was no way in hell he was taking her down without a blazing fight. She'd let him keep thinking she wanted the gun. She wasn't stupid. Sydney knew the gun might slow him down, but it wouldn't kill him. No, he'd just be even more pissed. She needed to use the stake; that was the only thing that would kill him. She just needed to get him closer so she could drive the stake into his heart. Closer without getting herself killed in the process.

"You want me, huh? How about you bring it. And while you're at it, I got a little message for that bitch of a Mistress who has you leashed." With those words, she fake-lunged for the gun, hoping to draw him to her.

In a flash, he flew across the room and grabbed her by the throat with one hand; he smashed her head several times against the refrigerator, jamming her up against the wall, leaving her feet dangling off the floor.

"I'm goin' to enjoy this. Nice and slow," he grunted, the spray of his saliva hitting her face. He weakened his grip around her neck and reached for his groin.

As he fumbled to unbutton his pants, Sydney quickly kneed him in the *cojones*, she'd remembered that much from Spanish.

"Puta." He slammed her head hard against the wall.

Sydney saw stars, her eyes teared as the pain sliced through her skull. Using every last bit of strength, she yanked the stake out of her pocket. Choking, she prepared to strike.

"Tell your Mistress," she spat, "tell that bitch that I said I'll see her in hell!" Sydney drove the stake up into his heart, and he instantly disintegrated into a pile of ash. Her body crashed to the floor as she lost consciousness.

Kade had argued with Luca on the way over to Sydney's. He knew his friend hated disagreeing with him, never wanting to appear disrespectful or insubordinate. Luca had always been respectful of Kade, having owed him his very life ten times over. But Kade knew Luca would never forget they'd discovered the girls in the barn. If Simone was back in the country, they both knew there was no time to stop and play kissy face with the nice detective. It wasn't as if he didn't understand Luca's point, but he wanted to say goodbye in person, alone.

When they pulled up to Sydney's condo, Kade insisted Luca stay in the limo. He went to push the buzzer, but no one answered. He rang Sydney's cell phone, but no one answered. *Where is she?* As someone opened the door to leave the building, Kade slid into the condo complex unnoticed. When he approached the door and knocked, it swung wide open. Tearing into her condo, he yelled for her and searched her apartment.

"Sydney! Where are you? Sydney!"

His heart sank as he entered the kitchen. Sydney was sprawled on the floor, wearing only a robe, which was spread wide open exposing her naked body. Next to her was a pile of ash. *Vampire.* Blood, he could smell blood, Sydney's blood. He could hear her heartbeat. She was alive. He knelt down and gently lifted her head, speaking to her softly.

"Sydney, love, can you hear me? Damn it to hell," he cursed when she didn't respond. Gently kissing her on the forehead, he thanked God she was still breathing. "It's going to be okay. I'm here now. I'll take care of you."

Needing to see where and how badly she was injured, he turned her head slightly to inspect her wound. A tiny cut bled from the back of her skull. Later she'd have a goose egg and a bad headache, but she'd be okay. Kade held a handkerchief to her wound. He shook his head, suspecting that Simone had sent a vampire to Philadelphia. And his girl had staked him well and dead. But if one vampire was here, more could be on their way. Kade needed the protection of his home and security team to keep her safe.

He had to get her out of here. Kade reached for his cell and texted Luca. They needed to collect Sydney, take her to the jet and get to New Orleans, now. Luca ran into the apartment, quickly finding Kade on the kitchen floor next to Sydney. Kade had forgotten her nudity. Glancing up to Luca then back to Sydney's naked body, he pulled her robe shut and covered her. She was his only.

"Grab a blanket and pillow from her bedroom and let's go. I'll carry her down," Kade told him.

Luca promptly did as he was asked. Within minutes, they'd all made it safely to the car and were on their way to the airport.

With Sydney in his arms, Kade gently brushed the hair away from her face, twirling a blond curl with his finger. He was overwhelmed with guilt. He'd known damn well what Simone was capable of, and he had left Sydney alone anyway. Kade's heart squeezed as he studied her face. She looked peaceful as she slept, vulnerable. He tucked the blanket around her neck, ensuring her warmth. Nothing would happen to her now that she was with him. She'd be spitting tacks when she woke up to find she was in New Orleans, but from now on, she wasn't getting to call the shots. Those days were over, and she would just need to deal with it. There was no way she was leaving him. She was his, and he would protect her with his life.

Chapter Nine

Sydney woke in a warm, soft bed that smelled of lilac. She stirred, her eyes fluttering as she was blinded by the light. She had a killer headache, and brought her hand to her head. *Where am I?* She wondered if she was dreaming. *Need Advil, now.* If she could only get out of bed and look for her pills, she'd be good. Sydney placed her palms flat against the bed and slowly pushed up. She felt soft but strong hands easing her back down into the bed as she heard Kade's smooth voice.

"Easy there, everything's okay. Just lie down, and I'll get you some water. You in pain, love?"

"Kade? Where am I?" Sydney was starting to panic as memories flashed into her head. She looked around, struggling to get her bearings. "Oh my God. A vampire. My condo."

"I know, but you're safe now..."

"Am I...in a plane? How the hell did I get in a plane? Where are we going?" She had traveled enough to recognize the hum of the engines.

Kade smiled. It didn't take her very long to try to control the situation. That was his girl. "Yes, we're in my plane, and we're on our way to my home in New Orleans. But you're safe now. The vampire who attacked you…not so much. You took care of him back there. He's dead."

Kade resisted asking details about her attack. He didn't want her to talk if she wasn't ready, but it was hard to ignore the fingerprint bruise marks that were starting to appear around her neck. She had been strangled.

"You have a small cut on the back of your head, but it's stopped bleeding. I iced it, but I can get you some more. Here, take these for your headache." He handed her pills and a bottle of water and sat down next to her. "Sydney, about what happened at the condo…I'm sorry."

"Considering that I can barely open my eyes, I'll forgive the fact that I'm in a plane heading to New Orleans. Couldn't you just take me to a hospital or something?" She was just too tired to fight, but when she regained her strength, Kade had some explaining to do. On the one hand, she would prefer to work the case in Philly, on the off chance more dead girls showed up. On the other hand, if Kade was going after Simone, she wanted to be there. Payback was a bitch, and after her little encounter with the sumo wrestler vamp, she was so up for it.

Sydney was starting to remember pieces of what had happened back in her home. It wasn't her first fight, but she'd be lying if she said it hadn't shaken her up a bit. She wasn't used to battling against vampires, or any other supernaturals, but she was a fighter and that was what counted. She lay her head back, closed her eyes, and took a deep breath. She glanced up at Kade.

"I was in the shower and heard a noise. He slammed me to the floor, before I had a chance to see who was in my condo. I always keep a spare gun hidden in the bathroom, and a few other places, you know, just in case. A girl can't be too careful. Anyway, the gun went flying into the kitchen. Before my shower, I'd been going through my weapons, and I was fooling around with a stake and shoved it in the pocket of my robe. But the gun I had in the bathroom…it didn't have silver bullets or anything, so I knew it wouldn't do much good. I played like I was going for the gun."

Sydney shook her head. She suddenly remembered the vampire saying something about Kade being his Mistress's mate. *Is Kade married? He said they were lovers, but did he marry her?* "He said Simone sent him to deal with me since, apparently, I was messing with her *mate*." She looked to Kade, hoping for a response. *He must be good at poker,* she thought, because he remained expressionless.

"He thought he could play a little before killing me. I don't even know how he got in…broke into my apartment." Her voice trailed off. She stared at the water bottle, unable to look at him when she said the words. "He…he was going to rape me. I staked him instead." She fought back tears, knowing how close she'd come to being violated, killed. Kade was about to interrupt, but she held up her hand, preventing him from speaking. "Kade, please. Don't say anything. You warned me. I'm a big girl who makes her own decisions. Rape, violence, it's not new to me. Every day this happens…just not to me."

Kade didn't want to show emotion, lest he freak the hell out right in front of Sydney. He was so furious that another vampire had dared to lay a hand on her that he wanted to break something. But he resisted, aware that any further violence would only demonstrate to Sydney what monsters vampires were. Now was not the time. What she needed was comfort. He needed to calm her, soothe her. He decided to save the anger, to harness it for when he obliterated his enemy. Simone, and whoever else was helping her, would pay dearly for hurting Sydney. As incensed as he was, he needed to help her heal, physically and emotionally.

He moved to lie down beside her, and held her in his arms, cradling her against his chest. Instead of fighting him, Sydney laid her head across his chest and allowed him to hold her, to care for her.

"Kade, I'm sorry. You need to know that this is who I am. I'm a fighter. And what just happened…I just can't forget it. I plan on finding this bitch and taking her out. The dead girls, and now this. I have a feeling that it'll only continue. Killers like Simone, they don't usually stop. They hone their craft, believing they're smarter than the cops, but we usually get them. She'll make a mistake, something…I sure as hell hope we get some clues about where she is down in New Orleans."

Kade kissed the top of her head. His heart swelled at his brave warrior's words. She'd just been attacked, and here she was ready to get back in the fight. He knew that telling her 'no' would be useless. He would put a security detail on her once they got home. *Home? His home. Their home.* He would protect her, so this never happened again. No matter how tough she thought she was, a vampire could easily kill her. She had gotten lucky back in the condo. She wasn't even trained to fight with vampires; a few stakes didn't make a human safe.

As he held her, Kade felt Sydney start to doze off to sleep and he considered how right it felt to have her in his arms. He heard a knock at the cabin door.

"Come in," he said. Kade continued to lie motionless in the bed with Sydney, unwilling to disturb her. He wasn't ready to let her go yet.

Luca stepped into the bedroom and raised an eyebrow at him. Kade knew his friend was wary of the woman he'd brought into their lives. Luca didn't trust humans, believing they were weak, easily broken.

"Kade, we're landing in about thirty minutes. How's the detective?"

"She'll be fine tomorrow. Right now, she needs rest. I will make sure she sleeps so she heals. Is security in place for when we land?"

"Yes, it's all in place. Etienne and Xavier are meeting us at the airport to help with the transfer. Dominique is at the compound securing things."

"Thanks, tell Dom that I'll need her help with Sydney when we get there. Make sure they all know she is arriving. Also, make sure they understand that she is under my protection and must not be touched. Am I clear?" Kade knew the other vampires might feel tempted with a new human on site. While they often had human donors and staff work at the compound, he did not want anyone to think she was available for their needs. She was his.

"Yes, it will all be ready. Do you need help with Miss Willows?"

"No thanks, I've got her. Just make sure Etienne and Xavier are ready to go. I don't want to waste time at the airport. Simone could have minions anywhere at this point. We need to get to a safe location. Any word from Ilsbeth?"

"Yes, she's been in seclusion with her coven. I summoned her to the compound, and she's expected to arrive tomorrow."

"Thanks. We'll need her assistance locating Simone. We also need to get details on what kind of magic is being used…why the girls were killed in the manner they were. Something is off."

As Luca left, Kade pulled the blanket up over Sydney's shoulders. He sighed, relieved that they'd soon be back in New Orleans. He could feel his power increasing, thrumming throughout his body as they got closer to the city. He breathed in the scent of the fragile woman who lay against his chest. He swore that no one was going to hurt Sydney again and live to talk about it.

Chapter Ten

Sydney woke in the middle of the night, finding herself naked in a strange bed. *Nice. This is turning out to be a fine damn week.* Not that she generally had a problem with nudity, but it was a little disconcerting to know someone had undressed her somewhere between thirty thousand feet and here…wherever 'here' was. She guessed she was at Kade's house…well, she sure as hell hoped that was where she was. She scanned her surroundings, surprised by the feminine décor. The violet bedroom was decorated with cream, shabby-chic furniture. If she hadn't known better, she would have thought she was in a Vermont bed and breakfast.

"Hey, Sunshine, 'bout time you woke up. My ass is getting sore sitting here playing nursemaid."

Sydney caught sight of a beautiful, tall, red-haired woman sitting in a large white leather chair.

"Nursemaid? Really? Okay, number one, I'm fine." Sydney winced as she sat up in bed, covering her chest with the sheet. She felt like shit, but she wasn't about to let

'Ginger' think that. The stranger's unearthly beauty and pale skin led her to surmise that her companion was a vampire. *Show no fear.* "Number two, where's Kade?"

"Yeah, okay. Well, Kade says you are not fine. And with Simone looking for your pretty little ass, I would be a little more grateful for a personal guard." The woman walked across the room, opened a large wardrobe, and held up a dress, giving Sydney a cold smile. "I guessed your size and brought over some clothes. Your purse is in the bathroom. Luca brought it…thought you might need it. Shoes are in the closet. As for Kade, he should be here soon. So you might as well know that you really don't look so great. Might want to go take a shower." She put the dress back into the wardrobe and opened another door. "Bathroom's here. Robe and slippers are in there too. Just like the freakin' Hilton, huh? So, guess that's about it. As soon as Kade gets here, I'm done. Xavier will be on next."

Sydney had had just about enough of the welcome speech. She felt as though she was in a bad horror movie.

"Thanks for the tour. But for the record, while it's true that Simone sent someone to attack me, I don't need a guard. You can ask the last vamp…oh, that's right, you can't, because he's now a pile of ash." Sydney sat up straighter, trying to appear as if she wasn't in pain. "I'm not planning on staying here long, but I appreciate the clothes."

The strange woman zipped across the room and was face to face with Sydney within seconds.

"Sydney, darling, I work for Kade, not you. If he says you need a guard, you get one. If you have a problem with that, take it up with Kade. I follow orders…that's how this goes. And if you like living, human, you should accept it." And with that, she strode out of the room and slammed the door.

Sydney shrugged, irritated with the encounter and left wondering what the stranger's relationship to Kade was. Her priorities at the moment were getting showered and fed. After that, she was leaving. There was no way in hell she was spending her days living in a house full of vampires. She recalled the compassionate way Kade had tenderly held her on the plane. There was no denying the desire he'd awakened inside her, but she wanted no part of his world. Living in his home wasn't an option. She reasoned that she could get a room at the Hotel Monteleone and work with Kade from there. She was willing to continue her partnership with him until they found Simone, or another dead girl showed up in Philly.

Sydney's thoughts moved to the case. There was so much to do. She needed to call into her office, let them know what happened. Panicked, she remembered that she had no weapons with her. *Where is my gun?* She walked over to the wardrobe and retrieved her purse, thankful that Kade's brooding friend had thought to bring it. Well, at least something had gone right; wallet, cell and charger were there, but no gun. Her weapons, that she'd so carefully prepared, were back in her condo. She felt naked, and it had nothing to do with her nudity. She clicked through her contacts and pressed the call button for Tristan. He picked up.

"Tristan! Thank God."

"Hey, Sydney. You okay? Kade called me and told me about the vampire. Listen, Syd…I need to talk to you." There was a period of silence as if he was seeking the right words. "Kade said that he told you everything about Simone. I know I should have told you, but I was just hoping that it wasn't her."

"Don't worry about it. I know you guys have a connection to her. But Tristan, this is just another killer. We'll get her."

"But, that's just it. You don't know what she's capable of…what she did. Aw hell. I just don't want to see you hurt. Before you even say it, I know it's your job to protect people, but there are forces that could easily kill you. You're human. She got my sister, and she was a strong wolf. If you could have seen what she did to those girls…you just need to be extra careful on this case." He sounded exasperated. "Look, I'm coming down there. My brother, Marcel, is the Alpha in the region, and before you say anything, which I know you will, don't argue. It's not negotiable."

"Okay, Tristan. I get it. Simone - evil vampire. Me - weak human." She rolled her eyes. *Men.* "I won't argue…well, not now anyway. But I need a favor. I need you to stop by my place and bring my weapons. You know, the special gifts you gave me a few years ago. I also need my guns. I left them in the condo. I might need them down here."

"Okay Syd. I'll bring the weapons, but please just stay with Kade until I get down there. You'll be safe with him at his compound. We can talk about next steps when I arrive."

"Okay, Tris, call me when you get down here. Thanks for bringing my stuff."

As she hung up, she sighed, resigned to the fact that it was going to be even more difficult working with both Kade and Tristan. Both men, the Alpha and vampire, thought they could boss her around. It was their nature to dominate, but it wouldn't deter her from her task. It might be a challenge to navigate around their domineering ways, but she was determined to catch the killer.

After taking a shower, Sydney gingerly brushed out her hair, still feeling the goose egg on the back of her head. At least the headache was gone. She dressed in a pair of black leggings and pink workout top, both of which clung to her figure, revealing a hint of cleavage. Her stomach growled. She recalled eating dinner with Kade, but she wondered what nourishment, if any, they kept in their own homes. She cringed, thinking about what they really ate: people. She wasn't stupid. She knew that human donors, both women and men, served themselves up on platters at

Eden, but Sydney had never witnessed a 'feeding'. And in a house full of vampires, she didn't plan on offering herself. *Just play it cool, get your weapons, and you'll get a hotel room in the French Quarter. You'll be fine.*

Deciding not to wait for Kade, she ventured out in search of food. A hand gently blocked her way as she took her first step out of her room. She looked up to see a good-looking, African American man smiling down at her. He must have been at least six-five, lean and strong. He was dressed in casual black sweatpants and a white sleeveless, spandex shirt that showed every hard line of the muscles in his arms. He was statuesque and reminded her of a Greek god.

"Where do you think you're going without me, cher?" He grinned knowingly.

Sydney smiled back. She didn't know this man, but her gut told her that he had good intentions. "I take it that you're Xavier? Hi there, I'm Sydney Willows, Detective Sydney Willows. Nice to meet you."

"Ah, so very nice to meet you." He reached for her hand and kissed the top of it. "Yes, I'm Xavier. I've been assigned to accompany you during your stay at the Issacson Estate. I'm a good friend of Kade's, and we do intend to keep you safe." He let go of her hand.

Okay, here we go again with the chivalrous hand kissing; so polite, so deadly. Sydney sensed he was a nice guy, so she decided just to go with the flow, no use fighting with the hunky, vampire guard. She would save her energy and deal with Kade once she found him. "Xavier, I really need something to eat." She laughed a little. "You know, like human food. Also, I really need to talk with Kade."

"This is N'awlins, girl. You kidding? We've got plenty of food." He laughed as if she was crazy. "Come on, you must be famished after your ordeal. We heard all about it, tough girl you are."

They made their way to the kitchen table where an older woman served bread, eggs and andouille. Sydney was pleasantly surprised that they had a human cook in the house. As she ate her meal, enjoying her hot, chicory coffee, she wondered exactly how many people lived here. She talked with Xavier and learned that the mansion was located in the Garden District. She was pleased to learn that she was in a place where she could easily get to the French Quarter without needing directions. On one of her previous trips to the city, she had stayed in a lavish bed and breakfast in the area and knew exactly where she was.

Xavier told her how he'd come to know Kade in the year of 1868. His father was of Acadian descent and married his mother, who was an African American freed slave. He grew up in Lafayette Parish on the bayou, learning to fish and trap as his forefathers had done. Around his twenty-eighth birthday, he was attacked by the Southern Cross KKK and left to die in a field. As he struggled for his last breath, Kade had found and turned him. Soon after, he'd come to live with Kade, Luca and the others. He was a loyal friend to Kade and currently worked for him as a technology specialist.

After she finished eating, Sydney explored the lower level of the home, discovering a large sunroom, which was filled with orchids, lilies, and various other flowers. Someone had designed this room as if it were an indoor garden. Moonlight poured into it through glass walls, and she found herself resting in a large, overstuffed chair. Xavier had told her she could wait there for Kade and that he would be nearby if she needed his assistance. Even though she thought there were other vampires living in this home, the house was curiously quiet. All she heard was the rhythmic serenade of the cicadas.

A familiar tingle danced up her spine, and Sydney quickly turned her head, aware of his presence. *Kade.* She blinked, and as if by magic, he stood in front of her. Seeing him again, her stomach filled with butterflies. Her breath caught as he reached for her, taking her hands in his, bringing her to her feet. Face to face, mere inches apart, this was the first time she would really get to talk to him since he held her in the bed on the plane…since *the kiss.* She wanted to be mad at him for bringing her down here, yet her body reacted as he placed a chaste kiss to her lips. Aroused, her nipples hardened in anticipation of his touch. She wanted more, but it was clear he wasn't about to give it to her yet. Kade sighed, and sat down on the ottoman. Sydney followed, resting back down into her chair. He placed his hands on her knees.

"Sydney, love, so sorry to have left you alone for the past hour. I have much business to catch up on since I've been to Philadelphia. Please forgive me." He appeared relaxed, as if his home was the one place they'd be safe.

"Thanks again for getting me out of the condo," she began, her voice soft. Sydney found it impossible to keep from touching him as she reached for his hands. "As much as I love New Orleans, this was not how I expected to return. I…I don't think it's a good idea that I stay here in your home. It makes me really nervous…all these vampires roaming around your house. Besides, I know this city. I'd be okay on my own in a hotel. I don't know it as well as I know Philly, but I can get around, and we can still work together. I talked to Tristan this morning and…"

Kade removed his hands from hers, stood, and walked across the room. He turned to her, astonished that she'd said she was leaving. Unbelievable. This woman had been in his home for less than twenty-four hours and was thinking about leaving already. And damn it all, she'd talked to Tristan about it. Sure, Tristan was a good friend, but he would not have her going to another man for protection, no fucking way. It was time he set her straight.

"Sydney, I'm not sure what you talked to Tristan about, but while you are in my city, in my home, you will abide by my rules. We will catch Simone together, but you will do this my way. I am completely serious. And before you open that lovely mouth of yours, I will not have any arguments about it. I've already called your captain and given him my assessment of what happened back at your condo. There is agreement between P-CAP and your department that you are here on a consultation basis only. That means no leaving this house without my knowledge and protection from me or someone from my security team. On the case, I tell you what to do and when to do it. I will not have you getting yourself killed while you are here."

Kade blew out a breath, steaming with anger and arousal. *That lovely little mouth*; he wanted to kiss it, to make love to it, to feel himself surrounded by her lips. But she wouldn't listen to reason, and he'd had enough of this 'I am a cop' nonsense. Simone would hang her from her wrists and skin her alive…he'd seen her do it before. They could work the case together, but Kade refused to let Sydney go it alone anymore.

"How dare you go and talk to my captain without my knowledge!" she yelled, jumping to her feet. She began to pace. "You don't get to tell me when to leave this house! I'm not waiting around while you go off and do business, or whatever you do. I'm the detective. You are…you are…I don't even know what the hell you are. I sure as shit know that you aren't a freakin' detective!"

Kade frowned. She was the most stubborn woman on the face of the earth. She was hot, sexy, beautiful, and damn hardheaded.

"I run this city, love. All of the supernatural activity in this town, including any P-CAP investigations, only happen with my approval and permission. That is all you need to know about my business. I am the law in New

Orleans." He moved toward her, closing the distance. "So unless you'd like to be tied to a bed, and believe me, I would love to have you tied to mine, you had better follow my rules."

"Okay. Fine. No going out on investigations without you, but I'm not staying in a house full of vampires. This just isn't practical or safe. I'm not going to end up a happy meal because someone got the munchies. And I'm not going to waste my time sitting around here while you do business. Where you go, I go. We work this case, get the bad guy, and I go home. Seriously, I can't stay forever, so I want to make the most of my time."

Finally, capitulation.

"Sydney, I want you to know that I admire your independence and tenacity. I just want to keep you safe. I want all my people safe." Kade didn't want her to know how deeply he was starting to care about her. He was pissed as hell knowing that she'd called Tristan instead of talking to him first. Hell, he wasn't sure he even liked that he was so captivated by her. After all, he'd been alone for a few centuries now. He didn't lack for female attention, and he had enough to keep him busy in life without complications. And Sydney was a huge complication. Yet he could not deny that he was very much connected to her and she to him. He gave a small smile as she backed away from him, making her way back into her chair. It was as if he could almost see the wheels spinning in her head.

Sydney pulled her legs up underneath her, glancing up toward her dominant but ever so sexy vampire, feeling conflicted about her situation. *Tied to his bed? Duly noted and under consideration.* She hated that she was starting to care about him, hoping that he'd kiss her again. He acted like he cared about her, like he wanted her, but she questioned his motivation. Was he making her stay here, because he was some kind of a control freak? After all, he didn't just want to keep her safe…no, he'd said that he wanted to keep everyone safe. And he hadn't kissed her either. It upset her to think about how disappointed she'd be if he really was just trying to manipulate her. It wasn't as if she hadn't accepted long ago that she would spend her life alone. That was how she wanted it. Sydney averted her gaze, attempting once again to pull up her emotional wall, nice and high.

"Don't worry about stroking my ego, Kade. I get it, you are the protector, and I am the consultant. No problem. So what's next? Where do *we* find Simone?"

As she was about to make a suggestion, Luca entered the room. "Kade." He nodded and turned to Sydney. "Sydney. I've got a lead on Simone. There's been rumblings that she was seen collecting donors downtown at Sangre Dulce."

"Sangre Dulce?" Sydney asked.

"Sangre Dulce is a local club specializing in…how would you say?" Luca looked over to Kade, clearly hoping for some assistance. Finding none, he continued. "It is a fetish club. S&M. Caters to the supernaturals and humans alike. If Simone was looking for someone to torture, she could easily find a submissive there who would go off with her. I talked to Miguel, the owner, and he said a bartender reported that a woman who looked like Simone was in the club well over a month ago. We cannot be certain it was her, but we could ask around. And Kade, if we do go to Sangre Dulce, I would advise against taking the human."

Sydney wanted to smack Luca. Why did he always have to be such a condescending ass? "Hello? Luca? That human is right here. I already established with Kade that we're going together."

"Kade, she serves no purpose on this trip," Luca commented, stone-faced. "Simone will have spies, and they will see her. And others…vampires…they'll view her as available. She is not marked, nor claimed, nor does she work for us. They will recognize her as an outsider. It's not wise to bring her. I must insist that you reconsider."

"Luca, your concern is taken under advisement. Effective immediately, Miss Sydney Willows is my employee." Sydney shot him a look of surprise. "I'm pleased to introduce my new Director of Security. She's in charge of my Philadelphia operations and arrived yesterday to learn from you about security operations in New Orleans. She is known to accompany me to events. After introductions to Miguel, no one will touch her."

"But how will she fit in? They'll sense she does not belong. It'll be bad enough that we have no business that would even call us there."

"What if we were there for some kind of inspection? If it's true that Kade approves all activities in this town, could we tell Miguel we were there because of a complaint? Cops do it all the time for other businesses when we suspect criminal activity. Or, we could just say I was there to see New Orleans. Lord knows there are plenty of freaky things going on in this city. What's a little S&M in this town? Seriously you two…have you ever been to Bourbon Street on Halloween? Everyone lets their freak flag fly."

Kade burst out laughing. A hearty, sexy laugh that made Sydney want to let her freak flag fly right there, right then, on the floor with him.

"You bring up a good point. But going in under the guise of an inspection will only put people off. You must understand that the people who frequent this club, go there for privacy. Any complaints would be handled directly by Miguel. We don't want people on the defensive. But if we go in as mere patrons? A date even? Now that would work, and I am more than willing to get freaky with you." Kade smiled at Luca who he could tell had resigned himself to the fact that they were taking the human. He knew that Luca felt indifferent towards her, having learned long ago that humans simply could not be trusted. They both knew that Simone was dangerous. If she went after Sydney, it would put them all at risk. He didn't like the fact that Voodoo and magic were involved either. They needed Ilsbeth.

"Kade, I need to get out tomorrow. And before you say no, which I know is coming, I need clothes and shoes. This has got to be believable. I need to look like the kind of girl who is looking for a little adventure, if you know what I mean. These sweats aren't going to cut it."

"Okay, you'll go shopping in the morning," he began. Kade knew she was correct, but she could not go alone. Unfortunately, he had a few meetings that he must attend. "But you go with someone. I will send Xavier with you. Even though vampires have weakened powers during daylight, Simone could be out looking for you, or have human minions spying about."

"I'll need a few weapons too: stakes, crossbow. Tristan is bringing my gear, but he may not be down before we leave tomorrow night."

"They will not allow weapons into the club. For your shopping trip tomorrow, Luca will give you a gun with silver bullets and a few stakes that you can easily stash in your purse." Kade approached her and sat on the ottoman. "Tomorrow night, we'll need to give you a few *special accessories* before we leave…undetectable weapons that you can wear into the club. You should be safe with us, but should you have any issues, you'll have the protection you need."

After Luca had left them alone, Kade's eyes met Sydney's. She'd gone silent, yet had adjusted her legs so that they were inches from his. For several seconds, they gazed upon each other. His hand touched her knee. When she didn't protest, his palm glided up her thigh until he'd captured her hand. Standing, he brought her up to him, so that they stood close, his hand on her waist.

"Sydney, I know you're mad that I called your boss. But if you want to stay on the case, we need to do this my way. I'm sorry I have to put so many restrictions in place. We'll go downtown tomorrow night and get more information about Simone's whereabouts. I promise that this will be over soon."

Sydney's body came alive as she felt the strength of his hands on her. She didn't want to forgive him so quickly for bossing her around, but my God, she yearned for his touch. Although she'd questioned what he'd done, she found herself justifying it. Deep down, she believed that he'd meant what he'd said; he'd keep her safe too. For so long, she'd had no one, but for now, it felt like she had him. Her body responded to his as she allowed the palms of her hands to lie flat on his chest. She wanted to know what it would be like to be flesh to flesh with him, tasting him.

He leaned into her and held her tight against his chest. She breathed in his clean masculine scent, allowing herself to imagine what it would be like to have him inside her. A rush of heat caused her sex to ache. He looked down at her wantonly, searching her eyes for permission.

"Kade, this thing between us…I don't know what to think…" She didn't get a chance to finish her thoughts.

"Don't think, Sydney, just feel." Kade brought his mouth to hers and she opened for him, allowing him to sweep his tongue into, over and around hers. He was demanding, passionate.

Kade was tired of waiting. He wanted this human woman so badly, and he was finding it difficult to make excuses for why he shouldn't just take her. Sydney moaned and kept pace with him as she ran her fingers through his hair, possessively pulling his head down to meet hers.

Refusing her the control she sought, Kade slowly pushed her back up against the wall and held her hands above her head with one of his. With the other, he pushed up her shirt, feeling the soft skin of her belly, and then slid his hand up, slowly cupping her breast. Shoving up her bra, he freed her breast from its confines. Kade's breath quickened, overwhelmed with excitement that he'd finally touched her silky peaks. He tore his mouth away from hers, lowered his head to her ripe flesh and licked her rosy tip.

Sydney shivered and groaned under his touch, submitting to his need to dominate. She wanted to be dominated by him; he was so strong, intoxicating.

"Kade, yes, please," Sydney begged, unable to keep silent in the throes of their passion.

Kade sucked the nipple harder until Sydney felt a twinge of pain, then pleasure. She couldn't believe she was letting him do this to her, but she felt helpless to stop him. The desire she felt overrode any sense of logic she had. He pushed up the other side of her bra and gave her other hardened peak equal attention. As he released her hands, she held onto his shoulders for dear life as he made love to her breasts.

"I want you so much, Kade," she confessed. "Please, don't stop."

The sound of clicking heels on the floor broke her concentration. Dazed and swollen-lipped, she opened her eyes to see the redheaded vampire watching her and Kade. *Voyeur much?* Refusing to be intimidated, Sydney glared at her. Interrupted by the intrusion, Kade slowly lowered Sydney's shirt.

"Dominique, you must learn to knock," he growled. Irritated, he blew out a breath. "This is my home, not the office. And as you can see, I am quite busy. What do you want?"

"Kade darling, I just came by to see how things were going with your lovely human."

"As you can see, she is quite well. Now it's getting late, anything else?"

"Yes, Ilsbeth contacted Luca. He asked me to tell you. She's coming in to see you tomorrow night before we go to the club. She's nervous about coming here, so Luca and I will go to her coven, secure her and bring her in safely. We should be here around seven. I would like to discuss the details, if you have time."

Sydney felt oddly out of place during this discussion. Instead of getting pushed out of the conversation, she decided to remove herself. She was tired again anyway and needed a break from the vampires who seemed to be crawling everywhere in this house.

"Kade, uh, I think I am going to head upstairs. I wanna give Ada a call." She placed a kiss to his cheek and pulled away from him.

"Okay, love. Oh and Sydney, remember our discussion earlier. No running off without me," he warned.

Sydney smiled without necessarily agreeing and began to leave. As she passed Dominique, she purposefully avoided eye contact. She wasn't sure what kind of relationship Kade had with her, but that woman irritated Sydney. Dominique had made it apparent that she wasn't going to go out of her way to make Sydney comfortable. If anything, Sydney suspected that she'd interrupted them on purpose. As she rounded the corner, she caught Kade's warm smile. Unconsciously, she brought her fingers to her lips, his kiss still seared on them. She closed her eyes briefly, leaving the room. Sydney wasn't sure how she and Kade would ever have a relationship. It seemed impossible. Yet, with the sweet taste of him fresh in her mind, she could feel her heart melting.

Chapter Eleven

Sydney locked the door to her bedroom and began searching for her phone. Logically, she knew a locked door was not enough to keep a vampire out of her room, but it gave her a small comfort knowing she wouldn't make it easy for them. Even though no one had tried to bite her yet, strange vampires milling about the house made her a little nervous. Finally locating her cell in her purse, she dialed Adalee at the lab. Sydney wanted to get the latest autopsy results and hoped they'd get an additional clue to help stop the killings.

"Hi ya, Sydney girl," Adalee said cheerfully as she picked up on the other end.

"Hey, Ada, sorry I didn't make it into the station last night."

"Yes, I heard all about it. And are you just gonna act like you aren't down in New Orleans with that fine piece of vampire who you've been working with? I mean really…do tell. I heard from the captain that you're down there with him. And what did he call it? Oh yeah, consulting? Is that what they call it these days? I'd like a consulting job in a romantic city with a hot hunk of vampire goodness." Sydney could hear Adalee laughing hard on the other end of the line.

"Very funny. But seriously, I nearly got killed back in my condo, and Kade brought me down here to…ugh…help him. I'm the detective on this case. So yeah, I am consulting, that's it."

"Whatever you say, Syd. You just keep telling yourself that, okay?" Adalee chuckled. "Now listen, I'm glad you finally called in. Got some new information on the second girl. Same cause of death, exsanguination. Again, no marks indicating fangs. No sexual assault either. This girl was tortured though. Looks like someone was using her for a pincushion, and I'm not talking tiny push pins either." There was a pregnant pause before she continued. "Syd, I've never seen anything like this. I can't be sure what made these holes, but I'm guessing right now maybe knitting needles or possibly large surgical needles. There are two holes in the chest region, two in the stomach, and one behind the ear. It looks like these were inflicted antemortem."

"The girl was alive during it. Anything else?"

"Yeah, we found traces of lemongrass oil again on the head and also on the wrists. Also, there were traces of human hair and hemp embedded in her wrists. Syd, I'm not sure what's going on down there but the person who's doing this…it's downright disturbing." Adalee sounded disgusted.

"I know, Ada. Isn't this some shit? Kade thinks he knows who's doing this. We're following a lead tomorrow night, so hopefully that will yield some good results. In the meantime, text or call me with any updates. Thanks."

"You take care, Syd. Talk to you soon. And hope you enjoy your…um…consulting gig," Adalee teased.

Sydney considered getting some more sleep after the call, but then she thought she'd better go tell Kade about what Adalee had discovered. Why the hell did the killer use needles on the girl? It had to be related to Voodoo. Was Simone making some kind of human Voodoo doll? Sydney didn't know the least bit about Voodoo dolls except for the fact they sold the little trinkets in the tourist shops. She knew a little bit about the background of Marie Laveau, the renowned Voodoo priestess of New Orleans. Sydney and a friend had once taken a walking "Voodoo tour" on one of her many vacations to the Big Easy, and they'd toured a Voodoo museum, even visited the mausoleum where Marie Laveau was buried. But aside from the legends, she was no expert on the subject and suspected Kade would have answers.

Leaving her room and quietly descending the large, spiral staircase, Sydney heard familiar voices in the great room. As she entered, Kade, Luca, Xavier, Etienne, and Dominique were sitting around discussing the witch. *No time like the present to interrupt the family fun.* She thought about being serious, all vampire-like, but then decided that flippant was more her style.

"Hey guys. Forget to invite the human to the party?" They all looked up at her at once as if she had three heads. Maybe serious would have been the best approach, grumpy vampires.

"Okay, guess the party is over. I have some news, if you're interested." Not waiting for an invitation, Sydney deliberately sat next to Luca, knowing it would irritate him. He seemed to have a stick up his ass, and she was about to dislodge it. "Hey, Luca, how's it shaking? What, no big hello for me?" She smiled up at him, knowing he was itching to remove her from his side.

Kade grinned in response to her antics.

"Sydney love, please refrain from poking the bear." Both Xavier and Dominique laughed.

Okay, things were loosening up a bit…at least with a couple of these vamps. Sydney decided to keep pushing.

"Let's play a game, Luca. You show me yours, I'll show you mine."

As Luca lifted one corner of his mouth, suppressing a grin, Sydney sensed that his hard exterior was showing a few cracks.

"I guess as long as Kade doesn't mind, I have no problem showing you mine," he replied, eyeing his friend.

"As if half this town hasn't seen it," Dominique snorted.

"We were just discussing Ilsbeth. It appears that instead of Luca and Dominique escorting her tomorrow night, she will be arriving within the hour with her own escort. Ilsbeth said she has important information for us, and feels it is a bit of an emergency. I would like you to meet her so you can review the evidence that was found on the two victims. She should be here soon," Kade told her. He gave her a smile. "And Sydney..."

"Yes?"

"Just so we're clear we understand each other. In my home, should you decide to share, you will only be showing *yours* to me."

Sydney's cheeks heated, and she resisted bringing her hands to her face. Kade's words were not lost on her. *Possessive? Jealous? Maybe I've misread what he said? Definitely not.* She had almost made love to him earlier in the sunroom, and he knew damn well that she wanted to show him...well, everything. But he'd had no problem dismissing her upstairs in lieu of Dominique and business.

"Kade, you had the opportunity a few hours ago to see all of mine, and if you recall, you chose business," she said, referring to Dominque. "Luca on the other hand, needs some loosening up."

Sydney patted Luca's thigh and stood up. She considered pretending like she was going to remove her clothes just to tease him a bit more, but thought better of it. Kade did not look amused. She glanced at Luca to find him actually smiling at her.

"Okay, here it is." With one hand on her hip, she rubbed her forehead with the other hand, pushing a stray hair out of her face. "Ada said the last vic had the same hemp and human hair fibers and same lemongrass oil on her. This time, there were no whip marks on the body.

But what is really sick is that someone was playing human Voodoo doll with this girl. She had five holes in her. Ada thinks they were made with knitting or surgical needles. To be honest, they are not really sure yet what made the holes. And to top off the shit sandwich, all the needles were inserted antemortem."

As Sydney observed their expressions, she could tell the vampires appeared to know something she didn't. Before she got a chance to ask and insist that they get a Voodoo expert in on the case, the doorbell rang. The witch was here.

As Ilsbeth entered the room, the air lightened; it was almost dizzying. Sydney was surprised by the witch's nearly ethereal arrival, her escort trailing behind. Ilsbeth's long, platinum hair flowed well below her waist, accentuating her petite figure. She was dressed in a purple velvet blouse that was complemented by a fitted, black leather jacket and pants. Ilsbeth took Kade's hand as they headed toward the dining room. She seated herself at the head of the table, as if she'd been there before, gesturing to Sydney to sit beside her.

Not sure about witch etiquette, Sydney followed Ilsbeth's nonverbal cue and sat down next to her. She couldn't help but admire the woman's deep violet eyes. Sydney was not sure what she'd thought a witch would look like, but she certainly wasn't expecting this. Maybe a green nose and a broomstick? No, but she was expecting someone a little scarier looking, certainly older. But Ilsbeth was anything but scary, or old. She looked barely twenty-one years old, with an angelic face.

Once everyone was seated at the table, Ilsbeth spoke a protection prayer. Sydney guessed it was your basic, 'keep evil spirits out of this house' prayer, from what she could tell. Hell, she wasn't even sure she believed in witchcraft mojo, but in order to catch the killer, she would give angel girl the benefit of the doubt. Sydney was getting anxious, but could tell that the witch was running the show. All the vampires at the table stayed silent as they listened to Ilsbeth finish her prayer.

Sydney nearly jumped out of her seat as Ilsbeth's eyes flew open and all the candles on the table and along the shelves in the room flared to life. *Okay, nice trick.* She glanced at Sydney and then to Kade.

"My dearest friends, there is a great evil in our city. She may have initially come for you, Kade, but now she is here for all of us. I felt it a week ago when I was working. It was a rumbling at first, but now there is a constant state of unease. The wind of evil has blown throughout our streets. Something bad is coming for all of us…something that wants to take over this city. I will help if I can, Kade, but I must know why this evil woman is here for you."

Kade recounted the story of Simone to Ilsbeth, including her banishment and the recent killings in Philadelphia. Sydney filled in the missing pieces with regards to the oil, the rope fibers, and needle marks. Ilsbeth listened carefully before speaking with great seriousness.

"If all that you told me is true, there must be someone helping Simone, a witch or mage perhaps, or possibly a Voodoo priestess. Simone may have some of this knowledge, but a practitioner would need supplies to help to carry out these killings and spells. It is possible that Simone is experimenting…using a living girl as a Voodoo doll. She seeks the assistance of evil spirits to help her with her goals." Ilsbeth stared deep into Kade's eyes. "Kade, Simone may have started off with a simple goal of revenge, but the darkness of her practices points to a monumental goal, perhaps to have power…power over all the supernaturals in the city. If her experiment showed any promise the first time, she'll kill again until she takes over this town."

"Thank you for your insight, Ilsbeth. As always, you bring profound knowledge and perspective to the problems we face. Tomorrow night, we are going to follow a lead on Simone. Do you have any recommendations about how to proceed with regards to the witchcraft? More importantly, do you know anyone in the witch community who would want to help her? Someone must know. It is hard to keep secrets within covens."

"You are correct in your assumptions. I plan to scour the books, seeing who made the purchases necessary to create the oil and rope. These ingredients are widely available online, but any self-respecting witch or mage from New Orleans would buy them in our shop. We certify the authenticity of ingredients for all our products and supplies, which includes Van Van oil as well as hemp and hair. And if a vampire attempted purchasing these supplies at any stores in the city, I am confident someone would remember. That would not go unnoticed."

"Thanks, Ilsbeth," Sydney interjected. "Look back a year or two in your records, just to be safe. We aren't sure how long she's been in the city. If you send us the list of possible suspects, Kade and I can check it out from there. We really appreciate your help on this. If you saw what was done to those girls…well, we've got to stop it." While she didn't understand witchcraft, Sydney had to admit that she felt glad the witch was helping them. It was possible Ilsbeth could lead them to tangible clues so they could nab the killer.

Ilsbeth nodded. "I will contact you if I find anything. Like I said, I have been with my coven the past week. I will need to go back to the shop for the records. My escort, Zin, has been with me. He is my cousin, a practicing warlock, but most importantly, he's trained in security. I will be going everywhere with him. We cannot be too careful. I must go, but I will be in touch."

After everyone had said their goodbyes, Sydney quietly retreated to her room. She wanted to give in to her desire to be with Kade, but she was on business and had to get up early. Being around him was beginning to cloud her judgment. If she could only get some sleep and shopping therapy, she'd be good…okay, maybe not good, but she'd be ready to go out tomorrow night. They needed to catch a break on this case.

Chapter Twelve

Dressing up to fit into a vampire fetish club was a bitch. Sydney spent the better part of the morning shopping for clothes that would say, 'I roll with kinky vampires'. She hoped she'd fit in. She knew better than anyone that people had a tendency to clam up around cops, and the supernatural crowd was even more tight-lipped when it came to revealing secrets. They had their own code of honor and laws.

Xavier had accompanied her on her shopping expedition to help her choose just the right outfit. She wasn't above letting Kade pay for everything; after all he was the one who had dragged her ass down here to New Orleans. Xavier had promised not to reveal the details of her 'costume' to Kade. Oh yeah, baby, she wanted this one to shock him. They all needed a good laugh, she supposed; a human girl dressing like some kind of sex-crazed dominatrix. She was planning on cracking the whip all right.

She finally managed to get the damn, thigh-high, fishnet stockings attached. Garters were not as easy to put on as they looked. She had to admit, glancing at herself in the mirror, that she looked smokin' hot. She would have preferred to look dangerous, but tonight she was playing a part; sexy, wanton, open to handcuffs, whips and paddles.

She had chosen a tight black fishnet camisette with garters, and a black leather miniskirt. The fishnet cami was tightly woven and see-through, so it showed off her pert, rosy nipples underneath. She topped the outfit off with a sexy pair of Christian Louboutin, black leather over-the-knee boots that were adorned with silver zippers that ran all the way up from the back of her ankle to the back of her thigh. Xavier had given her slim, silver stakes that fitted into the boots nicely. No one would feel them even if they patted her down. She also concealed a small silver knife and chain in her right boot that she could easily pull out if necessary.

Sydney conceded that she could not do much about her long blonde hair. There was no way she was dyeing her hair black, or any other freaky color just for one night. She tried on a few wigs, but they were too hot, so she stopped by a local salon and had them tightly curl her long locks. Her perfectly spiraled, golden curls flowed over her shoulders.

Sydney fingered the mask she'd purchased in Jackson Square. Its swirling diamond rhinestones added an enigmatic flair to her sexy, fetish look. She held the delicate black metal to her face and fastened the ribbon behind her hair. With one last glance in the mirror, she left her room, wishing she was home going to a Halloween party instead, but this was her life. There was no room for games or mistakes tonight. She would play the part and do everything she could to glean information about where Simone was and who else was helping her. She knew from experience that seedy bars were good places to get intel, as long as you had sources who were either afraid of you or trusted you; either worked. Unfortunately, in this town, she had neither.

Kade gaped at Sydney as she descended the staircase. *Holy mother of God. What is she wearing?* His cock jerked to attention and his eyes widened as he struggled to remain composed in front of his fellow vampires. In all his life, he had never wanted one woman so badly. He immediately noticed how her tight, hard peaks pressed against the fishnet weave. He could not believe she would freaking wear a see-through top to a vampire club. What was she thinking? Every supernatural in the place would want her. *Let them try*, he laughed to himself. She belonged to him and no other.

"So, who wants a spanking?" she asked seductively. Despite her bravado, her face flushed, aware that she was half naked in front of a group of free-loving vampires. "Mistress Sydney is here to make your fantasy come true."

Everyone started laughing, except Kade. He strode across the room, possessively grabbing Sydney's waist. Pulling her flush against him, he captured her mouth. It was a hard, dominating kiss, one that let everyone know she was his. His tongue forced its way into her mouth, and Sydney opened for him. She kissed him back, letting him know that she would not simply be taken. No, she would take as well. Her hands snaked up his back, feeling the soft leather of his jacket. She breathed in his masculine scent, feeling controlled in his arms, seeking all of him.

Dominique coughed loudly from across the room.

"Okay, you two, ya want to get a room and fuck, or go catch bad guys? Come on!"

Interrupted, Sydney and Kade broke their heated connection.

"Uh…yeah, that would be 'go catch bad guys'," Sydney responded, dazed from Kade's kiss.

Sydney glanced away from Kade to Dominique. She wore a dark purple bustier with matching leather pencil skirt and calf-high, patent-leather lace-front boots.

"Nice leather. And those boots…We need to go shoe shopping together someday, seriously," she suggested, attempting to bond with the vampire.

Dominique smiled at the compliment. "Okay, girl, so we actually do have something in common. I'll take a rain check. It may be nice to have another woman around all this testosterone."

"Listen up everyone," Kade ordered. All eyes fell on him. "Before we go in, Luca will be clearing the site.

Sydney, you will enter with the second group. I will approach Miguel and introduce you as my director of Philadelphia security. Luca and Sydney, stay close in the club. You are supposed to be working together. The rest of you work the club and try to find out anything about Simone's whereabouts, or accomplices. The witch who is helping her may also frequent the club. Stay on your toes, and try to fit in. It cannot look like we are there investigating, or people won't talk. Luca, please run down the security situation."

"We've got two limos. Xavier, Dominique and I will take the first one. We'll go in and case things out before we give you the all clear. We need to make sure Simone is not in the club. If she is, Kade will enter. *You*," he said, pointing to Sydney, "will stay in the car. Under no circumstances are you to enter the club if Simone is in there. I am serious, Sydney. What happened with the vampire in Philly is child's play compared to what Simone could do to you." Sydney rolled her eyes.

"Once the go ahead is given, we can all enter the club. Spread out. Like Kade said, we are not there to investigate, so it can't look that way. Play, feed, gather information. Kade will give the signal when it is time to go. Kade and Sydney will leave first."

Kade put his hand around Sydney's waist, clutching her to his side.

"Okay, everyone, let's roll. Sydney love, stay close to Luca or me. Remember, while you carry my scent at the moment, other vampires will most definitely try to lure you."

Sydney shot Kade a defiant look, growing annoyed with his rules. Kade might be the boss of his vampires, but he was not the boss of her. She would play nice so long as she was on the case, but no man, not even a sexy as hell vampire, was going to run her life.

Chapter Thirteen

After Luca had given the all clear, Kade entered Sangre Dulce with Etienne and Sydney flanking him. A tall, thin man with jet-black hair and a goatee rushed up to greet them. He almost looked like a pirate with the black leather pants and white ruffled linen open-chested shirt he wore.

"Sir, I am honored to have you here. We have a special VIP table set up for you and your guests, which provides a wonderful view of the dance floor as well as the public play area," he explained.

Sydney struggled to keep her mouth shut. *Public play area? What the hell?*

Miguel was soon joined by a naked petite woman with long bright red hair, which was braided down her back. The woman wore a small chain around her neck that Sydney assumed was some kind of a collar. Sydney didn't know much about fetishes, but assumed this pixie of a woman was a submissive. Miguel placed his hand on the woman's back, gently pushing her toward Kade.

"Sir, this is Rhea. She will serve you and your party tonight, in any way you wish. She is human and has agreed to be a donor. Rhea can procure additional donors, submissives or Doms for your party, should you need these services. And of course, she will be your waitress for the evening. She is new to Sangre Dulce, but as you will experience, she was born to serve others. She is quite the little obedient sub. I am certain you will enjoy her."

Studying Sydney, he extended his hand. She reluctantly allowed him to take it, cringing as he kissed it. Before letting her go, he turned her arm over and smelled her inner wrist. Sydney snatched her hand away from him, shooting Kade a pointed look.

Miguel didn't seem to notice.

"Sir, what a lovely human you have brought to my club tonight. Shall we expect a public performance from her? I would most enjoy seeing her tan skin turn pink." He licked his lips and smiled, displaying his fangs to Sydney.

Showing very little emotion, Kade approached Miguel in an authoritative manner. "Miguel, this is Miss Willows. She is director of my security operations in the Philadelphia area. She is being mentored by Luca." Kade's eyes narrowed. "Miss Willows is in my employ, and is not to be touched or seen by anyone but me." He paused and winked at Sydney. "That is, unless I grant permission for her to be touched."

Sydney fought for self-control as blood rushed to her face. She was pretty sure Kade was teasing her. Wasn't he? Oh my God. She *so* needed to get this case over with so she could get back to her less than exciting life in Philadelphia. What the hell was wrong with these freaky vampires? She took a deep breath in an effort to gain her composure before she said anything she'd regret. She tried to remind herself she was just playing a part…here on a case.

"So sorry, sir, it is just that she is so very beautiful and so very human. She smells lovely." Miguel bowed his head. "Please forgive me."

"No harm done. Rhea, please show my guests to our table. I have business that I need to discuss with Miguel."

Sydney was about to lose it. What was Kade doing? He was not just sending her off with some naked waitress? Etienne gestured for Sydney to follow Rhea. She reluctantly followed the submissive up onto a raised platform area to a large table, where she agreed, the view was great. They'd be able to see pretty much everything that was going on in the club, except for the private rooms. She took a seat and Etienne sat down next to her. He looked at the wine menu and ordered.

"Please bring us three bottles of Salon Le Mesnil, 1997. We are expecting additional guests." Rhea bowed her head and scuttled off.

Sydney straightened in her chair, trying to appear as if she regularly frequented kinky, BDSM, vampire clubs. Trying not to look surprised, she noticed several dominatrix-type women at a table across from them. They were drinking and laughing while naked men with collars knelt at their feet. The dance floor appeared to be rhythmically moving as one. Waves of bodies in various forms of dress - from fully clothed to no clothing at all, danced.

Observing what they referred to as the public play area, she saw a large naked bald man who was tied to a bench. He writhed in pleasure and pain as an older woman dressed in red leather spanked him relentlessly with a pink paddle. Sydney shook her head. To each his own, she supposed. Not that she was totally opposed to spanking, or being tied up every now and then, but tied to a bench in the middle of a dance club? Guess it took a lot to get that guy's adrenaline going.

Dominique, Luca, and Xavier approached the table and sat down to discuss the next steps. Kade was the last to arrive, and he sat next to Sydney.

"So, curious thing, our friend Miguel said the bartender who reported Simone's appearance, quit. He's gone. So we've got no one specific to question. Sydney, what are your impressions?"

"I say we question the submissives first." Sydney scanned the room, focusing on Rhea who was all the way across the club waiting for drinks at the bar. "I know we can't act like we're investigating, but we could ask around to see who they've played with. Maybe some prefer women Doms and would remember her. It's likely that if Simone was here she could easily have shopped for a victim. We should also question the Doms and find out if there are any new ones on the scene who match her description. We need to do it in a subtle way, so they don't suspect we're investigating. I have to say, as kinky as this place is, it only looks like maybe fifty percent of the people in here are regulars. Is it possible that some of them are tourists?" Sydney took note of the several patrons who appeared out of place. A casually dressed couple sat at a table, nervously playing with their drink straws.

"Yes, I'm sure some are, but there are also regulars," Kade agreed. "We'll need to spread out. Etienne and Xavier, start with questioning the submissives. Go ask Miguel to line them up and pretend you are looking for a sub. Be discreet. Do not make it seem as though we are conducting an investigation. Dominique, take on Rhea. Something seems off with her. Miguel said she just started, yet he assigned his least experienced server to our important party? It doesn't make sense."

As the other vampires left the table, Kade, Luca and Sydney moved together so they could more easily talk.

"I don't like this thing with the bartender going missing. If Simone found out that he told someone she was here, why wouldn't she take out Miguel too? She expected to have this reported, so why kill him?" Sydney asked.

"Good question, indeed." Kade took notice of Miguel, whose gaze lingered too long on Sydney. "Right now, I want you and Luca to go dance. You are supposed to be close. I don't want anyone questioning our intentions. I will join you in a few minutes then we will retire to the private rooms to investigate."

"As you wish...Sydney?" Luca stood and gestured for her to take his hand.

Sydney knew she wasn't Luca's favorite person, but he was polite, she'd give him that. She stood, glancing from Kade to Luca, finally going to him. He led her onto the dance floor and as she went, Sydney's eyes never left Kade's. She'd stopped counting how many times a day she wanted Kade to make love to her. She had never felt so connected to one man in her life, but she couldn't admit to herself that this might be a real opportunity for a long-lasting relationship.

Luca took Sydney in his arms, pushing his thigh between her knees. Sydney felt his strength against her, his muscular, lethal body brushing hers. She leaned into him and put one arm around his neck, swaying to the music. As Luca pressed his hips to hers, Sydney's eyes flashed open, surprised to feel his hardness against her belly.

"So, Luca, is that a stake in your pocket or are you just happy to see me?" she joked.

"Sydney darling, let's just say that you are starting to grow on me, and that outfit of yours is delectable. I may be a vampire, but I'm not dead." Luca grabbed the back of her head, pulling it toward his and whispered in her ear. "Even though you belong to Kade, it doesn't stop me from appreciating you...all of you."

Horny vampires, geez. Sydney had been somewhat unnerved at his sudden sexuality on display for all to see in the club. She kept trying to remember that she was there playing a part. They were supposed to be acting, and it was easy to do. She was attracted to Luca as well, as most women would be. He was ruggedly handsome, but not a pretty boy. Despite his forward comments, she felt, oddly, as though she could trust him. But she also wondered what Kade's reaction would be to having another man's hands all over her. But he'd told her to be with him. *Look like you are close to Luca.*

Just as she was beginning to relax, Luca spun her around straight into Kade's arms. Her breath caught as his lips met hers. She expected Luca to leave, but instead he sandwiched her in the middle, grazing his erection against Sydney's ass, reaching his arms around her waist. His hands slowly inched up under Sydney's breasts as Kade kissed her passionately.

Sydney's senses were overwhelmed. *What the fuck is going on?* She was letting two vampires monopolize her body, loving every minute of it. Kissing Kade took her away into a headspace that she rarely went, one of pure pleasure. Yet it scared her that she was letting him see her raw, so exposed. And worst of all, she felt the tingle all over her body, leaving her wishing the situation could be permanent.

Kade tore his lips from hers, leaving her breathless. He grasped the nape of her neck and leaned in to speak sensually in her ear.

"You are stunning tonight. Indeed, I am going to find it hard to let you go after this dance." He pressed his lips to the lobe of her ear. "You seem to like playing with two men. Enjoying our dance with Luca, aren't you, love? But remember this, Sydney, I don't share, and at the end of tonight, you will be mine." *Mine?* He could not believe he'd used the word but at the same time, he could not deny the all-consuming need to claim Sydney as his. He had every intention of making love to her over and over again, and was looking forward to hearing her scream his name in ecstasy.

As the song ended, Sydney was relieved to put some space between her and the boys. She ached between her legs, extraordinarily aroused from their dance. She longed for Kade's strong arms and wished he'd take her out of the club. He'd told her that she would be his tonight. She found herself wanting to let him take control and make love to her until dawn. She was conflicted, knowing that she was an independent woman, yet she could not deny wanting to belong to him.

As Sydney tried to regain her composure, she watched Luca leave the dance floor. Deciding to take control of the situation, she reached over and laced her fingers with Kade's.

"Come on, let's go check out the private rooms. My take is that some of the rooms may not be that private. Maybe everyone in our group is back there with the subs and Doms. We could help, or at least look for suspicious activity and clues to where Simone is. Even though this place is screaming 'erotic experience', I just have a feeling that sex isn't the only thing happening in this club. If Simone has spies here, they'll be watching for us…and may slip up by looking just a little too long."

"Let's make our rounds and see who's interested in our visit." Kade led them off the floor toward the back of the club.

Sydney braced herself for whatever kinky sights they'd see along the way. She wasn't a prude, but she wasn't used to seeing so many naked people prancing around in collars and leather. As they approached the back, they pushed through a red metallic beaded fringed curtain door. A sensual, hard, driving pulse of music spread throughout the hallway, which was dimly lit with black light.

A crowd gathered at the entrance of one of the rooms where a couple was performing. As Sydney pushed her way to the front, Kade settled behind, letting his hands fall protectively around her waist. A tall, lithe, gothic-looking woman stood spread-eagle with her hands secured by leather cuffs to an upright, wooden contraption that looked like an X. Although the woman was blindfolded and bound, she appeared to quiver in euphoria as her male partner teased her bottom with a blue leather whip.

The crowd silently watched as the woman begged her partner for release. It appeared that she had somehow earned her reward, because her partner unzipped his pants and entered the woman from behind. He was thrusting over and over into the bound woman while she screamed. Sydney could not believe she was watching such an intimate act with Kade and was growing embarrassed by her own arousal. Yet she knew this was why people came here…to arouse and be aroused. Concerned by her reaction, Sydney pushed back slightly in order to turn away. Kade's arms tightened, holding her still against him, forcing her to watch. She could feel his rock-hard cock pressed into her back, and knew he wanted her to see this.

Kade chose to make Sydney watch the lovers in the room, so she could experience a taste of his world. He was not a frequent visitor to this club by any means, but this kind of activity was not uncommon in the supernatural world. It was a harsh reality, albeit arousing. If Sydney was going to be with him, she needed to be aware of the dangers and temptations that lurked in his city. He could smell her arousal as she watched the strangers make love. His rock-hard cock strained against his leather pants, begging to take her in the same manner. He could not resist the opportunity to tease his normally self-composed detective. He leaned his mouth down to her ear, making sure she heard his every word.

"Do you like this, Sydney? Would you like me to tie you up and take you from behind? I promise not to be gentle with you, detective." He smiled, knowing he'd ruffled her feathers. "Now don't lie to me…I smell your desire."

Damn vampire senses. Sydney was mortified and had had enough of this crazy sex show. She pulled herself out of his strong grip, knowing he'd chosen to let go of her. It was time to get back to business. There wasn't anything suspicious going on in that area. Just a couple having sex, and a dozen horny people watching. What had she gotten herself into on this case?

As they walked further down the dark hall, Miguel appeared out of nowhere, calling for Kade.

"Sir, I thought it might be a good idea for you to speak with Gia, a back bartender who works here. I remembered that she was friends with Freddy…you know the guy who quit? Maybe she has information about Simone's whereabouts? Please forgive me. I should have thought of this earlier."

"Sydney, come with me. We can talk to her together."

"No, you go. I'm fine. I want to find Dominique and perhaps, *play* with Rhea." Sydney did not intend to play, but she did want to question the waitress. She also didn't trust Miguel. She wanted him to think she was only here for fun, not to investigate.

"But as my director of security, you may find my questioning of interest. Please come with me." Kade's lips tightened, anticipating her refusal.

"But you said we're here to have a little fun, not work. I promise I'll catch up with you later. As you know, I like to play with the girls. Dominique should be back here somewhere. When you're finished, come find me. We can play later," she purred, rubbing her hands up and down his chest.

"As you wish, my love. But know this, we will play later," he said in warning, blowing out a breath. "I can sense both Xavier and Etienne back here, so give them a shout should you run into any issues, okay?"

"I promise. I'll be fine," she assured Kade as she pressed her lips to his cheek.

"Be careful," he whispered.

She winked at Kade as he and Miguel headed toward the light at the end of the hallway. Something about Miguel made her skin crawl. He wasn't lying, but he wasn't exactly telling the whole truth. She wanted Kade to go find out what the bartender knew. They could not leave any stones unturned, and so far this evening was a bust. Besides kinky sex, there didn't seem to be anything dangerous going on at the club.

She sobered at the thought of what had happened to those girls in Philadelphia, renewing her purpose. She considered that Dominique had been gone with Rhea a little too long. She'd like the opportunity to interview her as well. Sydney scanned the hallways, trying to decide which way to go next. *How the hell am I going to find them in this labyrinth?* Putting one foot in front of the other seemed the only way, so she continued walking and glancing in rooms that were open to public viewing. Nothing seemed amiss. She could see a blue light coming out of one of the rooms at the far end of the hallway on the right. It was so dark in this area she really hoped there weren't any bugs or mice back here, or she'd freak out.

Caution told Sydney she might want to check her weapons, so she reached down into her boots, making sure the silver stake, knife and chain were still there. As she looked up again toward the end of the hallway, someone slammed her hard against the wall. She could barely see the outline of a bearded man who smelled of stale cigarettes and whiskey. He firmly held her to the wall with a stubby hand on each of her bare arms. She struggled but was unable to dislodge him.

"Hey, missy, what ya doing back here all by yourself in the dark? Your blood," he leaned in to sniff her neck, "oh yes. It smells so good. What kind of a master would let his human run around back here unprotected? You need a real master to get you in line. How I'd love to spank that pretty ass of yours and drown in your sweet blood. Come on now, this is going to be fun."

Sydney recoiled from the putrid smell emanating from the vampire. She could see the fine points of his teeth glinting off the black light. Should she play innocent? Or pretend she belonged to him? But then again, Sydney was Sydney. She did not do damsel in distress well. *Fuck that. This foul-assed vampire is so going down.*

"Listen, pal. I'm giving you fair warning, get your fucking hands off me or you're going to regret it, last chance." She stared at him defiantly, planning her next move.

The vampire cackled in response, undeterred.

"Feisty one, aren't you? It's going to be a pleasure whipping you into submission."

He barely got his last word out when Sydney kicked him in the balls. Yep, no matter how supernatural you were, testicles were always vulnerable. Tried and true, Sydney loved how that worked. The vampire let go of her to clutch himself, and she whipped out the silver knife from her boot and held it to his throat.

"Sorry, pal. I must admit this has been fun…whipping your ass into submission and all…it's been a laugh riot. Now down to the floor, on your stomach, hands up over your head, or you're going to eat silver. And in case you feel like trying again, you best remember that I have a few vampire friends of my own back here, not to mention the silver stakes in my boot that I'm just itching to try out."

The vampire stretched out his hands and Sydney wrapped a thin silver chain around his wrists, effectively immobilizing him for the night.

"Now listen here, be a good little vampire and I'll let Miguel know you're waiting to be freed. I know you vamps have your own laws, so I'll let Kade know what you did to me, and he can decide what to do with your ass."

As she strode further down the hallway, Sydney stopped in her tracks on hearing the cry of a woman's voice coming from one of the rooms. It was familiar and in pain. Although several people might be in pain in a place like this, the hair on her arms stood straight up as she heard the woman scream again. *Dominique.* Sydney started running down the hallway, screaming Dominique's name. She turned left, then right until she found a closed metal door. Shit, it was locked and wouldn't open. She wished that she had some of those vampire super-strength skills about now. She shoved against the door, and then tried kicking it, but it wouldn't budge. *How am I going to get this open?*

Sydney pulled out the thin silver stake and her knife. Slowly manipulating them, she picked the lock and the door clicked open. As Sydney burst through into the room, she found Dominique handcuffed, lying on a large padded table. Sydney rushed over to help her. "Dominique, what happened? I thought vampires could easily break cuffs. Where's the key?"

"Sydney, please." Tears streaked down her face through a black blindfold. "Silver. The handcuffs…it's burning, please help me."

"It's going to be okay, Dominique. Just take a few deep breaths. I don't see the key anywhere, but I have a knife. Just hang in there."

Sydney finally picked the lock and broke the last handcuff off of Dominique, horrified by the oozing and third degree burns they left on her skin. Dominique was too weak to get off the table. Sydney cut off a piece of her skirt and began to dry Dominique's face.

"Thank you. I thought no one would find me back here. That little bitch Rhea did this to me. I was questioning her about Simone when she said her master wanted to play with me. I let her blindfold me, thinking it was a game and I could earn her trust enough so she'd talk. But when she cuffed me in silver, I fell onto the table." Dominique slowly sat up inspecting her burned wrists and ankles and then fell back onto the table, unable to stand, woozy from the silver. "Damn, now that's gonna leave a mark. Listen, Sydney, I need one of the guys to bring me a donor. I can feel them coming now. But I can't get up yet. I need blood."

"You'll be okay, Dominique. Just lie back until they get here. Are you sure Rhea was the only one here with you? Did she bring someone else into the room?" Sydney asked, determined to find out what had happened. A noise caught her attention and she observed an opened back door that led out to an alley. As much as she wanted to go investigate, she was not about to leave Dominique alone.

"I'm not sure if someone else was here." Dominique shook her head in confusion. "Usually we can sense such things, but the silver, it doesn't just burn like a motherfucker; it weakens all of our abilities. I was screaming at Rhea, but there could have been someone else. The fact is that Rhea is a human, possibly a witch cloaking her talent, but most definitely human. So she could have been thralled into doing this to me, but the vampire or mage would have needed to be close. But I didn't feel anyone when I entered the room with her."

The conversation with Gia, the bartender, garnered no tangible leads except the last known address of the staff member who had reported seeing Simone. Kade was getting frustrated. Simone was somewhere in this city and had been at this very club. They needed to find her before she killed another girl. After getting the address, Miguel stalled Kade at the bar and seemed to talk endlessly about nothing. Kade thanked him for his help and started to make his way through the crowd back to Sydney. By the time he reached the dance floor near the entrance to the back, he sensed something was wrong. He sped down the darkened hallway to find a male vampire attempting to escape silver chains. He could feel something was wrong with Dominique, but halted as he smelled Sydney on the dirty predator.

"Where is Sydney?" Kade growled.

The vampire strained to get a look at Kade. "Who? You mean that human bitch who chained me? Get me out of these. You really need to teach your slave girl better manners. I will be honored to watch you beat her. She needs to learn a lesson. Look what she did to me!"

Kade, furious beyond words, reached down with one hand and grabbed the vampire by his throat, bashing his head into the wall. "You touched her? You insolent fledgling. She's mine. You're going to pay for your misguided actions!"

"What, that human girl? You are kidding, right? You can find pussy anywhere you like in this city and you would seek to punish me for being who I am? A vampire?" he sneered at Kade.

With restrained emotion, Kade slammed him again, holding him up so far against the wall that his feet no longer touched the floor.

"No, I will punish you for being an animal who doesn't know his place in our society. You will never touch her or any other woman ever again. Your time on Earth has officially come to an end." In a swift move, Kade pulled a small thin wooden stake from his back pocket that telescoped like an antenna and snapped into place. With precision, he jammed the stake into the heart of the vampire. The hallway filled with ash as Kade ran forward in search of Sydney.

Kade rushed into the room followed by Luca and Xavier. Spinning Sydney around, he hugged her tightly.

"Sydney love, I leave you for ten minutes and you manage to find trouble? Are you okay? He didn't hurt you, did he?"

"Who, stubby vamp boy in the hallway?" Backing out of his embrace, Sydney laughed it off. "He may have left a bruise on my oh-so-delicate skin, but as you probably noticed, he won't be messing with me anymore. Don't worry about me....Dominique's the one who needs help. She said she needs a donor, and as much as I would love to help her I'm kind of attached to my blood."

Sydney and Dominique explained what had happened with Rhea. While a vampire could have been responsible for Rhea's actions, Kade suspected that Rhea was a witch who was working with Simone.

"Luca, Xavier, go sweep the alley. She's probably gone, but we should check anyway."

Sydney was strangely touched as she watched Kade hold Dominique's hand. He felt something for this female vampire, but she wasn't sure what it was. Love? Responsibility? She questioned herself, wondering if she should be jealous, but she wasn't. No, what she felt was admiration for Kade, a leader taking care of his own, comforting Dominique as a father would a daughter.

Soon Etienne entered the room with a donor in tow. He was a ready and willing strapping young man, nearly twenty years of age. He appeared to be strong enough to feed her. Kade waved him over and held the man's wrist up to Dominique's mouth as she bit into him and sucked greedily.

As Sydney glanced away, she grew concerned that she should give them privacy. Such an intimate act, yet no one seemed to mind her presence. At that moment, she wondered what it would be like if Kade bit her, drank from her. Would it hurt? Would it bring pleasure? The word on the street was that women found it incredibly pleasurable, often orgasmic, but she wasn't just any woman. And Kade certainly wasn't just any vampire. Did he yearn to bite her? Would he try to bite her if they made love? As she contemplated the scenario, Sydney realized her thoughts were more than curiosity. No, she wanted Kade to bite her. As she stared at Dominique, latched to the donor's wrist, she glanced up to find Kade watching her, not smiling, but giving her a sultry, all-knowing look as if he knew what she was thinking. Sydney demurely averted her eyes; it was all too much.

When Dominique had healed and was strong enough to leave, their small group walked back through the dim hallway. Sydney stopped dead in the corridor as she kicked a pile of ash up into the air. Where was the chained vampire?

"Hey guys? Uh...did anyone see a vampire here? Silvered by the wrists? Smelly guy?" Without speaking another word, it clicked with Sydney that the vampire had not escaped. He was dead. She'd been kicking his ashes around with her boot. Yuck.

She looked down again at the floor and then up to Kade. He was dangerous; primal, unyielding. Sydney's breath hitched as he snaked his hand around her waist, holding her tight to his side.

"No one touches what is mine."

Sydney didn't flinch as she processed his words. He had killed the other vampire for attacking her. The police weren't called. No one even batted an eyelash that the guy was gone. Vampire justice. She shuddered at the power Kade held in this town and he drew her to him like a moth to a flame. She straightened her back and held her head high. If she was bothered or surprised by what he did to the vampire, she would not let him see it. Sydney gladly allowed Kade to usher her out of the club and into the limo. It had been a hell of a night, and she could not get out of there fast enough.

Chapter Fourteen

"Kade, what's going on?" Sydney asked as Kade shut the car door behind them. Only one limo had returned to the compound and Luca stayed in the car. "Where is everyone? I thought they lived here with you."

"No, love, they do not. While it is true that Luca lives on the compound, he doesn't live in the main house. His home is located next door, but is within the borders of the compound for safety." Kade trailed behind Sydney, appreciating her fine assets. Tonight she would be his. He smiled at the thought.

"Never a dull moment around here," she quipped, entering the foyer. Sydney unzipped her boots, took them off and started up the steps. "Just when you think you're shacking up with a bunch of vampires, you find out that there is really only one vampire. Lucky me."

Kade rushed toward Sydney, pinning her against the railing. His hands on her waist, he placed his forehead to hers. Their lips were mere inches apart.

"Sydney, there is only one vampire for you, and there is only one human for me, *you*. You are an incredibly courageous woman, fighting that vampire and saving Dominique. You never cease to amaze me, but you do worry me." He sniffed her neck. "I cannot bear the smell of that derelict on your sweet skin. We should both wash away the filthiness of the evening and rest ourselves for tomorrow night. A hot shower should relax your muscles nicely. Go on up. I'm going to get us something to drink, and then I will be up to massage your neck in a few minutes." Kade released Sydney, turned, and walked away into the kitchen. Wanting to kiss her, he'd make her wait until she craved his touch, begging for mercy.

For once in her life, Sydney was speechless. Her body was humming with excitement, she wanted, no needed, Kade to make love to her, but he hadn't. Where was her trusty vibrator when she needed it? What a crazy night, and now this. She sighed. Kade was right about one thing, she needed to relax, and apart from him or her battery-operated friend, a shower was the second best option. She was disgusted by her experience with the vampire; she could still smell the odors of cigarette smoke, sex, blood, and sweat from the club clinging to her clothes and hair.

As Sydney undressed and walked into the guest bathroom, she admired her surroundings. A bathroom like this would take up half her condo. The huge granite shower had several nozzles that sprayed overhead as well as sideways. Jumping into the spray, she shut the glass doors.

The hot water rushed over her hair and body. Sydney closed her eyes, willing her mind and muscles to relax.

Her eyes flew open when she heard the bathroom door click open and shut. *Kade.* He was in here with her? Her heartbeat sped up knowing that he was near. She leaned further into the pulsing rain, anticipating his touch. Her body awakened, tingling with the knowledge he'd come for her.

With her face to the wall, she sighed as Kade came up behind her, his erection brushing against her back. As his hands worked their way into her hair, she smiled. He gently scrubbed her hair with shampoo, letting the bubbles sluice down her body. She let him tease her, drawing out the tension.

Holy fuck. Sydney could barely take it. The man finally had her naked, and he was driving her crazy with need by simply washing her hair. She laid her hands flat against the granite tiles and rolled her head back to give him better access. She couldn't stop herself from moaning out loud as she felt his hands rubbing the soapy bubbles across her shoulders and down around her waist. She hungered for his touch, feeling his strong hands slide over her wet, shivering skin.

"Kade, please. We've waited so long. I just…I can't wait anymore."

"Sydney," he whispered. "Goddess, you're so soft. Do you remember when I told you that you would be mine tonight? I meant it. Are you ready?"

His cock stood to attention at the sight of her shapely ass. Unable to abstain any longer, Kade glided his palms up across her belly, pulling her toward him until his hard length rested firmly above her bottom. His hands roamed over her soft breasts, gently caressing them and rolling her nipples between his thumb and forefinger. He moaned in pleasure at the feel of her soft body against his.

"Yes. I'm more than ready," Sydney replied.

"I have waited centuries for the right woman, and you are most definitely the one." He breathed in deeply, trying to resist burying himself in her right there.

"Please, Kade, please," she begged.

Kade massaged her breast with one hand, letting his other hand drop down between her legs. She opened her thighs, allowing him better access. Sydney screamed his name as he reached into her slick center, exploring every inch of her warmth. He circled her clit and then plunged a thick finger deep inside her. She rested her forehead against the cool tile, panting with desire.

"That's it, Sydney, feel me in you. Let it go. You are a beautiful, amazing woman, my woman." The one? In the heat of the moment, she wanted to believe that what he was saying was true, but she couldn't think clearly when her senses were so delightfully assaulted. As Kade pinched her nipples, blood rushed to her clitoris. She ached to be touched. She wanted him inside her, now.

As Kade added a second finger inside of her, she cried out loud. A crescendo of pleasure built up in her that was about to come crashing down. Kade coaxed her on, encouraging her to reach her climax.

"Yes, love. Come for me. That's it."

His fingers stimulated her sensitive nerves inside, and she couldn't hold back any longer. Sydney's orgasm crashed over her in waves as she trembled at Kade's hand. She thought she would collapse in the shower except for the fact that he turned her in his arms and held onto her tightly.

Reaching over, Kade turned the water off. Sydney protested.

"No Kade, don't leave. Please, make love to me now."

"I have every intention of doing just that, but I want our first time to be special. I plan to take my time with you slowly savoring every part of you. Come here…with me." He wrapped a warm, fluffy towel around her. After drying their bodies, he took her hand in his and led her into the bedroom.

Sydney's heart squeezed as she noticed at least two dozen lit candles scattered all over her room. The bedspread had been turned down, and there were rose petals on the sheets. Her vampire was a romantic. No one had ever done anything like this for her.

"Kade…it's beautiful," she gasped.

Smiling back at her, Kade wrapped his hands around her waist, drawing her into him so her breasts crushed against his hard chest.

"I am glad you like it. Now I intend to show how special you are to me, every last inch of you," he said suggestively.

They both stood naked at the foot of the bed. With reckless abandon, Kade speared his fingers through Sydney's hair, grasping her locks in his hands, and he kissed her. Not a soft kiss, but a hard, demanding, possessive kiss. Sydney welcomed his tongue, tasting him, lost in his dark embrace.

Kade yearned for this woman like no other. He planned to claim her tonight, but knew she was the one claiming his heart. They fell upon the bed together, their arms entangled, reaching, touching. Struggling for dominance, Kade pinned Sydney on her back. He dipped his head down, his mouth seeking her rosy tips. He finally found what he was looking for, laving her peaks and gently biting down. Sydney moaned and arched her back at the erotic pleasure and twinge of pain.

Reaching up, Kade caressed her breasts with his hands as he slowly kissed his way down her stomach. Sydney writhed on the bed in anticipation. She felt a kiss to her hip, a kiss to her thigh, a kiss below her belly button. He slowly spread her legs, feasting upon the sight of her waxed, bare beauty. He ran a hand down her mound and felt her shiver underneath his touch. He planned to tease her again and pleasure her beyond her wildest dreams. Lowering his head, he kissed along the crease of her legs. Not being able to resist any longer, his tongue ran up and down her lips. He pressed his mouth into the core of her, sucking her tender nub.

Sydney splayed her arms to each side of the bed and grasped the sheets in a tight hold. Her reaction to his mouth on her delicate skin was so intense she thought she would fly off the bed. Colors danced in her head as Kade licked and suckled her sex. Sydney began to beg him again as her body filled with overpowering sensations.

"Oh my God. That feels so good. I…I…please."

Kade slowly plunged a finger, then two into her pussy while continuing to lick her, concentrating on her soft bundle of nerves. He slipped in and out of her as he drank her luscious essence, bringing her closer and closer to release. He loved hearing her beg and longed to reward her. He gently curved his fingers inside, stroking her thin line of sensitive fibers. As he stroked her, he flattened his tongue, pressing down hard, then sucking, tantalizing her over the cliff of arousal.

Sydney convulsed in orgasm as she felt his fingers stroke her while he continued to kiss her sex. Wave after wave of orgasm descended upon her as she screamed Kade's name over and over. She curled over to her side for a minute, feeling as if every nerve of her skin was on fire. She was exhausted but ready to take Kade inside her. She needed him, in her arms, making love to her.

"That was incredible…oh my God."

Kade stalked above her like a hungry panther. She reached up, sliding her palms over his hard, lean muscles. She hungered to lick every bulge of his ripped abs. As he rested on his arms above her, they gazed into each other's eyes. Kade's focus fell to her lips, and he kissed her gently, their tongues dancing with each other. Loving. Caring.

"Sydney, you are exquisite…I look forward to tasting you over and over through eternity."

"Please, make love to me. I can't stand it…I ache for you."

"Are you sure, love? After tonight, there is no going back."

Sydney quietly nodded.

Kade grasped her wrists with one hand, pushed her arms up over her head, and pressed his lips to hers in a passionate kiss. Confident that she was ready for him, he thrust his cock into her core in one primal stroke. Pumping slowly in and out of her, he reveled in how wonderful her tight, warm sheath felt around him. He wanted so badly to make it last but was struggling to hold his orgasm at bay. Sydney was finally his. The resplendent woman beneath him provoked an appetite that he hadn't known existed. For all of his physical strength, she simply had no idea how much power she wielded over his heart.

Sydney stretched to accommodate Kade's ample size. Allowing him to hold her arms above her made it possible for her to give in to her most carnal desire to submit to him. She arched her hips up into him, her clitoris grazing his nest of curls. Shuddering in pleasure with every stroke, Sydney wrapped her legs around his waist, pulling him closer.

Kade slowed his pace, his eyes locked on hers.

"Kade, need more. Please, God, don't stop."

"Things will never be the same for either one of us after tonight," Kade growled, his fangs elongating. He licked the curve of her neck, losing himself in the lusciousness of her warm skin. There was no going back. He couldn't hold on any longer. "You. Are. Mine." He pulled back his hips and drove into her hard as he bit into the soft flesh of her neck.

Sydney's sweet blood filled his mouth as he continued to pump voraciously into her body, spilling his seed deep within her. Releasing her hands, he rolled onto his back pulling her to him, embracing her closely. Kade closed his eyes, overwhelmed by his response to her. Not just her body and blood, but her mind as well. Without a doubt, he knew this woman was the one, and he had just claimed her. Forever.

Chapter Fifteen

Sydney awakened to the sounds of birds chirping outside. Kade lay unnervingly still next to her. She reached over and stroked the hard lines of his chest, reminiscing about their lovemaking. He'd insisted that she was his, and Sydney struggled to understand what that meant to a modern woman like her. *How many women belong to him?* She knew he'd been around for a very long time, but he'd told her that he'd only loved a few women.

Sydney's heart constricted at the thought that there could be anyone else in his life. Then she knew in an instant that meant she was in trouble. *Shit. I'm falling for him. No, no, and hell no.* This couldn't be happening, yet it was. No one in her entire life had made her feel the way she had last night: wicked, euphoric, loved. That was it…loved. Did he love her? Was that what he meant when he kept saying she belonged to him? Eventually they would need to talk about what this all meant.

How was she supposed to have a relationship with a vampire? First, there were location issues. She lived in

Philadelphia, he lived in New Orleans. She had a job, commitments. Second, he would totally outlive her. She'd be an old woman, and he'd still be looking like he stepped off the cover of GQ. Third…third? Why was she even running through these scenarios? She wasn't even sure he was serious about her. For all she knew, being 'his' meant he thought she was one of many women. *A harem? A bloody vampire harem. Stop worrying, Syd!*

Needing to clear her head, she tiptoed away from the bed into the bathroom, convinced that a nice, hot shower would make everything okay. An ache grew in her chest as she stepped under the hot spray. *Nice job, Sydney. You're falling in love with a vampire. A hot, sexy, romantic vampire.* Shaking her head in disbelief, she quickly washed her hair, soaped her skin, rinsed, hopped out of the shower, and dried herself.

When she opened the door to the bedroom, disappointment washed across her face. The bed was sadly empty. Where had Kade gone? Feeling a sense of loss, she dressed, avoiding looking at the bed where they'd made love. Hearing a familiar buzzing, she frantically searched for her cell phone. *Why can't I be more organized?* Finding it in a pile of clothes, she answered the call. "Hey." It was all she could manage amid her confusing thoughts.

"Hey to you too," Tristan replied. "I got down early this morning. I'm staying at my brother's condo on Royal Street. How about you grab a taxi and meet me for beignets?"

"Now, that's what the doctor ordered. You've got my weapons?" Sydney felt as if she was suffocating in the guest room. A little time away from vampires would be good for her.

"Sure thing. I packed them up in a backpack so no one will notice. It's about four o'clock now. Can you get down here in about forty-five minutes?" he asked.

"Yes, sounds great. Meet you there. Thanks Tris!" Sydney sighed, clicking off her cell. She and Kade would have to talk later, but for now, it was back to reality. She desperately wanted her weapons, especially after last night's incident with the vampire in the hallway.

Sydney slid on a flirty, purple sundress and adjusted the thin straps that supported her C cupped breasts. She slipped on a sexy black lace thong on the off chance she'd get surprised by Kade later. Thank goodness she'd been able to find a pair of comfortable sandals on her shopping trip the other day. Comfort was a must for running around in the city. Glancing in the mirror, she pulled her long, blonde hair into a ponytail and added pink shimmer lip gloss. She almost left the room without grabbing her silver knife. With nowhere to conceal it on her body, she quickly slid it into her purse on her way out of her room.

Walking through the house, she noticed it was quiet, too quiet. Nothing but silence filled the great room. Where did Kade get off to now? She steeled her emotions, afraid that he might not be serious about her. What man leaves a woman's bed while she's in the shower, wet, naked? Sydney peeked down the long hallway past the kitchen and heard Kade's voice coming from one of the rooms. Even though the door was cracked open, she didn't want to intrude on his business. But then again, why the hell not? He did leave her bedroom after the most fabulous night of making love, ever.

Brimming with confidence, Sydney swung the door open and leaned against the doorjamb. With a hand on her hip, she watched Kade intently as he leaned back in a black leather chair, his feet propped on an antique, cherry desk. *Nice desk,* she thought…a picture formed in her mind of her bent over it, with Kade taking her from behind. She gave him a wicked smile. He grinned, blew her a kiss, but kept on conversing about Issacson's company investments while she stood there waiting for him to get off the phone. God, that man was sexy as hell…but infuriating. *He's not hanging up for me, really?* Sydney gave him an innocent wave, turned on her heels, and trudged back toward the kitchen. She decided that since he was busy, then the man was getting a note.

She quickly scrawled a message, letting him know she was going to meet Tristan and that she'd be back in a couple of hours. Convinced that Kade wasn't getting off the phone any time soon, she taped it to the inside of the front door. Patience wasn't her strong suit, but at least she'd let him know where she was going. Sydney loved New Orleans and was hoping she'd get a chance to window shop for antiques on Royal Street on her way back. She really wanted to go over and check out the address they got last night, but she knew that the other vampires wouldn't be at full strength until sunset. And after last night, she hadn't planned on going to the address by herself without backup.

Deciding against a taxi on a warm summer day, Sydney opted for a ride on the St. Charles Streetcar from the Garden District to the French Quarter and then grabbed the Canal Streetcar over to the Riverfront Streetcar to meet Tristan. She loved taking in the sights of the city, while riding on the train. Within a half hour, she arrived at her stop and hustled down the riverfront steps to Café du Monde.

Tristan was already seated at a corner table under the open-air canopy with a large platter of beignets sprinkled with powder sugar and a café au lait awaiting her. Sneaking up behind him, she wrapped her hands around his neck and planted a chaste kiss to his cheek.

"Hey, mon loup, you want some company?" she teased seductively.

"You really are looking to get me killed down here in New Orleans, aren't you, Syd?" Tristan laughed.

"What are you talking about? Can't I give a wolf a little love? I missed you. You don't know what it's like being surrounded by vampires twenty-four-seven. You have to come back with me to Kade's. We have an address we're checking out as soon as the sun goes down."

Tristan handed her a mug, sliding the plate of beignets in front of her. "First things first, you really don't get how a little wolf lovin' could get me killed, do you, mon chaton?" he asked. "Look, Kade and I go way back, we're close. And let me tell you that in all the years that I've known him, he has never expressed his desire to claim a woman. I can smell him on you. Remember? Super-wolf sniffer? And as hard as you tried to hide it with makeup, I can see that he marked you. You may not know it, sweet Syd, but you are his." He grinned, bringing his cup to his lips.

Sydney nearly spilled her coffee, slamming it down on the table. "Marked? Claimed? What the hell is that supposed to mean, Tristan? Claimed like luggage? I'm sick as shit of all this supernatural lingo, and rules! Rules that don't even apply to me, by the way, as everyone down here keeps reminding me that I'm human, which I pretty much take to mean 'less'." She picked up another beignet, fully intending to shove it into her mouth. "You know what; don't even explain it to me. I'm sorry I asked. As much as I love the Big Easy, I am so ready to get back to Philly where I'm appreciated for my kick-ass human qualities." She bit into the beignet, and powder sugar sprayed over her plate.

Tristan laughed out loud. Poor Sydney just had no idea what was going on with her and Kade. And Kade didn't seem to be doing a very good job communicating it. He had a tiger by its tail, one that had sharp teeth and bit. This was going to be fun to watch.

"Listen Syd, I didn't come all the way down here to get you riled up. Look what your Alpha brought you…a pretty pink backpack with all kinds of fun toys." He held up the bag and smiled.

"Now, that's what I'm talking about. Thanks." She took out her cell and glanced down at the time. "As much as I'd like to soak up the sounds of the city, we'd better start making our way back to Kade's. The sun will be down in an hour or so, and I don't want to waste time finding this bastard."

Tristan stood and left money on the table.

"Okay, let's roll," Tristan suggested. As he went to leave, he caught sight of her weaving her way through the maze of tables, smiling as if she hadn't a care in the world. *Oh yeah, this is going to be fun all right.*

Kade finished talking with his overseas contacts and sighed. As much as he'd wanted to hang up the phone and go make love to Sydney again, he needed to take care of Issacson's investments. Issacson Securities was a firm he'd built over the years, one that catered to supernaturals. He'd been neglecting business while in Philadelphia, so completing the call was a necessity. Kade was a man who honored his commitments and his clients trusted him with their finances.

Just as he was about to go look for Sydney, Luca entered his office. Waving a piece of paper in the air, he seated himself in the chair across from Kade's desk.

"So, did you hear from the witch?"

Kade nodded. "Yes, and interesting news, the address she gave me matches the one we got from the bartender last night. A mage by the name of Asgear bought Vin Vin oil around six months ago…fits our time frame. So maybe we'll get lucky tonight and find Simone. When is everyone coming over here? We should prep Sydney and the others."

"Yeah, about your girl." Luca smirked knowingly. "Do you happen to know where she is?"

"She is here in the house. I just saw her a few minutes ago standing at my door. Why do you ask?" Kade's lips tightened.

"Well, you might be interested to know that she took off to meet Tristan in the French Quarter, alone." He threw the note across Kade's desk. "You must have been on your conference call a little longer than you thought."

Kade read the note, feeling blood rushing to his face.

"Damn, stubborn woman. I specifically told her not to go out alone. She does not follow instructions," he muttered.

"Or simply does not wish to and ignores them on purpose. She's with Tristan, though. Surely he will protect her?" Luca could not resist stirring the pot.

"She is mine," Kade barked.

"I see," Luca said quietly. "I must inquire, Kade, does she understand how you feel? Does she know that she has been claimed, or what that means? That she is yours? She is only human after all."

"Hell, I don't know. You know me better than anyone. I've had many women over the centuries, but only a handful of actual lovers, women I cared about. But this human woman, she…she makes me crazy. Crazy with lust, crazy frustrated, infuriated at times. She won't obey orders, putting herself in danger left and right. Worse, danger is part of her job, so she acts like it is perfectly normal. And as insane as she makes me, I cannot resist her. There has been no one like her, ever." He rubbed his brow with one hand and stretched his neck from side to side. "I must talk with her when she returns. This nonsense has got to stop. And if she has been with Tristan…" He could not even go there. He loved Tristan, but would rip out his heart if he touched her today. He knew they had a past relationship, but he had informed Tristan of his intentions with Sydney, which Tristan had agreed to honor.

"Listen, I'm sure she'll return safely." Luca rose and patted Kade's shoulder. "It's daytime, and Tristan will escort her back here. Even I must admit that Sydney is a very capable woman. You know that I'm generally opposed to getting humans involved in vampire business; their weakness puts us all in danger. But the woman has staked two vampires so far and rescued Dominique, so I have to give her that. I'm still not crazy about having a human working the case with us, but she is proving her worth.

"As for Tristan, you are friends." Luca crossed the room to the doorway, knowing he needed distance for what he was about to say to Kade. "He will honor your intentions with Sydney…as will I."

Kade listened, already aware of what Luca was thinking.

"Last night, on the dance floor, dancing with Sydney, with you and her. It was intimate. I have not danced with a woman in a very long time. She is…" He lowered his eyes in submission. "She is very desirable, but Tristan and I are your friends. Even if Sydney doesn't yet understand the extent of your feelings, we have a pretty good idea. None of us will pursue her, knowing she is yours. Well, not unless you invite me in on the fun again," he joked, trying to diffuse the tension. Kade knew Luca had been aroused the previous night. But he'd controlled the situation, had given Luca permission. He'd felt no jealousy, as he danced erotically with them both. It wasn't as if he and Luca hadn't shared women in the past. But there would be no sharing Sydney. Dancing was one thing, making love was another. Kade was falling in love with her. Sydney was his, and he needed to make her understand they could have a future together.

Sydney pushed through the front door feeling refreshed. Kade stood waiting in the foyer, his arms crossed, aiming a menacing glare at her and Tristan.

"Look, man, I told her you'd be pissed for not telling you where she was going. And before you vamp out on me, no, I did not touch her." Tristan retreated a few steps and held his hands up in surrender. "So, looks like you guys have a lot to talk about. I'm gonna get something to eat."

Kade shot his friend a look of irritation as Tristan waved, making his way toward the kitchen.

"Listen, Kade, I'm not sure why you're boring holes into me, but I just went out for beignets and I needed to get my weapons and..." Sydney began.

Kade tore across the room, possessively grasping her arms and pulling her into him closely. Her bag dropped to her feet. They were so very close, chest to chest, face to face, forehead to forehead. He would never hurt a single hair on her head, but she needed to understand the seriousness of running around in this city alone. Most importantly, she needed to understand that she belonged to him for the rest of time.

"Sydney, love, what don't you understand about my directions? I told you not to go out alone. Outside this house, Simone can get to you, any time, any place. You scared the life out of me," he growled.

"You said that I was expected to consult on this case, not pursue leads on my own, and follow your directions...all of which I've been doing. Furthermore, you do not get to tell me what to do in my spare time," she said, pointing a finger at his chest. Showing no remorse, Sydney defiantly wrenched out of his arms. "I would have been more than happy to tell you where I was going today had you actually stuck around in my bed this afternoon to find out, or if you had taken the time to talk to me when I came looking for you. You did neither of those two things, so I left you a note. Which by the way, I believe was a perfectly acceptable alternative considering how you treated me."

This woman was trying to make him insane. Her full, lush lips beckoned to him, as did her engorged tips straining against her tight, purple sundress. She needed to be taught a lesson all right, but his cock grew in instant arousal, with a very different activity in mind.

"You, me, now. My office." He pointed down the hallway and took her by her hand. He was not having this conversation out in the middle of the house where Tristan and Luca could hear every last word, not to mention the others who would soon be here.

Sydney winced as Kade slammed the office door shut, plowing his fingers through his hair. He paced the room, finally positioning himself directly in front of her chair, and her eyes drifted to his groin. *I did not just look there. Okay, I did.* Averting her eyes to his desk, which also brought dirty thoughts to mind, she huffed.

"I didn't deliberately set out to make you angry, but you've got to look at this from my perspective. It's not my first time in New Orleans. You were busy; I left a note and went directly to meet Tristan. I was perfectly safe."

"Sydney, first, let's get something clear, until Simone is caught, you cannot go out on your own. We found a mage suspect who happens to reside at the same address the bartender gave us. Said mage would not be limited during the daylight hours. So even though you thought you may have been safe, you could have been bespelled at any time."

"Okay, point taken," Sydney conceded. *Spells? Witches? Mage?* The last thing she needed was for someone to put a whammy on her while she was looking to get her beignet on. "I promise. No going out alone, but in my defense, I did leave a note. So, it wasn't as if I just went missing." She'd known he'd be angry but hadn't expected the intensity of his reaction. The cop in her told her to be mad at him, but his pure masculine strength reverberated throughout the room, making her grow wet with desire.

"No going anywhere without me," he repeated. Like a predator, he deliberately locked in on his prey, closing her knees together as he straddled her legs, dominating her personal space.

Sydney nodded in agreement. As he towered above her, she could feel the heat of him upon her. Blood rushed to her face as she became swollen below with need. The man was so sexy, delicious, and all hers.

"Last night was electrifying," he continued, twirling a strand of her hair. "Making love to you…I have never felt for a woman what I feel for you. You must understand that we are halfway bonded to each other. When I bit you…" He trailed his finger along the mark on her neck. She shivered in anticipation, wanting more. "When I bit you, I claimed you as my own, my woman. I am falling for you, Miss Willows, and I don't intend to let you go…not after this case is over…not ever."

Sydney's heart ached, finally hearing him say that he wanted to be with her. She gazed up into his piercing eyes and felt as if he could see into her very soul.

"Kade, I'm falling for you too. I…I don't know what this all means, but I want to explore this with you…our feelings, our relationship. I can't believe I'm even saying this, but us…last night…it was amazing. You overwhelm me. I want you so much I can't think straight."

Sydney craved him; his kiss, the taste of him. Reaching up his hard, muscular thighs, she let the palms of her hands roam toward his growing arousal. Ripping his belt off within seconds, she unzipped his pants, releasing his straining masculinity.

"Yes," he groaned as she took him into her hands.

"I have to taste you now, can't wait." Stroking his throbbing shaft, she licked the underside of him, laving it from root to tip. Drawing out the pleasure, she pressed the crown between her lips.

"Sydney, you're killing me." Kade's head lolled back.

That was exactly what she was planning…to bring him to his knees. Pumping his stiff, wet shaft in her hand, she gradually slid his thick hardness all the way into her warm, parted mouth. She pumped him in and out, sucking and relishing every hard inch of him, while sweeping her tongue along his length. Reaching under his rigidity, she caressed his tightened balls, tenderly rolling them in her hand.

"Sydney, stop, please, I want to make love to you...which I won't be able to do if you keep that up." Kade sucked a sharp breath, unable to endure the sweet torture of her moist, warm mouth.

Seductively, Sydney released him from her mouth pulling his pants down and off in the process. It was her turn to dominate, to take the initiative. God, she loved this man. She thirsted to enjoy his magnificent body. Standing up, she switched places with him, and pressed him down into the soft leather loveseat.

"I want to enjoy every inch of you, Mister Issacson, every hard inch," she purred. Climbing over him and yanking her dress up, she pulled off her thong and balanced her knees on either side of his thighs, hovering over his narrow hips, but not yet touching him. Kade clasped his strong hands around Sydney's waist, allowing her to direct the play.

The deep aching heat between her legs threatened to hasten her approach, but she wanted this to last. Desperately needing to taste Kade's skin, she slowly unbuttoned his shirt and threw it aside.

Kade reached under her dress to touch her, only to find the bare, silky skin of her soft flesh. "Aw...love...you're so very, very wicked. A naughty girl, my naughty girl. Truly, I cannot take waiting. Come here."

Placing his hand behind her neck, he pulled her toward him and fiercely kissed her. He captured her soft lips, his tongue finding hers. Sydney gave in to his intoxicating kiss, running her fingers through his hair. His fingertips dug into the smooth skin of her ass and massaged her toned muscles.

Allowing her hand to roam below, she rubbed his straining cock against her slick, wet crease, readying him for her. A burst of ecstasy shook her body as she guided him into her slowly, one incredible inch at a time. Slowly she sank all the way down on him, enveloping his entire length, joining their bodies as one.

"Yes! Kade, oh my God. You're so hard, so big. Please, oh yes!"

She arched her back, moving up and down in a rhythmic motion that stimulated her most tender nub. Sensing her increasing arousal, Kade reached a hand up and slid down the straps of her dress, freeing her full, heavy breasts. Leaning forward, he captured a nipple in his mouth, sucking and biting its tortured peak. Sydney moaned again, opened her heavy-lidded eyes and watched as he mastered her body.

The sight of him pushed her over the crest. She began forcefully riding him, both of them rocking to her rhythm. Sydney felt dizzy as her body started to shake intensely. He bit her softly on her breast, pushing her into an explosive climax. She cried out his name as she shuddered, riding out the last wave of her orgasm.

Kade reluctantly separated from her, dominantly lifting her from his lap. He glanced to the desk and raised an eyebrow at her.

"Desk. Now," he ordered.

"Yes," she breathed.

Kade gently bent her over it, placing her hands flat onto its surface. She grew hot as the cheek of her face settled on the cold leather desktop. He lifted her dress to expose the creamy flesh of her backside.

"You ready for me, love?"

"Please. I need you now. Inside me. Make love to me," she pleaded, her breath quickening as she anticipated his entrance.

Flattening his hands on her buttocks, Kade plunged inside of her core, filling her with his hardness. Her warm, moist sheath massaged his cock as he pumped in and out of her. He knew he wouldn't last long. Letting a hand slide up her back, he wrapped the long hair of her ponytail in his fist, tugging her back into him. She screamed his name in rapture, the pain and pleasure of the moment almost too much to bear.

Their bodies moved together as one. As he drove himself deep inside her, she pushed back on his shaft. Both Kade and Sydney fought for breath as they approached climax, moving in response to one another. Kade let go of her hair to tightly hold her by the waist, thrusting harder and harder. Knowing they were both close, he leaned over, pressing his chest to her back.

"I love you. Forever, you are mine," he whispered in her ear.

With those words, he slammed into her one last time while biting down on the back of her neck, releasing her divine blood into his mouth.

The slice of his teeth drove her into an uncontrollable orgasm. Pulsating waves of pleasure resounded throughout every square inch of her skin. Her contracting sex convulsed around Kade's cock, and he groaned loudly, erupting inside of her.

Sydney didn't resist as Kade slipped out of her, pulling her into his arms. He kissed the top of her head, and Sydney contemplated what he'd just told her. *I love you.* She could hardly believe that within days of meeting Kade, she'd fallen so hard for him. A vampire. Surreal as it was, she couldn't deny what was in her heart.

"Kade?" she whispered.

"Yes, love?"

"I'm not sure how it happened, or what kind of a future we can have…but," she began.

"Yes?"

"I love you, too." Sydney buried her face into his chest, surprised at the words that had spilled from her lips.

Sydney's heart raced as Kade lifted her chin and gazed into her eyes. He smiled in response, and she knew in that moment what he'd said was true, she'd forever be his.

Chapter Sixteen

Delightfully sore after making love with Kade in his office, Sydney sighed, reflecting on their night together. Her chest blossomed with the love she felt for this man. She couldn't believe she'd told him she loved him. She wasn't sure how it was going to work with her living in Philadelphia, but she decided not to dwell on the details.

Nothing was going to put a crimp in her day, except for Simone. Damn Voodoo, vampire bitch. Sydney sobered with the thought that they were about to go bust a mage, one who could very well put their lives in danger with dark magic. The address traced back to a large, abandoned building in the Warehouse District. Going in at night would give them a greater advantage, since the vampires would have the full use of their powers. Sydney, on the other hand, knew she'd be at risk, given her many human frailties, like not being able to see in the dark. Luca had provided her with a pair of state-of-the-art, night goggles so she could see better, but she still lacked the speed and power of the vampires.

After securing her hair in a neat French braid, Sydney pulled on a pair of black leather pants. The rugged fabric clung tightly to her finely toned figure. It might be a tad hot wearing leather on a warm, summer night in New Orleans, but her skin needed protection, given the abandoned building they planned on searching. She yanked a black cotton long-sleeved t-shirt over her head, but not before hiding a miniature curved sheathed Kerambit knife in a hidden compartment of her sports bra. Strapping on the bullet and stab proof Kevlar vest, she was almost ready to go. The clothing wasn't very comfortable. Sydney added a lightweight concealer jacket, which sported several hidden pockets and compartments where she could stash her ammunition: stakes, darts and silver chains. She strapped on both waist and leg holsters, loaded them up and paced the room, satisfied with the weight of her trusty Sigs. Before lacing up her military boots, she shoved a small, sheathed push dagger next to her ankle. The arrow-pointed knife was small, but effective in hand-to-hand combat.

Lastly, she pulled her pistol crossbow out of her backpack, checked and counted the wooden darts. Confident everything was in order, she strapped it across her chest, and it slung behind her back. Lifting the night goggles off the bed, she sucked in a breath, letting courage run through her veins. It was time to go kick some mage ass, and hopefully get one step closer to capturing Simone.

Entering the great room, Sydney steadied herself, taking in the sight of the vampires towering above her.

They were also dressed in black combat outfits, ready to fight. In the doorway, she was surprised to see a large black wolf with amber eyes staring at her. She was tempted to ask if someone brought their dog, but thought better of it, realizing it was Tristan. Sydney didn't think he'd appreciate the dog joke, so she just nodded at him, not sure of what to say to his wolf. He yelped in response, and padded over to her side, rubbing against her leg.

When Kade entered the room, his presence dominated the space, and the air shifted. The wolf retreated away from Sydney, sensing Kade advancing directly over to her. Her body tingled in response to the sight of him. Dressed in black leather, he approached her. Looking dangerous and formidable, he was an animal in pursuit; hot, menacing, enticing. Sydney's pulse raced as if she and Kade were the only two people in the room.

He leaned toward her and captured her soft lips. Releasing her, he whispered in her ear, "You are ravishing in all that leather, love. It makes me want to take you upstairs and show you how very much I appreciate your outfit." He kissed her once again, asserting his claim on his woman.

"Seriously, you guys?" Dominique snorted. She flicked her long red nails which had been filed into fine points. "Enough with the lovey-dovey crap. It's time to go kill some bad guys. I'm looking forward to finding that little bitch who silvered me to the table and drinking her dry."

"Hey Dominique, how are the wrists? Your nails look great, love the color." Sydney smirked at the sight of a badass vampire girl worried about how her nails looked when she was about to go into combat.

"Thanks, Syd. Wrists are great. Amazing what a little blood can do." She laughed and held out her hands, showing off her polished talons. "The color's Sanguine Red. Want to make sure I look my best when I tear open Rhea…if that's even her real name."

"Okay, then. Good plan." Sydney raised an eyebrow at her, grinning. She didn't ever want to be on Dominique's bad side. "Can't say that I blame you after what she did to you yesterday. Hopefully we'll find her there tonight."

Kade moved to the center of the group, commanding attention.

"So, here's the deal. We are going downtown to the Warehouse District. Even though the building is abandoned, the area is active with humans, so keep a low profile. That means no killing within sight of others. Keep it in house." His lips tightened. "All we know so far is that Asgear is the mage who purchased the Van Van oil. So it is a good possibility that he is the one who is helping Simone. Asgear may be harboring dark magic, so no going it alone…stay together. Watch your step for traps. We'll be partnering up…Luca and I will go in first, then Xavier and Sydney. Dominique and Etienne, you bring up the rear. Tristan will be monitoring the outside, making sure we don't get any surprises while we're in there. If possible, we need the mage alive so we can get Simone's location. Got it?"

A sea of nods erupted, and Luca coughed. "We need to take two vans so we have enough room for all of us when we bring Asgear back to the compound. As for Simone's fledglings, my advice is to stake them and put them out of their misery. They'll be unable to give us any information because of their blood tie to Simone. That's about it. Everyone stay safe tonight."

"Let's go," Kade ordered. As the sober group filed out the door and into the vans, Kade prayed they'd all be coming back tonight.

The abandoned building was located on the outskirts of the Warehouse District. Sprinkled with restaurants, galleries and bars, the 'SoHo of the South' bustled with people on summer nights. Luckily, the address was located a little off the beaten trail, far enough away from most activities, reducing the risk of human interference. From the outside, the two-story, large brick building appeared desolate, with indecipherable graffiti painted on the walls. Sydney noticed all the front windows had been boarded over, some with new plywood and some with old. Perhaps a recent tenant had made the repairs?

As they circled the block, Kade pointed to the front doors, double steel with small square windows that had been spray painted over in black. There was another single door lower down, which looked like it could possibly lead to a basement. Driving around to the back of the building, they parked the vans. Kade, Luca and the others silently exited, seeking an entrance. Sydney guessed the vampires might have been telepathically communicating, as they appeared well synchronized, quickly locating and shimmying open the rusted locks on the rotting, wooden warehouse door.

A rush of stale air choked Sydney's lungs as the door swung open. Many of these old buildings had been abandoned in the late 1800s, outliving their usefulness as factories or mills. But this building stank of stale blood, decaying bodies, urine, and garbage, smells she was all too familiar with, working the city streets of Philadelphia. She may not have been a vampire, but she was certain recent activity had happened in this place. A chill ran up her spine as she remembered the vampire who'd attacked her in her home. Were there more just like him waiting here for them?

Total darkness descended upon them as they entered the dark hallway. Sydney flipped on her night vision goggles, and swung her pistol crossbow to her chest. Looking behind her, she saw Dominique and Etienne moving in stealthy silence. A confining, steep staircase led to a gray steel state-of-the-art security door. Pivoting around to face the group, Kade silently signaled his intent to breach the door. Muscular vampires would have no difficulty breaking it down. Bracing himself for impact, Kade raised his fingers. One. Two. Three.

Sydney crouched as dust and debris flew ubiquitously throughout the stairwell. Coughing up dust, she charged after Kade. At least twenty vampires flew at the doorway, fangs drooling and snapping at Kade and Luca. Immediately, a fight ensued in the spacious area. Sydney backed against a wall and systematically began picking off vamps with wooden darts to the heart. She was a good shot and ashes flew as they disintegrated on the spot.

"Remind me to stay on your good side, woman. You're damn good with the darts," Luca commented, sidling up next to Sydney against the wall. "Kade and I are heading toward the basement. Etienne and Xavier are taking the second floor. Now! Cover me!"

Luca dashed across the room with unnatural speed, catching up with Kade who was already at the basement door. Sydney took aim at a vampire lunging after him. Pop! The hit to the leg slowed him down, but Luca was struggling to shake him off. She didn't want to come off the wall just yet, but two more vamps were descending on Luca and Kade. *Where the fuck are they all coming from?*

Hoping she'd be fast enough, Sydney sprinted across the room, nearing Luca. In a last minute decision, she leaped onto the vamp's back and shoved a silver stake deep into its heart. Luca struggled to his feet. Grabbing Sydney's arm, he pulled her up with him. Sydney shook off the ash and backed against the doorjamb next to Luca.

"Going old school?" Luca asked with a small grin. "I appreciate the save, but don't get reckless. Kade will whip both our asses if something happens to you. Looks like he's already headed downstairs. Let's go with him. Stay close. I go first," he ordered.

Kade was already three quarters of the way down the stairs when Luca and Sydney started after him. The air hung heavy, an audible hum resonated from the basement walls, yet no apparent source could be seen. Illuminated in candlelight, a thin wiry man, who wore a glowing crimson robe, sat perched upon a stone pedestal. *Asgear.*

Kade attempted to maneuver toward him, but slammed against an invisible barricade. *Dark magic.* Asgear released a wicked laugh.

"Foolish vampire. Did you really think it would be that easy to capture me? My Mistress has anticipated your every move thus far. And while I've had great fun playing with you, the time grows near. She will ascend. You will be no more."

"Your Mistress, Simone, was banished over a hundred years ago. She has no right to be here and will soon be exterminated as punishment for her crimes. Give it up, Asgear. Tell me where she is. I will be fair meting out your sentence," Kade demanded.

"You're an arrogant vampire." Asgear ascended from the pedestal, floating across the room toward Kade, his feet never touching the floor. "You know nothing of the strength of my magic. I've been honing my craft for decades. Now, my power is growing exponentially every day as does hers. Soon, you'll be begging on your knees in agony as she drains the blood of your whore!" His eyes shot daggers at Sydney.

Luca and Kade pounded their fists against the barrier seeking a weak point, but it was unyielding. Attempting to kick at the invisible blockage, Sydney unexpectedly penetrated it, falling to her knees. Her hands scraped the concrete floor and began to bleed. Asgear laughed maniacally, amused by how easily the spider had caught the fly.

"Ah, Sydney. Welcome to my inner sanctum. We have such plans for you. You will serve a greater purpose. We have almost perfected the ritual."

"You must be out of your fucking mind if you think I will be part of any plans you have. I'm gonna bring you down. There are a few girls back in Philly who have a message for you and that bitch you call a Mistress. Now, do you want to come willingly or are we going to do this the hard way? You should know that I'm more than pissed, and could care less which way it goes," she spat at him. Sydney aimed her dart at Asgear, guessing a few holes would loosen his lips.

"Tsk. Tsk. Must you be so vulgar? You're less than nothing, a simple harlot, one who will serve nicely in our next Voodoo ritual. The Mistress seeks revenge for taking her husband. She's going to consume your spirit as you writhe in pain. Oh yes...your life force will add to her power quite nicely. The spirits will reward her greatly for the ritual. Now, come to me, Sydney, the portal awaits...we will take hedonistic pleasure at the palace of Voodoo. The spirits will bless us!"

Asgear's demented, Sydney thought. *A portal? Hedonistic pleasure? What the hell is he talking about? Fuck that.* She had no plans of going anywhere with this psychopath, let alone to some pleasure playground for dead people. She caught a glimpse of Luca and Kade, who were still pummeling against an invisible enemy. Sydney drew her pistol crossbow and fired twice, score. The darts tore through Asgear's leg and shoulder. He tumbled to the ground, spitting obscenities at her. She went to approach him, but he rose off the floor wickedly grinning at her, unharmed.

"Did you really think a few darts would hurt me? You stupid, stupid little whore! I am done playing. This game is over!" He lifted his hands into the air, mumbling chants that Sydney couldn't understand.

A rush of confusion washed over her as she began to feel dizzy. What was he saying? More importantly, how the hell did he get back up? Sydney started to waver as she desperately tried to retreat to Kade, but the pull of the air whirled around her, immobilizing her limbs. *Shit. This can't be good.* She flailed her arms and legs, struggling against the air current, but it was of no use. The air spun around and around, stinging her face.

"Kade! Help me! I can't move! Please!" Screaming into nothingness, Sydney hoped Kade could hear her. She stole one last look at him before she faded into blackness.

Kade and Luca choked on the stale dust as they rushed to Sydney, but it was too late. She was gone.

"Shit!" Kade yelled, outraged. "She's gone. She's fucking gone. My God. Asgear took her. They must have transported through a portal of some kind. We've got to find her."

They quickly searched the basement, but found nothing.

"There is no trace of her or Asgear," Luca said. "Where would he take her?"

"Let's just think. He was babbling about Simone, her plans." Kade plowed his fingers through his hair, frustrated. "Voodoo. Simone wants to use her as a doll. Something about using her spirit. But what she really wants is me. And power. She won't be satisfied by killing Sydney. No, she wants more. Asgear and Simone both want more. They want control over all the supernatural beings in New Orleans." He started to pace, trying to think where Asgear could have taken Sydney. "But where? This city is a hotbed of supernatural activity. They could summon spirits literally anywhere."

"She wants us to find her, Kade, so she can get to you." Luca blew out a breath, as Tristan, Etienne, Xavier and Dominique joined them in the basement. "Asgear, he said, 'palace of Voodoo'. A Voodoo museum? Maybe he meant the field where you burnt down the barn where Simone tortured the girls?"

"The cemetery, St. Louis cemetery." With ferocious intensity, Kade's eyes met Luca's. "Marie Laveau. Her mausoleum. It is the one place in New Orleans where even humans go to give sacrifices in the name of Voodoo. They could be anywhere on the grounds. Don't ask me how she's using the sacred cemetery to garner evil spirits, but that is where she's going. I just know it."

Chapter Seventeen

Sydney moaned in pain, realizing her hands were shackled in rusted metal cuffs linked to a two-foot chain above her head. Her body, sans clothes, slumped against a cold steel wall. A surge of panic rushed through her veins as she struggled to remember what had happened. *Asgear. Portal. Where the hell am I?* She stretched her legs, thankful that she still had on her underwear. Unable to reach down to her torso, Sydney jostled, hoping to feel the Kerambit knife still hidden in her bra. *Hello, baby, still there.* Relieved she still had a weapon, she took a deep breath, but nearly gagged on the stench of urine and vomit that permeated the air.

As her eyes adjusted to the pitch-black room, she sensed she wasn't alone. Hearing a moan, she called out into the darkness.

"Hey, is there someone in here with me? Who's there?"

"Over here," a weak, feminine voice answered. "I'm Samantha."

"Samantha?"

"Please don't hurt me," she begged.

"Willows. Detective Sydney Willows. I'm with the police. Listen, it's okay. I won't hurt you. How long have you been here? Are you injured?"

"I've been here a few days. Lost count after being beaten. I think I can walk, but I'm bruised. The cuts are healing. It's hard to see," she whimpered.

"You remember how you got here?"

"I was taken. My friends and I went to Sangre Dulce for fun. I'm not even from New Orleans. I was at a computer conference. It was my first time at that kind of club. We were just dancing. Then I met him. James…he seemed so nice. He bought me a drink. I don't remember anything else except for being here…him beating me. Oh my God. I'm going to die in here."

Sydney heard her crying. "Listen, Samantha, this is not your fault. There're some sick people out there who do bad things. I'm going to get us out of here. If they take me, just stay calm, okay? I promise I'll come back for you." She sighed, knowing things were about to get worse before they got better, and she didn't want to lie to the young woman. "I'll be honest, I'm not sure how this is going to go down, but my colleagues are coming for me. I'm sure of it." *I sure as hell hope they come soon.* "I need your help though, okay? Who else is here? Who have you seen since you've been here?"

"James. He brings me crackers…water. I tried to hit him the first day, tried to escape. Then he beat me. I haven't seen anyone else. But I think there might be a woman. I think I've heard her voice. I don't know, though. I haven't seen anyone else. I feel like I'm going crazy…maybe dreaming it. Even though I hear her voice, I've only seen James."

"Good girl, Samantha. Listen, this is how I'm going to play this. When James comes for me, I'm going willingly. I don't want him using me as an excuse to hurt you. You stay quiet, okay? Just let him take me, got it?" Sydney had to keep the girl alive.

"Please don't leave me here. I've got to get out of here. He's going to kill me. You promise you'll come back for me?"

Sydney didn't want to freak the girl out, but she figured she'd better warn her that there were *others*, other supernaturals who were coming for her. "I promise. Now listen, I have some friends who are vampires. They won't hurt you, and there's a very large, black wolf. They are friends. You'll be safe. If they come for you…if I don't make it back, you go with them, okay? They're the good guys."

"All right," Samantha sniffled in the darkness. "Oh my God. Shhh. I hear him. The keys. You hear the keys? It's him. He's coming."

Silence fell over the small closet-like prison cell as the girls awaited their captor. Feigning sleep, Sydney lolled her head back against the wall and closed her eyes. The sound of clanging of keys was followed by a creaking door. *Asgear.*

"Wakey, wakey, little whore," he called.

Sydney shivered as his clammy hands clamped onto her skin. He briefly freed her from her shackles but her hopes of freedom were crushed as she heard the unmistakable click of handcuffs closing around her wrists. She stumbled as he jerked her up onto her bare feet.

"The Mistress is pleased with my success. You're going to make a fine offering. Your smooth skin…ahhhhh." He ran a wet finger over the swell of her breasts. She recoiled from his touch. "Now, now, little whore. You will not get away from me so easily. Consider yourself lucky that I cannot take your body for my own carnal pleasures before giving you to my Mistress. So greedy she is…she wants you all to herself."

Sydney resisted telling him to go fuck himself as he continued to run his palms over her belly. She needed to conserve her energy, to get him to release her from her bindings.

"Go," Asgear ordered, propelling her forward into the bright hallway. "No funny business. I'd hate to have to bruise that pretty skin of yours before Mistress has her way with you."

Shuffling ahead, Sydney squinted as her eyes adjusted to the light. The cold linoleum floor appeared oddly clean. She'd take small favors at this point, given her lack of shoes. The hallway was only about twenty feet long, which initially led her to believe the space was small. A frigidness chilled Sydney's nearly naked body. *What was this place? A basement?*

A small vestibule led into a large, cathedral-like room made entirely of smooth, grayish limestone. Large silk scarves in various shades of blacks, purples and greens draped the walls. A shiver of terror tingled up Sydney's neck as Asgear dragged her across the chilled stone floor. Sydney spied a long, planked table with ropes attached to its legs and an enormous white chalk pentagram drawn underneath it. *Hemp and human hair rope?* At the front of the room stood an altar of some sort. Black and green candles burned brightly, illuminating a modest wooden box covered in black cloth, a golden chalice, and a long, silver sword.

"Oh great Mistress!" Asgear grinned widely, as if he was high as a kite. With grandeur, he spoke into the open space. "Our offering has arrived. She will serve us nicely so that the spirits of the dead will grant us their powers."

"Delusional much?" Sydney said, unable to resist. Eyeing the table, she refused to let him sacrifice her without a fight. She held onto the thought that Kade would find her. She just needed more time. "Asgear, even if you do manage to conjure up some evil spirit, do you really think that bitch mistress of yours plans to share the power with you...little mage that you are? Get real! So not happening."

She attempted to yank her arm free from his firm grip, but he dug his fingers into her skin. Angered by her actions, he spun Sydney around by her shoulders and backhanded her across her face. She fell to the floor as blood sprayed out of her mouth.

"Now look what you made me do, little whore!" he screamed violently.

Sydney spat at him as he reeled her up and thrust her onto her back upon the splintered wood table. She struggled unsuccessfully as he uncuffed her wrists one at a time and bound each hand to the legs of the table. She flung a leg toward him as he went to bind her ankle. She landed a blow to his nose, his bone crunching upon impact. Sydney tugged her wrists, trying to free herself, but he rapidly recovered.

"Be still!" he yelled and landed a slap to her face.

Sydney refused to give up, wildly kicking her legs, hoping to make contact again. Within seconds, her eye began to swell, blurring her vision. Asgear continued his task. He wound the rope around her ankles, fully securing her to the table until she was laid out spread eagle.

"Wait until my Mistress sees what you made me do!" He glared at her in disgust. "Your skin is marred. She won't be pleased at all."

Sydney continued to writhe on the table, struggling to liberate her hands from the cutting rope. Twisting to the side, her adrenaline spiked as she spied several of Simone's vampires entering and assembling in a circle at the perimeter of the room. *Shit, shit, shit. Freaking bloodsuckers.*

Asgear knelt in front of the altar and started rhythmically chanting. The din of the crowd quieted and Sydney turned her head toward the antechamber. Her heart raced as a pale, thin, tall woman entered and approached the altar. *Simone.* Her flowing, alabaster silk skirt grazed the floor as a train of fabric streamed three feet behind her. A matching silk bustier bolstered her small, ashen breasts. Simone's long raven tresses were pulled and parted down the middle flat on her head with a full, massive ponytail of tight ringlet curls, a late eighteenth century hairstyle. Sydney cringed at the overwhelming scent of gardenia perfume as Simone floated past her.

"Hey you!" Sydney screamed at Simone. Blood trickled from her eye and mouth. "That's right, I'm talking to you…you lily white, vampire bitch."

Simone glided over to the altar, scanning her worthy sacrifice.

"Silence, human! So, it is you who attempted to steal my husband. You are nothing more than a mere dollymop…a whore for his liking. You are nothing. I shall take my vengeance tonight and the torture will be sweet. The spirits will infuse me with gifts, supremacy. This city will return to its greatness under my rule."

"Fuck you! This isn't the eighteenth century, and Kade is not your husband. He doesn't love you. You are an evil, sick bitch who will regret the day you ever met me."

"I said SILENCE! It is time for the offering. I sentence this human to death in the name of Satan and all the spirits who wish to grant me their gifts. She is guilty of crimes against me, the high priestess vampire." She waved her hand, and the candlelight flickered as a cold breeze blew throughout the room. The circling vampires hissed at Sydney, their fangs dripping saliva.

Sydney tried to speak, tried to move, but she was completely paralyzed except for her breathing. Her eyes peered wide open, feeling the chill across her flesh. *This is not good.*

Through her peripheral vision, she could see Simone preparing some kind of concoction at the altar. Asgear spread oil on Sydney's forehead, chest, and abdomen while he continued his chanting. He pivoted, cupping the golden chalice with both hands, and hovered it above Sydney's head. Panic began to set in as Simone laid the cold, flat surface of a silver sword against Sydney's belly, dragging the sword crosswise. Blood pooled on Sydney's skin as Simone drew an X on the soft flesh.

"Your blood is my blood. Your life force is my life force. You give it to me freely as a punishment for your crimes. We shall drink your essence in preparation for the sacrifice." Simone spoke in a monotone, as the room fell into total silence. "Now, whore. I want to hear you scream!" She sliced deeply into the underside of Sydney's forearm, cutting so far through the tendons that the blood flowed freely. Crimson liquid rapidly filled the chalice to the brim. Asgear watched in exhilaration as Simone licked Sydney's arm, sealing the wound.

Released momentarily from paralysis, Sydney cried out in pain, yet refused to give in to tears as her arm was slit open. She fought the vomit that rose in her throat as she watched Simone's acid tongue lick over her bloodied skin. Asgear began offering the chalice to the vampires to drink as some kind of a preparatory, bloody communion. One by one, they drank of her blood, passing the chalice to the next vampire.

Fear washed over Sydney as she spied the tool she suspected was used on the second murder victim. Simone inspected the twelve-inch-long needle, holding it to the candlelight. She raised the instrument into the air, and both Simone and Asgear began to chant in tongues. Vampires swayed in a trance to the nonsensical vocalizations. A strong hum started to vibrate the room and the wooden table shook.

In the middle of the chaos, Sydney felt him. *Kade.* She wasn't sure how she knew, but she did. He was here for her. *I love him.* It was her last coherent thought before Simone shrieked and slammed the full hilt of the needle down into Sydney's torso, penetrating her belly clear down into the table.

Chapter Eighteen

"What in the hell just happened?" Tristan questioned his friends accusingly. "Goddammit! You were supposed to keep her safe! I should have gone with you instead of guarding the perimeter!" Tristan felt guilty, knowing he too had planned this failed operation with Kade and Luca. Although she wasn't wolf, he considered her under his protection since the day he'd met her. Former lover, good friend, Sydney was his one link to the human world that he trusted with his life. Now, because of their miscalculations, she might be dead. Tristan howled loudly, frustrated with their defeat and the potential loss of his friend.

"You're right. Luca and I lost her, but we cannot focus on failure right now. We need to plan on how we are going to kill Simone and extract Sydney safely. You know our girl is not going to go down without a fight. She is strong." Kade deliberately called her, 'our girl', trying to get the group focused on the task that needed to be done. They needed to find her quickly and kill Simone. Sydney was no one's but his and everyone knew it, but he was a leader and could not let them dwell on their defeat. No, he needed to get Sydney back safely into his arms. He had not lived through centuries only to lose his chance with her, his one true love. "Tristan, take Luca's cell phone and call your brother, Marcel. Let him know the situation has escalated, and that we need his pack's assistance with backup."

As they arrived at the cemetery, Kade stiffened, sensing Sydney's presence.

"I feel her. She's here."

"Kade, please forgive my question, but I sense no human or paranormal presence in the area. Are you certain she is here?" Etienne asked.

"Yes. Do you forget? I have claimed her. I'm certain that she is here. Quickly, search the grounds. Stay in pairs," Kade ordered.

A high-pitched howl emanated across the darkness; Tristan. Weaving through the tenebrous labyrinth of crypts, Kade and the others converged on a nondescript tomb that no one would give a second glance to, compared to its ornamental counterparts. *Sydney.* Like Tristan, Kade could smell the sweet scent of her blood everywhere in the vicinity, as well the repugnant odors of Asgear and Simone.

"She's here, but Asgear and Simone are also present. We must move with caution. Simone will be expecting us," Kade warned. He'd need to rely on his friend to distract them so he could get to Sydney. "Tristan, you go in first and disable Asgear. We cannot be certain if he will conjure a thaumaturgical barrier like the one we experienced back in the warehouse, so make sure to cover the whole area. If Simone is in there, then it is likely that all vampires can pass. We won't know for sure until we get in."

Tristan transformed back into his naked male form, extending his claws, planning to pry open the stone door. A chorus of wolves howled in the distance.

"Ah, Marcel and the pack are here. They will come in behind us, and kill any of Simone's vampires who try to escape."

"Now, let's see what is in this tomb." Tristan ran his claws up and down the hard, smooth stone, loosening it. "Open up for papa."

"Back off, Tristan," Kade commanded. *Wolves always think they are so damn smart.* "Watch and learn, wolf." He smiled, unfolding his Smith & Wesson tactical knife. "Sometimes a vampire is well suited going old school, now is one of those times."

Plunging the edge of the knife far into the dusty stone seam, he jerked it upward, disengaging the primitive lock mechanism. The heavy mason door creaked open as it revealed a limestone staircase. The tunnel was illuminated by candles that sat on small wall shelves. Transforming back into his wolf, Tristan padded down the steps tilting his head back up toward Kade, awaiting his orders at the door at the bottom of the stairs.

A blood-curdling scream resonated throughout Kade's mind. Sydney's scream, Sydney's blood. He kicked the door open, letting Tristan run first into the madness. The wolf narrowly escaped being clawed by several vampires converging toward him. Slipping between their legs, he targeted Asgear who was holding a chalice above Sydney, who appeared to be strapped to a table. Razor-sharp teeth shredded Asgear's right shoulder and arm as Tristan pinned him to the cold floor. The wolf held him down, allowing Kade and the others to enter the chamber in order to get to Simone.

Scarlet body fluid sprayed the walls as Kade, Luca, and the other vampires tore into Simone's fanged puppets. Kade caught sight of Sydney, who was bound and bleeding. Enraged, he slashed through a sea of vampires, advancing toward her.

"You will die!" he spat at Simone, who ran at Tristan with a knife.

As Kade reached Sydney, he sliced at the rope, freeing one of her wrists. She lay bleeding on the table, her life's essence spilling out onto the floor with the thin spear lodged inside her gut.

"Sydney, I'm here. Just hang on…stay with me. I've got to get this out of you. Please don't leave me," Kade begged. He gently kissed her cool, pale lips and clutched the needle. Realizing it was jammed into the wooden table, Kade wrenched it out in one quick stroke, hoping to minimize the pain. "I'm so sorry, love."

Sydney arched in agony, screaming uncontrollably as the pain slammed into her once again. Her eyes flew open, and she stared up at the cold, gray vaulted stone ceiling above her.

Kade licked the small hole, sealing her wound. It wouldn't stop the internal bleeding, but it might buy her time. Knowing he would need to give her blood for a full healing, he sought her permission.

"You're going to be okay, but love…" He paused. He shook his head. This was all wrong, but she needed his blood to heal. "You're bleeding internally. I can give you my blood, but you must understand you will be bound to me forever. I will not do it without your agreement. I love you as much as life itself. You have no idea how much I wanted to give of myself to you, but not like this."

"Do it," she whimpered. Sydney's eyes fluttered as tears spilled over her cheeks. "I love you, Kade. I want to live."

"Are you sure?"

"Yes, but Kade?"

"Yes, love?"

"That woman of yours from the 1800s? She's a real bitch." She cracked a small smile. "Now, I just need to sit up. The rope…cut the rope."

As Kade pulled out his knife to free her, a vampire smacked him clear across the room.

"No! No! No! This is not going down this way! Get me off this fucking table!" Sydney screamed in frustration.

Remembering her knife hidden away in her bra, she felt around with her hand. *Thank you, baby Jesus. Still there.* Blood sprayed her face as she cut the rope and released herself from the table. Wolves and vampires bit and slashed each other as she gently eased herself onto the floor.

She looked over to see Dominique tearing the heart out of one of the vampires and silently cheered her on. Both Etienne and Xavier were also fighting, slashing through the crowd of vampires with wooden stakes. Ash started to cloud the room as one by one they staked their foes.

Sydney was shocked to see Simone fighting Tristan against the far wall. She sliced his wolf with a knife as he bit tightly into her other arm. Sydney struggled to locate Asgear. *Where is he?* Tilting her head upward, she spied the gleaming face of a sword on the altar. Pain shot throughout her entire body as she stretched her arm up to reach it. Blindly fingering the altar, her hand clasped around the hilt of the sword. She slowly lowered her arm, clutching the cool blade flat against her chest.

Kade honed his eyes on Sydney's, seeing she'd gotten free. He needed to get her out of the melee, but there seemed to be no end to the vampires who were attacking from all sides. Tristan was yelping in agony; several small knives stuck out of his bloody fur. Luca, Dominique, and the others were engaged in battle as well.

"Your little whore is going to die tonight, vampire. You cannot stop us." Blindsiding Kade, Asgear struck him in the head with the heavy metal chalice.

"You are the one who will die tonight. Even your magic wanes in the light of war." Kade shifted and delivered a side kick to Asgear's thorax, pounding him into the floor.

"She tried to fight me. I think she likes it rough." Asgear crawled toward Kade, trying to push himself upright. "She bled nicely when I beat her. When you die, I'm goin' to take her for my own. She'll serve me on her knees!"

Kade had had enough of Asgear's venomous words. He stood erect over the mage and kicked his face hard. Once, twice. Blood spritzed out of Asgear's mouth as he rolled onto his back.

"This is not the end, vampire!" Asgear hissed.

"Wrong again. This is the end of the road." Kade smirked at him. "Rot in hell!"

Kade pinned him to the floor, cracking his neck and wrenching his head off its spine. He bared his fangs, shredding Asgear's throat until there was not a single drop of blood left in the mage.

Sydney couldn't see Kade, but heard him arguing with Asgear. She grabbed the edge of the table, pulled upward and steadied herself on her feet. As Tristan came into sight, she screamed. Simone repeatedly stabbed the wolf.

"Hey bitch! Over here! Leave the wolf alone! It's me you want," she baited.

"You! You! You distracted me from my purpose!" Simone turned from Tristan, all her focus on Sydney. She tore across the room, grabbing Sydney's throat with one hand. "All my hard work. The girls' deaths ...it was all for him. I was practicing. My power was growing. And you had to stick your nose into my business...ruin my ritual!" She spat at Sydney's face. "I will make him watch as I drain every last drop of your whorish blood. I will rule this city! Nothing will stop me! Nothing!"

Sydney choked and struggled to breathe under the pressure of Simone's strong, bony fingers. Her eyes darted to Kade, who stealthily approached Simone.

"Let her go, Simone. She is a mere human. This animosity is between you and me."

Simone's eyes darted to Kade, but she didn't release her prey from her deathly grip. Sydney felt herself starting to lose consciousness. Even as both her arms fell to her sides, she fought to hold on to the sword.

"I do not love you, Simone. I never did." Stepping a hair closer to Simone, Kade refused to relent. "You'll never rule this town. You're finished."

"You do love me." Simone threw Sydney to the floor, and rushed over to him. "I'm here now. I am your queen. My power, I will share it with you. We shall rule together." She laid a pale hand upon his chest. "This is our time. You are mine."

Reaching for the table's edge, Sydney quietly pulled herself up so she was standing once again. Her abdomen throbbed, and she felt dizzy with pain. *Never give up.* The sword hummed underneath the warmth of her grip. She quietly approached Simone. *Time for the bitch to go.* With a final thrust of strength, Sydney whirled the heavy sword above her head. As the sword hissed, it sliced through the blood-tinted air and Simone's fine, pallid neck. Simone's dismembered head went flying across the room as blood and ash sprayed Kade's face. A clank of the sword on the ground was followed by silence in the room, as Simone's spell was broken.

Sydney fainted and her head cracked loudly against the ebon floor, blood covering her golden braid. Kade fell on his knees screaming her name. Biting into his wrist, he pressed it to her still lips hoping she would swallow the precious fluid.

"Sydney! You cannot bloody well leave me!" He laid her head in his lap, smoothing her hair across her head. Sydney's swollen lips began suctioning against his wrist. "I love you so much. Please, drink. That's it, love. Don't give up."

Kade kissed her forehead, knowing she would survive. He delicately lifted her frail body into his arms, carefully cradling her head against his chest. As he ascended the stairs, a healing breeze grazed his face. He sighed in relief, finally exiting Simone's diabolical stone creation. He called to Dominique to beckon Ilsbeth. Whatever demonic forces held the walls from the water table, they needed to be dismantled. The tomb and its rooms needed to be destroyed and blessed so that nothing remained of the malignant force within.

Luca approached him, carrying a small, unconscious woman with long, red hair. Kade immediately recognized the woman as Rhea.

"Where did you find her?" he asked.

"She was cuffed to a wall. The room was barbaric." Luca took a deep breath. "She's been recently beaten. Bloody whip marks all over her body, black eye...the works. She said her name is Samantha. Kade, something strange is going on here...it was as if she had no recollection of the club or the night she silvered Dominique. When we released her cuffs, she fainted. Exhaustion maybe?"

"Take her to my compound," Kade told him. He glanced to Sydney in his arms, concerned with getting her home as soon as possible. "Clean up the girl, make sure she's healing, and lock her in the downstairs security room until I get a chance to read her thoughts. It is possible that she was under Simone's thrall, or that Asgear bespelled her, but we need to make sure she holds no culpability before we return her to her home. And whatever you do, don't let Dominique see her yet. She is looking for payback, and will ask questions later. Now go."

Luca sped off across the cemetery, human in tow. Kade scanned the area and found Etienne kneeling on the ground, holding a naked Tristan, who drank at his wrist.

"How's Tristan?"

"Simone stabbed the hell out of him. He'll survive, but we need to get him back to the compound before his brother comes sniffing about. He will be pissed beyond belief. Marcel means well, but Tristan needs more vampire blood if he is going to make it." Etienne winced as Tristan continued suckling his wrist.

Kade caught sight of Dominique and Xavier exiting the tomb, and yelled over to them. "Let's get moving. Xavier, help Etienne with Tristan. Get him out of here now. Dominique, I need you to wait for Ilsbeth to get here. She needs to clean up this mess. You know what to do."

Kade was tired and angry. How could this have gone so very wrong? Sydney had been beaten, stabbed. He should never have let her leave Philadelphia. She was human, a strong human, yes, but still very human at that. She could have died tonight. His heart ached knowing she might need several days to recover from this ordeal. And then, would she still want to be with a vampire? The blood, the violence, the danger?

He trudged back to the van, his mind swirling with doubt. The only thing he knew for certain was that she was his. He was fooling himself to think he would let her go without a fight. He kissed her forehead as she slept peacefully in his arms. He prayed his beautiful, fighting warrior woman would be okay and that she would forgive him for involving her in this mess.

Chapter Nineteen

Sydney slowly opened her eyes to a candlelit room. *Kade's room?* Peering up, she noticed the intricate carving of the dark stained mahogany on the ceiling of the four poster, Tutor bed. Luxurious black velvet curtains were tied to the elaborately patterned posts, held back by red silk tiebacks with tassels. *Nice bed, Kade.* She smiled and turned her head toward the center of the bed where Kade slept soundly on his side with his hand possessively touching her stomach.

She moved to get out of bed when Kade pulled her into his arms and rested her head against his chest.

"Now exactly where do you think you are going, love?" He pressed his lips to her hair. "How are you feeling?"

"I don't know. It's weird. All that's happened…but I feel energized…as if I hadn't been beaten and stabbed to a wooden table by some crazy vampire bitch." Sydney vividly remembered her last vision before blacking out…blood spraying profusely as Simone's head flew off her shoulders clear across the room. She shuddered, thinking about the torture she'd endured, but felt strangely rejuvenated. "Seriously, though, I feel great; no bruises, no soreness. I take it you gave me your blood? Pretty potent stuff, huh? Hey, do I need to worry about turning into a vampire?" she teased. She nuzzled into his chest, taking a deep breath of his masculine scent.

"No, you are not a vampire. You would have to essentially lose every last drop of blood and then have me replace it with mine. But, Sydney…we are bonded now. You have taken my blood. I wanted it to be special, but it is done." Kade sighed.

"I know you asked me before you gave me your blood, and I really do appreciate that, given we exchanged bodily fluids and all, but what do you exactly mean by bonded?" Sydney questioned.

"You are mine. I am yours. When we made love before, I bit you. Your blood runs through my veins. And now, my blood has been introduced into your human body. We are formally bonded for eternity. I will always know where you are and be able to sense you. As our bond becomes stronger, you and I will be able to speak telepathically like I can with some of the others. And as long as you continue to take my blood, you will not age. We are linked." He lifted her chin to look into her eyes. "I want you to stay with me, Sydney. Here with me in New Orleans. You belong to me now."

A rush of emotion flooded Sydney's mind. She felt as though she could deal with being linked to Kade. She'd never loved anyone the way she loved him. He made her feel womanly, empowered, and erotic all at once. He'd fought with his life to save her, never giving up on her. He was everything to her. After so many years of frivolous sex and meaningless relationships, Kade filled her soul, captivating both her mind and body. She wanted to submit to him. To give herself over to him, becoming one heart with his. But seeds of doubt grew in the pit of her stomach. He hadn't said he wanted to marry her. He said he wanted her to move in with him.

And for eternity? What about her job? She'd worked so hard over the years to make it through the ranks to where she was in her division, and now he expected her to give up everything on a whim and move down here? And what about the children's center? How could she just leave the kids and give up all the work she'd done at the center? And her condo…was she just supposed to abandon it? As much as Sydney wanted to think with her heart, her mind was jolting her back into reality.

"Kade, you know I love you, but I have commitments back at home and my job and…."

"Yes, but you'll stay here with me." He softly pressed his lips to hers, stifling any rejection she might give him. "All the things you mention are minor details…we will work it out. Now come…come to me. Let me show you how much I love you."

"Kade…"

"Sydney," he interrupted, capturing her lips once again. Kade slid his hand across the healed, smooth skin of her stomach until he found what he sought, gently cupping her breast. He deliberately chose to be gentle with her, acutely aware of the trauma she'd been through in the past week. Although her physical wounds had healed overnight, it would be a long time before either of them forgot the evil they'd faced and defeated. As he kissed her, he reveled in her strength and beauty. This woman, his woman, she was everything in life; his warrior mate, his friend, his lover.

Sydney squirmed under him, impatiently awaiting his next touch. Her skin tingled with anticipation, knowing he was capable of providing her immeasurable pleasure. She let her hands explore the hard smoothness of his chest. Ripping her mouth from his, she licked her tongue across the hollow of his neck and bit down on the flesh of his shoulder.

"My girl likes to bite?" He growled in ecstasy.

She laughed in response, gliding her tongue down his muscled flesh, licking and sucking his nipple.

Releasing one of her breasts, Kade allowed his hand to delve into the slick, wet heat of her sex. Sydney sucked in a startled breath as she felt a finger slip deep into her pussy. She bucked into the rhythmic intrusion, needing more.

"Oh God, that feels so good."

Responding to her erotic desire, Kade pumped another finger into her while circling her clitoris. With quickening gasps, Sydney arched toward his hand as she spiraled hopelessly into orgasm, shattering in a million pleasurable pieces. Screaming Kade's name repeatedly, Sydney curled into him, quivering in his arms.

"You're the most incredible, fascinating woman I have known in all my years; so responsive, so soft. I love you so much." Kade gently rolled her onto her back, straddled her and held her arms down with his strong hands. "Look at me. Watch me love you."

Dipping his head, he captured a rosy, hardened tip in his mouth, gently taking it between his teeth. She moaned as he alternately bit and laved her hard peaks, driving her mad with need.

"I can't take it anymore. Please. I need you…in me now."

Kade smiled and kissed the pink point one more time before settling himself at her entrance.

"I want you to see the pleasure you bring me. I want to look into your soul as we join as one."

Kade shifted the weight of his body, supporting his hands on the bed, and Sydney opened her thighs wide, inviting him into her. Frantic with desire, she lifted her hips up to Kade, moving to accept him. He groaned in blinding delight as he slid his rock-hard cock into her warmth. He moved slowly, letting her stretch to accommodate him. Sydney gazed into the depths of Kade's eyes, acknowledging the love in every thrust.

"I love you," she whispered.

He smiled as he continued to plunge in and out of her, increasing the pace, building the sexual tension. The slick heat of her center massaged his manhood as he leaned in to kiss her swollen lips.

Sensing the nearness of her climax, Sydney lightly circled her hips into him, stimulating her most tender flesh. She was quickly losing control.

"Kade, yes, Kade, I'm coming. Don't stop. Yes, please."

"That's it, love. Come for me. You're beautiful," he told her as she climaxed.

At his direction, the crescendo rose to the edge of ecstasy.

"Fuck yes. Oh my God. I'm coming! I'm coming! Yes! Yes!" Sydney rocked frantically against him as her orgasm slammed into her.

As her hot channel convulsed, making it impossible for him to hold back, Kade sank his fangs into the soft flesh of her neck. Thrusting deeply into her one last time, he exploded inside her as pulsating waves of pleasure washed over him. *Mine.*

Kade fell back into the bed off of Sydney, rolling her with him so she lay upon his chest once again. He would never let her go. She would stay here and build a future with him. He knew she was worried about her job, but he would get her one here if that's what she wanted. He'd spare no expense making sure she had everything she needed to stay.

Sydney fought back the tears, overwhelmed by the emotions from making love. God, she loved him. He was everything she could ever want in a man; masculine, honorable, sexy, and intelligent. She'd never met a man like him before in her life and was pretty sure she'd never meet another. Kade made her feel loved, desired, wanted.

Hell, he made her *feel,* period. It had been years since she'd dated anyone for more than a month, let alone someone who made her consider moving hundreds of miles away to live with him.

But give up her entire life for a man she met less than a week ago? Could she really just move all her stuff down here, not knowing if they had a real commitment? It was true that she had bonded with him, but as a human, she still wasn't exactly sure of the implications. As much as she was tempted to tell him 'yes' right away, she had responsibilities waiting for her at home; her job, the center, friends, a life. Okay, so she didn't have that many friends or family, but still, it was her life.

Her chest tightened as she wondered if what they had was real. She knew that working long hours with a partner often caused simple emotions to escalate. With Kade it had gone so much further; she'd fallen deeply and utterly in love with him, a vampire. There was no going back. If she left New Orleans, hoping for a long distance relationship, it would crush her. She reasoned that she needed time to think about how she could make it work. She'd been held up in this dark, fantasy world for days. She knew life and death situations had a way of skewing one's perspective. If she could just get some fresh air…maybe a Philly cheesesteak…get back to the office, she'd be able to make hard decisions with a clear head. The thought of leaving him, even for a few days, caused her heart to break.

"Kade," she whispered, "I need to take a shower."

"Okay, love. You sure you don't want me to join you?"

"I would love you to, but I really think I just need to take a nice, relaxing bath. You know…decompress after the past few days."

"As much as I would like to wait for you, I really should get downstairs to help Luca. The woman in the cell…she needs to be questioned."

"Samantha?" Sydney asked.

"I'm not sure what her real name is, but we need to find out before we release her."

"I was in that cell with her. Now granted, I couldn't read her facial expressions, but her story rang true with me. I didn't even recognize her as Rhea. I mean, how will you know the truth?"

"It shouldn't be hard. I'll try to scan her mind. See if she shows any signs of deception. I called Ilsbeth over here to see if she's been bespelled. It is possible Asgear put a spell on her that could enable her to lie so well even she would think she's telling the truth."

"But he's dead," she countered.

"True. But Jane Doe down there may still harbor dark magic. If Ilsbeth senses any residue, she will take her to the coven to be cleared of spells and blessed. We cannot be too careful, considering Asgear may have schooled others in his dark ways."

"Others?" Sydney shivered at the possibility that Asgear had spawned other mages.

"I sense your fear, Sydney. I would tell you not to worry, but you and I both know the truth of the situation.

All I can say is that supernaturals sometimes are not all that different from humans. Evil has no boundaries. And you and I…we both seek justice, albeit in very different worlds."

"Yes. Crime is everywhere, that's for sure." *There is crime waiting for me back in Philadelphia.* "I hope Samantha is okay. She deserves a lot better than what happened to her. Please, Kade…just go easy on her."

"I'll try, but we have to be safe. I promise that if she's innocent, she'll get her life back."

"Thank you," she replied, convinced he'd treat the girl with compassion. Not wanting to end their time thinking of leaving, she kissed Kade, savoring his warmth once more. She knew what she had to do. She also knew he'd be really pissed, more like infuriated, but she needed to clear her head. Not looking back, tears pricked at her eyes as she scurried off to the shower.

Chapter Twenty

Luca shot Kade a look of desperation as he entered the safe room in the basement. The girl was crying again. Shit, no man liked crying. Kade felt a pang of guilt for essentially saving the girl from Simone, only to imprison her yet again, in his home. Granted, the room was a large, comfortable guest room with its own private bathroom. It didn't scream 'prison cell'. No, if anything, it looked like a luxurious room at the Four Seasons. Regardless, the girl was scared and confused. She crouched on the bed with her knees pulled up against her chest, glaring at him as he went to sit in an overstuffed guest chair. He needed to get control over the situation, but fast. Taking a deep breath, he readied himself for the interrogation.

"Samantha, my name's Kade. Now listen, we are not here to hurt you. I'm sorry that we needed to keep you here with us, but we need to make sure it is safe to let you return home. The people who took you were an evil pair of criminals who apparently used you to further their exploits. You may not be aware, but you attacked a very good friend of mine a few nights ago at Sangre Dulce. Do you have any recollection of this activity?"

"No. I…I don't know what you're talking about," the girl sniffled. "Where is Sydney? She said she'd come for me."

"Sydney is recovering." Kade glanced at Luca, who passed Kade a snapshot of Rhea standing naked serving drinks at the club. He flipped over the photo, not yet wanting to shock the girl. "I need to ask you some questions, Samantha. The faster we do this, the faster you get out of here."

"Do you remember being at Sangre Dulce?"

"Yes, I told Sydney. I'm so stupid. It was my first time. I went there with friends. I don't even live here in New Orleans. I was at a computer conference. My friends and I went there, you know, just to have fun…see what it was like. There was this guy…James…he seemed so nice. I remember having a drink with him. Then…all I remember after that is being in that cell…he beat me…I couldn't get out. I told Sydney," she sobbed, tears spilling down her face.

Not detecting deception in her words, Kade needed her to understand what had happened, and unfortunately what was about to happen. She wasn't going home.

"Okay, listen, Samantha. Here's the thing. James, the man you mentioned, was a powerful mage. His real name was Asgear, and he practiced dark magic. I'm very sorry to tell you that you were bespelled by him. I have someone who can help you, but I've got to be honest with you. You need to know what happened. I have a photo here." He held it up to her. "This is you in Sangre Dulce serving drinks and engaging in various other duties." He coughed, not knowing how to tell her. "Miguel, the owner, introduced you to us as a submissive. You know what that is, right?"

"Yes." Nodding her head, Samantha whimpered. "Oh dear God. No, no, I would never do that. I just went there with friends for fun. Oh my God. How did this happen to me? What did I do?"

"That night, you took one of my friends. You silvered her to a table. Now, before you get too upset, it's entirely possible Asgear did most of the silvering. You see, my friend was blindfolded. At any rate, you helped this man. So we need to make sure whatever he did to you is lifted and cleansed, so you don't do it again."

"What do you mean? I promise I won't ever do anything like that again. Am I going home now? I need to get home. My family, my job." She wiped the tears from her eyes.

"I would love to send you home, Samantha, but like I said, we need to make sure you are free of the dark magic. A friend of mine," he hesitated, "a friend of mine and Sydney's, she is a witch, a good witch. Her name is Ilsbeth. She is coming here and taking you to her coven. Now, I am not sure how long it will take, but I promise you that you will return to your home…soon enough."

Samantha put her face into her hands, crying softly. Lifting her chin, she wiped her tears.

"I'm sorry. I want you to know that I am normally a very strong person, but this past week...I feel quite shattered right now. But I will be fine. I just need to get home."

Luca glided across the room, put a hand on her shoulder and gave her a tissue. This frail human stirred something in his cold, dark heart. Over the centuries, he'd seen many a human cry. It was the hard reality of life. But this fragile woman with long, fiery red hair ignited a small, caring flame inside of him.

"Samantha, it'll be okay." He ran a hand over her soft hair and patted her shoulder, attempting to provide comfort. "Ilsbeth is a strong and kind witch. If you have been given magic, she will cleanse you. All will be well again."

Kade raised an eyebrow at Luca, wondering what was going on with his old friend. Luca didn't do comfort, or sympathy, or humans. There was a long list of all kinds of things Luca did not do. Kade wondered if some kind of magic was rubbing off on his second. *Where the fuck is Ilsbeth?*

A loud knock at the door jolted Luca away from Samantha. Kade shook his head in confusion at his friend's actions.

"Enter," he ordered. A blinding glow shone through the doorway as Ilsbeth opened the door. "Please come in, Ilsbeth." Kade gestured for her to sit in a guest chair, but Ilsbeth wandered over to sit next to Samantha on the bed. "Ilsbeth, this is Samantha. She has no recollection of her actions in the club the night she silvered Dominique. I sense no deception, but we need to be sure she is safe to be around others…and herself."

"Samantha, I am Ilsbeth." She ran her lithe, pale fingers across Samantha's cheek. "You understand you have been in contact with a great evil, yes?"

Samantha nodded silently.

"This evil, it made you do things, things against your will, things you do not recollect?"

She nodded again.

"Do I have your permission to read you…your aura? Do you come to me willingly?" Ilsbeth asked in a soft, lilting voice.

"Yes, I am so sorry. Please help me," she begged.

The air thickened as Ilsbeth closed her eyes and raised her hands, palms up above the crown of Samantha's head. She hummed a cyclical melody as she lowered her hands around the girl. Opening her eyes, she blew out a breath.

"This young woman, dark magic tints the edges of her aura." A somber look crossed her face as she locked her vision on Kade. "She must come with me to the coven where my sisters and I can purge the darkness and cleanse her soul." She was holding back.

Kade knew there was something else. What was it? He'd promised this girl she could return home. "Ilsbeth, thank you for your reading. As always, I am appreciative of your magical insight. Yet, I sense there is something else."

"It is the magic." In disgust, she shook her head. "It has been infused."

"Meaning?" he questioned.

"The magic has been infused. We can cleanse her aura and remove the darkness, but the magic, it will stay. In short, Samantha is now a witch. She will need to stay with the coven, learn the craft, grow into the light." She regarded Samantha. "Do you understand, dear girl? You are now a witch."

"I am a witch?" she asked, saying the words back to Ilsbeth as if it would get easier if she spoke them aloud. "I have to be honest with you. I'm not sure what that really means, but I will try. I want this evil out of my body now. I promise to do whatever you say…just please help me get on with my life."

"It will be okay, Samantha. I will help you," Ilsbeth reassured her. She hugged her, knowing this would be an uphill battle. It was not an easy life being a witch, let alone being turned into one so late in life. Being thrown into the supernatural world after spending your entire life as human was difficult to comprehend.

Samantha pulled out of Ilsbeth's arms and looked up to Kade. "Sir, one thing before I leave. Please…I want to see Sydney. I owe her my life. I just want to thank her."

"Go get Sydney." Kade motioned to Luca. "I know she'll want to see the girl before she leaves."

Luca nodded and left the room, giving Samantha one last glance.

"Thank you again, Ilsbeth. We do seem to make good allies, don't we?" Kade hoped to lighten the mood before Sydney arrived. She had been through enough this past week, and didn't need to come into a room full of serious faces.

"Ah yes, that we do. The coven is in your debt for eradicating Simone and Asgear. If we hear of any other activity related to Asgear, I'll make sure to contact you immediately."

Within minutes, Luca returned to the room sans Sydney. He gave Kade a hard stare, needing to speak to him in private. He glanced to Samantha, who stared back at him with wide eyes.

"I'm sorry, darlin', but Sydney isn't available to come down to see you at this time," Luca explained in a gentle tone. "She promised that she'll visit you at the coven as soon as possible. Now, if you don't mind, a vampire situation has come up that Kade and I need to attend to. Etienne will see you up to the foyer, and then I will escort you back to Ilsbeth's."

Upon hearing Luca's words, Kade sent out mental feelers to locate Sydney within the house. When he was unable to detect her presence, his jaw tightened in anger.

"Where is she?" he demanded.

"Kade, please, you must understand, no one saw her go, and there's been no evidence of foul play. It appears she just left. The maid saw her jump in a cab about an hour ago. Maybe she went downtown to get beignets again?" Luca sighed.

No, Goddammit. Kade knew that she wasn't shopping or sightseeing. His woman was running, running from her feelings, running from him. Sydney Willows could run, but she could not hide. He would find her any place on the face of the Earth. What exactly did the woman not get about them being bonded?

"That woman is going to be the death of me. Seriously, Luca. I ask her to stay here and move in with me and she takes off? What the hell? Get Tristan on the damn phone, and then call the airport and gas up the jet. We, my friend, are going to Philadelphia tonight. She is mine, and it is damn well time she starts to understand precisely what that means."

Chapter Twenty-One

Sydney felt sick as soon as she got in the cab. She kept telling herself she just needed time to think, time to figure out how she could have a relationship with a vampire, one who lived a thousand miles away. She'd call Kade as soon as she got to Philadelphia, tell him that she loved him, and that she just needed space. If she called him before she got on the plane, she would fold and return to him. If she just had some time to make a decision without Kade tempting her with his sex-on-a-stick gorgeous body and demanding presence, then she'd know she was making the right choice. She couldn't trust herself to think clearly around him. Her libido had officially taken over in New Orleans. She had lost the capability to make intelligent decisions with her brain when she was thinking with her wanton, aching loins.

Sydney had to call Tristan before boarding the plane. There was no way she was staying in her condo after the attempted rape. She needed to repaint and decorate it anyhow, since the place had been trashed.

"Tristan," she began as Tristan picked up the phone. "It's Sydney. Listen, I need to talk. Um…I mean I need a favor."

"Syd, uh…what's going on?" Tristan responded, suspicion in his voice. "Why do I hear airplanes? Where's Kade?"

"Please, Tristan, just hear me out." Sydney sighed heavily. *Damn Alpha wolf.* She couldn't keep secrets from him on a good day. "Okay, here it is. I ran out of Kade's house, hopped a cab to the airport, and I'm about to board a flight to Philly." She silently cringed, guessing what Tristan's response would be.

"Sydney dearest, excuse me for saying so, but are you fucking crazy? Kade is going to go ballistic when he discovers you just left without telling him. Hell, even if you told him, he'd freak out. You do get that he claimed you? And then there is the whole completing of the blood bond, not to mention he keeps telling everyone that you are freakin' his! My God, woman, have you lost your ever-lovin' mind?"

"Thanks for the lecture, Dad. And yeah, I know he's going to be mad. I understand everything… yadda, yadda, yadda…blood bond. I love him too, more than life itself. But I need some time to think. I need to get back to my job, the kids. Things are too intense down here. I need to make sure that I'm making the right decisions."

"What is there to think about? No, forget it. You human women are irrational…unreasonable…whatever. I just want you to know that when this all goes down, I reserve the right to tell you, 'I told ya so'. Now what do you need?" When push came to shove, Tristan would always be there for her. She was part of his pack…wolf or no wolf.

"My condo. The vampire. You know what happened." She didn't want to even say the words. "I need some time to get the place back together. I'm going to sell it…especially given the fact I might, and that is a big might, move to New Orleans. So, can I stay at your place for a while?"

"Mon chaton, you're truly trying to get me killed, aren't you?" He laughed. "Since I do not have a death wish, I will politely refuse to let you stay at my house, but I have several rental properties. I've got one that'll work. It's an empty, furnished apartment and most importantly, it's in a safe part of town, okay? You're welcome to stay there. When are you getting in? Do you need a ride from the airport?"

"Thanks, Tris. You're a lifesaver. And no, I don't need a ride. Tony's picking me up and taking me to the Hilton. If you could get the keys and address to the station by tomorrow, I'd be forever grateful."

"Yeah, you better be, girl. Kade's goin' to be supremely pissed when he finds out you're gone. I love you like family, but I'm not going to lie when he comes a-knockin'. And he will, just warning you."

"Fair enough." Sydney slumped in her chair, knowing he was right. Too late now. She already took off…might as well see this thing through. "Hey…I just wanted to say thanks for saving my ass the other night."

"And what a fine ass you have. You know that I should be the one thanking you. If that vamp bitch had stabbed me one more time, it could have been the last howl for the wolf. You were pretty badass with that sword. Listen, call me when you get settled, okay? I'm worried about you."

"I will," she promised.

"Can I give you a bit of advice? You know, from a wise, old Alpha?"

She laughed softly. "Sure, Tris."

"You think too much. Open your heart to him, Syd. You deserve love. You get me? Stop thinking, start living," he told her. "You take care. Safe travels."

She hung up the phone. Tristan's words resonated throughout her very being. *You deserve love.* She loved Kade with every cell of her body. And he loved her. Maybe Tristan was right. Maybe she did think too much. As she boarded the plane, tears welled in her eyes. *A mistake.* She shouldn't have left Kade's house. Taking a deep breath, she held the emotion back. She just needed time to get her life in order, and if she still felt like she did today, then she'd return to Kade, the love of her life.

Chapter Twenty-Two

Tony glanced over at Sydney, who silently stared out the window, looking a million miles away. Something seemed off with his partner.

"I'm glad you're back. The cases are piling up, and it sure will be good to have you back here." Sydney continued gazing out the window, oblivious to his words. "Hello? Sydney Willows? What's up, Syd? You seem really out of it. Are you sure you're ready to come back to work?"

"Sorry," Sydney sighed. "I just...was thinking, that's all...about work. Yeah well, I want to finish up the paperwork on the Death Doll case, even if it officially belongs to P-CAP. Just want to clean it up a little, tie up loose ends."

She rubbed her eyes. *What next?* She was supposed to be clearing her head, but thoughts of Kade consumed her.

"I think I'm gonna take a few days off after that. My condo is a mess, so I've got to get it cleaned up. I'm going to sell it...maybe. I don't know. Anyway, I'll spend tonight at the hotel and then go over and get my stuff in the morning…pack a bag. My friend Tristan is letting me stay for a while in one of his rental properties."

Tony rolled his eyes. He knew she wasn't telling him everything, but they'd been partners long enough that he knew when to push her and when to just let it go. He could tell she was on edge, that she'd been crying recently. Pulling the car into the hotel entrance, he put it in park.

"Syd," he paused. "You and I. We've been partners a long time. I know something's going on, and if you don't want to talk about it, that's okay. But I'm just a phone call away. If you need me, just call and I'll come running. You sure you don't want to stay in my guest room? I feel kind of bad just dropping you off at a hotel." He placed his hand on her shoulder, trying to comfort her.

Sydney put her hand on the car door handle ready to bolt. She turned to him. "I'm okay. I promise… I just need some time to myself. A lot went down in New Orleans. Now, get going. I'll see you at the station tomorrow afternoon. Thanks."

Sydney reached over and quickly hugged him. Releasing her partner, she popped the car door open and headed into the hotel.

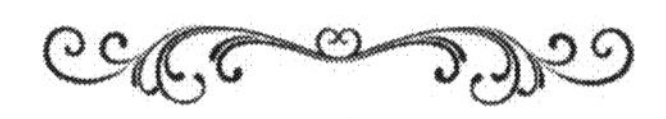

Sydney felt even worse the next day. She was in misery knowing she'd left Kade. What had she been thinking?

She would have given anything to wake up in his arms this morning. Instead, she awoke to strange voices talking though the paper-thin walls and an air conditioner on the fritz. She checked her cell phone for the hundredth time hoping Kade would call or text her. Nothing.

Dammit to hell. She'd left New Orleans in order to think clearly, but all she could think about was Kade. She almost took a cab back to the airport, but reason won out, and she landed back at her condo. She breathed in deeply as she laid a hand against her door. Memories of the attempted rape flooded her thoughts, but she let a small smile grow, knowing that she'd won out in the end. She was the one still alive and kicking, and that asshole vampire was nothing more than ash. Her thoughts drifted back to Kade, thinking of how he saved her butt…waking up on a jet? *What kind of a world does that guy live in?* Certainly not the gritty, very real, paycheck earning world she lived in.

She gave the door a shove, and it squeaked open. Thank God, Luca and Kade had thought to lock the place when they left. Not that she had too many valuables, but one couldn't be too careful in the city. Scanning the room, she felt nauseated, taking sight of the dried blood. She dreaded straightening up the mess. The station had offered to pick up crime scene cleaning expenses since the incident had occurred while she was working a case. Not having the emotional strength to pick up even one broken vase, she decided right then and there that she'd hire a service to do it.

Ignoring the overthrown furniture, and bits of glass, Sydney strode down the hallway into the guest room, hauling out the largest travel bag she owned. She emptied her drawers, underwear, sweatpants, and t-shirts spilling into her luggage. *Nothing like summing my life up in a suitcase.* Instead of folding up clothes that were hanging in her closet, she grabbed them by the hangers and threw them onto the bed. Scooping up several pairs of shoes, she dumped them haphazardly into a duffel bag.

Rifling through her guest room chest, she gathered up any weapons Tristan had left and stowed them with her clothes...including her guns. Sydney's skin pricked with discomfort being in this condo. *Goddamn vampires.* If she hadn't insisted on working this case, nothing would have happened, and she could have gone about life not knowing all the evils that existed in the supernatural world. But she also wouldn't have known love...desire...ecstasy...Kade.

She gathered a few treasured pictures of her family and friends, and looked around once again to see if there was anything else she wanted to take with her. Deciding that she'd packed enough, she collected her possessions and left her apartment. After making her way down to her car, she carefully laid her hanging clothes flat in the tiny trunk of her convertible and squeezed the large suitcase into the passenger seat. Tight fit, but it would have to work. Silently saying goodbye to her home of seven years, she took off toward the station.

The parking lot buzzed with activity as she parked her car. She checked twice to make sure it was locked, before she padded into the station. Waving hello to her fellow officers, she slumped into her chair and flipped on her laptop. Her plan was to bury herself in her work for the next few hours. She wanted to forget New Orleans for a little while; to forget evil vampires and mages, and most of all, to forget the ache that was burning a hole through her gut from missing Kade.

Hours later, after a mountain of paperwork, she sighed in exhaustion. She was startled as Tony slammed a cheesesteak down on her desk.

"Hey. What's up? Thought you could use one of these. Now, I know they don't have these babies down in the Big Easy." He grinned.

"Oh. My. God." Her mouth watered as the scent of fried onions and cheese teased her nostrils. She couldn't wait to tear into it. "Thank you, Tony."

"Yeah, I have been called a god by certain women. And funny you say so…women do usually like my ten inch…just not a steak sandwich." He busted out laughing.

Sydney punched him in the arm. "Real nice, Tone. You're a smooth talker, you." She bit down into the sandwich, letting the grease, soft bread and steak entice her senses. "Okay, Tony. Did I ever tell you how much I love you?" she grinned, wiping her mouth.

"Yeah baby. I know you want it." He smiled, seeing that she was starting to get back to normal. "Hey, if I knew all you needed was a steak sandwich, I would have fed you last night." He straightened in his chair, a serious expression washed over his face. "Seriously, Syd. You need something, I'm here. There's no going it alone. We all get pummeled down by this job every now and then. You and I both know it. I don't know all what happened down there in New Orleans, but this is just a bump in the road. You're tough. It'll be all right."

Sydney avoided the heavy conversation by nodding and stuffing her mouth full of steak and pickles. She wished lifting her spirits was as easy as eating a sandwich…although the cheesesteak was pretty damn good.

"Delivery!" The station secretary dropped a small Fed Ex envelope on her desk. *Kade?* She ripped open the package only to find a key and a small, engraved card. *Tristan. The key and address to the rental property.* Shoving away the rising disappointment, she fingered the black shiny key, which was attached to a copper Liberty Bell key chain. Only in Philly, she grinned to herself.

What was she thinking…that Kade would call her? Text her? Send her a card? She was the one who had up and left without saying goodbye…after making love, at that. Waves of guilt flooded her mind. Why did she do that to him? He said he loved her, wanted her to stay. Why wasn't that enough for her? But he didn't seem to really understand that she had responsibilities. She did recall him saying that they'd work out the details, but she'd been so freaking impatient as usual. She didn't even try to talk to him. No, she just panicked, overwhelmed by emotions, and ran back to Philly. *Shit.* She needed to call him tonight and set things right. In the past twenty-four hours, she may not have cleared her mind entirely, but she knew one thing to be true, Kade was hers. She loved him. With each passing hour, her heart cried out for him as she yearned to be in his arms.

Rubbing the key, she shut down her laptop, deciding she couldn't wait one more hour to call him. Once she got to her new place, she'd sit down, call him, apologize for leaving, and possibly beg for his forgiveness–okay, only if necessary–and figure out a way to make this work. Maybe she could get a job at the NOLA PD. Myriad thoughts and solutions swirled in her head. Before she lost her nerve, she needed to get out of the station and make the call.

Tapping Tony on the shoulder, not wanting to interrupt his phone call, she mouthed the words "thank you" and waved goodbye. Jumping into her convertible, she pulled the top down, cranked up the radio, and set the GPS to the address on the card. Her heart sang in joy knowing that it wouldn't be long before she heard the loving tone of Kade's voice again.

Chapter Twenty-Three

Sydney gasped at the sight of the newly built, Penn's Landing riverfront condo building. *Swanky.* She could not believe Tristan would let her live in this place rent-free for a week or so, let alone the couple of months she'd initially planned on. She had a feeling she'd never want to leave, considering the incredible view of the river and city. Why wasn't Tristan living in this fabulous location? She knew he dabbled in real estate, but had no idea that he owned a place down on the waterfront. She double checked the address before pulling her car into the valet parking.

"Excuse me, Miss," A bellman approached her car and leaned forward, "but do you need assistance with your luggage?"

Sydney coughed, trying desperately to compose herself, hoping she was in the right place. "Uh…yes. I have some clothing in the trunk, a few bags. My friend, Tristan Livingston, is letting me stay in his condo for a while."

"Of course, Miss. We've been expecting you. I'll take your keys, park your car, and bring your things to you shortly." Smiling, he opened her car door, gesturing for her to get out.

She gave him the keys, confidently striding toward the door where another bellman awaited her.

"Hello…I'm Sydney Willows. I…."

"Greetings, Miss Willows. My name is Bernard. Welcome to Riverfront Estates. As Fred indicated, we've been expecting you. Please follow me, and I will escort you home."

Home? Sydney obediently followed Bernard, having no idea where she was going. It dawned on her that Tristan had failed to provide her with the condo number. She didn't want to appear as if she didn't belong, so she trusted that she'd figure it out from Bernard eventually. Standing in the elevator, Sydney noticed the numbers went up to forty floors. Nervously playing with the key, she tried to remember which button Bernard had pushed. The elevator was moving, but no numbers were illuminated.

As the elevator settled and the doors slid open, she saw a small foyer that led to a lone set of double doors.

"Your condo, Miss. Do you need me to open the door, or show you about? Your bags will be up in just a little bit via the service elevator."

"No thank you. Please, just leave my things in the hallway here. Seeing as this is the only condo on this floor, my things should be okay for a little while. I have a phone call to make, and it's important that I'm not interrupted. Thanks again." She stepped into the vestibule and reached into her purse.

"Thank you, but please, no tips. This is your home now." He waved as the elevator doors silently closed.

Finally alone, she blew out a deep breath. My God, this place was unbelievable. She could hardly wait to see the view of the river. Not knowing what floor she was on, she sensed she was up fairly high. She steadied the key, slid it into the lock and quickly opened the deadbolt. *Secure door, very nice.*

As Sydney clasped her palm around the door handle, she felt it. A warm, tingly sensation ran up her spine. *Kade. What is he doing here?* After everything she'd been through in the past week, she trusted her instincts enough to know that Kade was behind this door. Taking a deep breath, she tried desperately to gather her thoughts. *What can I say to him? Take it easy Sydney…apologize…just pretend he's on the end of the phone like you were planning.* But he wasn't on the phone in New Orleans. No, he was truly here in Philadelphia. In Tristan's condo. *Shit. Shit. Shit. Breathe, Sydney, breathe.* Feeling as if she could use an oxygen mask, she sucked in a deep breath, turned the handle and pushed the door open.

Across the great room, she spied Kade, who gazed at the river, the muscular frame of his silhouette darkly carved against the incandescent moonlight. Sydney's soul wrenched, begging her to go to him so she could lose herself in his embrace, but he was a dark, lethal predator who she'd wounded. She didn't have the courage to seek what she needed from him. No, she would approach him cautiously, thoughtfully. She needed to make things right with him.

"Kade, I'm sorry." Although he said nothing in response, as if he hadn't heard her, she knew he had. He would make her come to him, and she'd willingly go.

Sydney cautiously approached, walking into an open space. Moonlight shone through the sun lights of the cathedral ceiling, illuminating the entire room. As she passed the kitchen, the black, pearly granite countertops and stainless steel appliances sparkled. She crept slowly toward Kade, noticing the condo was completely void of furniture, save for patio furniture on the enormous, outdoor terrace. A stray thought passed through her mind as she wondered why Tristan would send her to an unfurnished property, a minor issue compared to the menacing, aggravated vampire standing in front of her.

Sydney's heels clicked softly on the hardwood floors. She extended her fingertips, letting them graze the hard planes of his back. Attraction did not begin to describe the intense desire that grew in her belly.

"Kade, please. What are you doing here?"

Kade silently waited as she came to him, sensing his prey ever closer. He could smell her desire. He fought the urge to ravage her right there on the floor, burying himself within her hot depths. But he needed to teach this stubborn, sexy woman a lesson she would not soon forget. She had run from him, not willing to discuss her emotions, her fears, or their life together. Not acceptable. No, she needed to learn that without a doubt they belonged together…forever. And that he loved her more than life itself, and was willing to do anything to keep her in his life. Not looking back at her, he took a deep breath, steeling himself for the conversation that would change his life.

"Ah, Sydney love, I am here…because this home is my home…our home." He pivoted around, pulling her toward him, settling her body so that she also faced the river. Grasping her hands, he rested them on the cool terrace railing. The view of the river was magnificent. Lights twinkled from the boats and the bridge spanning the rushing water.

"Your home?" Sydney asked, her voice shaken. "Wait…what do you mean, our home? This is Tristan's condo. He gave me a key. He's letting me stay here. Did Tristan tell you I was here?"

Snaking his hand around her waist, he pulled her into him so that their sides pressed against each other. At his demanding touch, he felt Sydney straighten, quivering as if electricity had run through her body. Every sensual cell in her body stood wide awake, ready to engage with him.

"Precisely what I meant." Smiling at her response, Kade continued. "This is our home. I bought this property last night after you so very cleverly left New Orleans." He turned her body so it was flush with his, hip to hip, their lips mere inches apart. She did not attempt to move away from him, allowing Kade to hold her tightly in his warm, muscular arms. His blue eyes pierced down into her soul as his lips tightened somberly. "You see, Sydney, you did not seem to quite understand what I meant when I said you are mine. I thought we established things in my office that fine day, but it appears you need another lesson."

"Kade, I…I…I," she stammered, her words caught in her throat.

"Don't say a word, not one word." He lifted a finger to her lips, silencing her excuses. "It's my turn to talk, your turn to listen. I want to be clear…*so* very clear…that you never misunderstand me again. You are mine, I am yours. We are bonded. I love you, Sydney, not just this minute, not just today, not just this year, I love you forever. This means the next time you get upset or confused, you do not run out on me. Never again will you do that, understand? We, us…we work on things together from here on out. You lean on me. You share with me. We are one together, no longer on our own. Together and always we shall figure out this world."

Kade smiled, twirling a strand of her hair with his finger.

"Now, before you say anything or even attempt to protest, I am going to tell you how this is going to work. Since you left me in New Orleans, instead of working together on answers to how we would make our relationship work, I took it upon myself to figure it out for us."

"But Kade," Sydney began, still trying to capture control over the situation. Something she was failing at miserably at the moment.

Kade jerked her closer into his body, grinding the hardness of his maleness into her belly. He leaned in close, almost touching her lips with his.

"Shhh. You really have trouble listening, don't you, woman?"

A small giggle escaped Sydney's lips, releasing a nervous energy.

Dominating her space, he parted her legs with his thigh. As her feminine scent called to him, he resisted the urge to take her right there and fuck her senseless. But he needed her to accept their future as it would be before he went any further.

"First, your career. I would never ask you to give up your job. You've worked hard to get where you are, and I'll support you in whatever you decide. That being said, I will not let you rush foolishly into supernatural cases again…at least not without me. I took the liberty of speaking with the powers that be, and your police department has graciously agreed to lend you to my security forces as a consultant whenever I see fit. Therefore, you can work here in Philadelphia for months at a time, should you choose to do so, and then we can go back to New Orleans and work down there for however long we need to remain. Your city is close to New York, and I frequently have business there, so this location is advantageous for me as well. We will live in both locations."

Sydney was about to interrupt, but she chewed her lip instead. Sensing her imminent interruption attempt, Kade raised an eyebrow at her, challenging her to disobey his earlier request to let him finish speaking.

"Secondly, you shall drink a scant amount of my blood…just often enough so that you do not age or become ill. In doing so, we can be together throughout eternity. I am quite sure that I'll be doing enough worrying about your safety due to the nature of your job. I certainly don't need to worry about you getting sick from human diseases. Likewise, I'll drink from you whenever possible, as I want no other woman for my sustenance. I am quite sure that you would agree to this point, given you would not want me with another woman, especially given the erotic, intimate nature of feeding."

Kade stopped speaking for a minute, drinking in the silence of the night. The crux of his argument rested solely upon point number three. He sighed, hoping he would say all the right words so she finally understood how very much she meant to him.

"Third, and most importantly, I love you, Miss Willows. When I asked you to move in with me and stay in New Orleans…let's just say, I do not take commitment lightly. I told you before that there have been few women in my long lifetime who I have considered a lover, but there has been no woman that I have ever considered a soul mate. Or a wife…until now." Kade pressed his forehead to Sydney's. He desired so deeply to make love with her, but he wanted her head clear of the throes of sexual passion so she never doubted his intentions…or her answer.

Tears ran down her face as he withdrew a small, blue and white box from his pocket. "You, Sydney…you came into my life unexpectedly. You are a stubborn woman, infuriating at times. A woman filled with a heart of courage so large…well, what can I say? Even though you feel fear, you continue to fight in the name of justice, giving everything you have…willing to give your life to save others. Blood, sweat, tears. Then there is the soft side of you…my woman…my lover: caring, sexy, beautiful. I am simply enchanted by you. More importantly, I love you. I want to be with you forever. I want you to be my wife. Marry me, Sydney."

Kade opened the small box, offering his gift to his bride-to-be. An enormous, princess-cut diamond sparkled in the moonlight.

"Yes, I would be honored to become your wife," Sydney cried.

As Kade slipped the ring on her finger, a tear ran down her face. Feeling guilty for how she'd run out on him, she pulled out of his embrace, but did not release his hands. "Kade, I'm so sorry I left without telling you. I was just so overwhelmed. You have to understand. I never thought I could love someone, let alone as much as I love you. I was scared. Worried about my job and the children's center. So when you asked me to move…I just panicked. It was wrong, and I am really, really sorry for hurting you. Please forgive me?" she purred.

"Ah my lovely future wife, I'll certainly forgive you but perhaps I should punish you first," he teased. "A spanking perhaps?"

"I guess I would agree to a consensual spanking every now and then." She winked. "But you know it goes both ways!"

"Both ways? I'm not sure I can agree to those terms. Let's say that some things aren't up for negotiation. Now come to me, my sweet fiancée. I plan to make love to you in every room of this penthouse."

No longer able to control his lust, Kade leaned forward and pressed his lips to Sydney's. Their tongues danced in delirium, finally sealing their future. He speared his fingers through Sydney's soft, blonde hair, pulling her head into his. She tasted like sweet honey on a fine summer day. His lover…soon to be his wife.

Sydney moaned in delight, breaking away from his lips for a second.

"Um, Kade, considering we have no furniture in our home yet," she glanced over to the oversized, outdoor day bed, "maybe we should start right here on our wonderful balcony." She grabbed his hand, led him over to the soft bedding and pushed him backward so he lay on his back at her mercy. "Kade, I plan to make it up to you and then some…over and over again for the rest of our lives." She straightened above him, seductively stripping off her clothes until she was completely naked in the moonlight.

"Love…oh…you are such a naughty woman." Kade groaned and massaged his rock-hard cock through his jeans. "The way your skin shines in the moonlight, I cannot resist you for one minute longer. Come here," he demanded.

Sydney moved over him, straddling his legs. Kneeling, she slowly leaned over, gently kissing him, her soft hair falling onto his face and shoulders. Without warning, she rose, resting her hands on his shoulders, rubbing her plump, ripe breasts into his face. He moaned as he cupped and suckled her soft peaks, teasing them until they hardened in pain.

"Yes, Kade. Oh my God. Yes…I want to taste you. Now," she begged.

Slithering down his body, she made quick work of his pants, freeing his straining manhood. Taking him into her mouth, she greedily sucked his shaft, moaning in pleasure as she tasted his salty essence. Sydney grazed her teeth along his hardness, teasing him, hoping to make him beg. Finally, her vampire cracked, his breath began to quicken into pants.

"I…I need to be inside you. Hurry…I want to come inside you. Please," he pleaded.

Sydney smiled. Her big, bad vampire's begging was music to her ears. She crawled up him slowly and lowered herself onto him until her sex settled fully onto his cock. Sydney's receptive body welcomed him, her hands clutching his shoulders for support.

"Yes, baby. That's it. You feel so good inside of me," she said, staring deep into his blue eyes. "I've never loved another man like I love you. You're everything to me."

Connecting on a higher level, Kade and Sydney slowly rocked together as one in total harmony, allowing their arousal to consume them both. Pressing her hips into his, she gradually increased the pace, her climax building as he stimulated her most sensitive area. Kade moved his hands, grasping her by the waist, supporting her while she seated herself upright onto him, taking every inch of his throbbing hardness. Throwing her head back, she moaned in pleasure, undulating against him with reckless abandon.

"Oh yes, Kade. I love you! Please…I'm coming," she cried out as her explosive orgasm washed over her. She splintered in glorious rapture, writhing above him.

In a swift move, never leaving her body, Kade brought her to him so they faced each other on their sides. He swung his leg possessively over hers, linking them together. In a delirious frenzy, Kade and Sydney passionately kissed while he thrust up into her again and again. Sydney surrendered to his rhythm, losing herself in his rich, intoxicating scent. She loved this man with all her heart. Kade slowed his movement within her warm sheath, reluctantly pulling his lips from hers. He pressed his forehead to hers once again, gazing into her eyes.

"You're everything to me. My future, my love, my wife. I love you."

Sydney bared her throat freely, offering her blood to him in anticipation of his erotic bite. Her gift of submission sparked a primal instinct deep within him. He growled possessively and powerfully thrust into her, and pierced her soft flesh with his fangs. Sydney excitedly drove her fingers through Kade's hair pressing his mouth into her neck. She screamed in sheer bliss as her release shattered simultaneously with his. He sated his thirst, losing control as he spilled his seed deep into her.

They lay still within each other's arms, embracing, not wanting the moment to end. Sydney was elated knowing that not only had he forgiven her for leaving, but he was totally committed to her in every way. She never thought in a million years she'd be the kind of woman who could fall in love so completely, but she had. And now, she would never let her vampire go.

"Mmmm....that was awesome. You're amazing, do you know that?"

Kade chuckled softly. "Ah...my love, it is you who are amazing. I am not sure how I ever survived all these centuries without you."

"Kade," Sydney smiled, realizing they'd just made love on the balcony, "as much as I love being naked in your arms outside on the terrace, the sun will be rising soon. People could see us out here. Where are we going to sleep?"

"Funny thing, since I was short on time," Kade laughed, "I only purchased the bare necessities for our penthouse. In doing so, I realized that most furniture is highly overrated. However, a bed, my love, is most definitely a necessity when it comes to you and me. And since I planned on making love to you all night and well into tomorrow, I purchased two beds: an outdoor bed, so we could make love under the stars, and a bed for the master bedroom. If you're ready, we can test that one out now. Shall we adjourn for the evening?"

"I would love that," Sydney agreed. She kissed him once again. Feeling light as a feather, she let Kade lift her up into his arms and carry her into their new home.

Epilogue

Sydney woke feeling optimistic, looking forward to her future with Kade. She gazed up at the stark white ceiling, dreaming of how she would decorate their new home. The open penthouse was quite a contrast to the historic, Garden District mansion in New Orleans. She wondered how Kade would adjust to the cold hard streets of Philadelphia, but guessed he could more than hold his own. She looked forward to living in both cities, in both of their homes.

She laughed to herself, thinking about how much she actually liked belonging to Kade, and having Kade belong to her. She moved to lay her head on his smooth chest, his vampire heartbeat resounding in her ear.

Letting her thoughts drift back to New Orleans, she wondered how Samantha was doing. She'd left the mansion before she had a chance to visit with the girl, and in the fray of taking off back to Philadelphia, she'd forgotten to ask Kade how she was.

Kade glanced to Sydney, having been awake for over an hour. Without a doubt, he knew that he was the only person Sydney had ever really loved, would ever love. Ecstatic that she had accepted his proposal, he looked forward to their life together. She was the woman of his dreams. Kade hugged her closer into his embrace and kissed the top of her head.

"What are you thinking about so hard this morning? I may not be able to read your thoughts clearly yet, but I certainly can sense you thinking…very loudly. Is something wrong?"

"Just wondering about Samantha, that's all. It's hard to believe that girl in the cell with me was the same girl we met in Sangre Dulce. Samantha seemed so innocent and scared, but not in a submissive kind of way. She was a fighter, no doubt about it."

"Don't worry." Kade sighed. "I promise Ilsbeth will take care of her. Your instincts are correct, though. She's not the person who was in that club. Not of her own accord, anyway. Ilsbeth detected dark magic on the girl's aura. Even though the coven can eliminate the darkness, the magic is infused within her. She is forever a witch." He shook his head, feeling frustrated about how he'd left things with Luca. "There is something else that bothered me, though. Before you left, Luca seemed off. I don't know if the dark magic emanating off of Samantha was affecting him or what, but he actually seemed…I don't know…caring?"

"Caring?"

"Yes. He seemed caring toward the young woman."

"What's wrong with that, Kade? I mean, Samantha has been through a lot. Asgear…did you see what he did to her? Anyone would show feelings after seeing what happened to her."

"I know. It's not caring that is a problem per se. It's just that…I've known Luca for nearly two centuries. Other than Tristan, he is my best friend. He has many good qualities. He's loyal, respectful, honest, a valiant warrior, but caring about the feelings of a crying, human woman? That is not something he does. Usually, he wouldn't care in the slightest. No way. That isn't his style. Honestly, I've never seen him in love with a woman in all our time together. Sex with a woman, yes, but never love. When we were with Samantha, he actually comforted her. It was strange…for him anyway. I don't know. It's probably nothing."

Sydney turned her naked body beneath the sheets, pressing her soft flesh against his chest. He leaned down, kissing her warm lips, parting them with his tongue. Growing hot with need, she reached down to explore the evidence of his arousal. They both jolted when Kade's cell phone rang loudly.

"Damn phone. I'll get it later. Don't stop."

"You sure?" She smiled. "Maybe you should just answer it this one time and then turn off the ringer so we can make love in peace."

Kade reluctantly pulled out of her arms and reached down to the floor, scavenging through his clothes. He glanced at the cell. *Ilsbeth?* Why was she calling? He shouldn't be hearing from her so quickly. Answering, he sensed that something was terribly wrong. They'd been attacked on the way to the coven. Ilsbeth and the girl had made it back safely, but Luca was missing.

Romance by Kym Grosso

The Immortals of New Orleans

Kade's Dark Embrace
(Immortals of New Orleans, Book 1)

Luca's Magic Embrace
(Immortals of New Orleans, Book 2)

Tristan's Lyceum Wolves
(Immortals of New Orleans, Book 3)

Logan's Acadian Wolves
(Immortals of New Orleans, Book 4)

Léopold's Wicked Embrace
(Immortals of New Orleans, Book 5)

Dimitri
(Immortals of New Orleans, Book 6)

Lost Embrace
(Immortals of New Orleans, Book 6.5)

Jax
(Immortals of New Orleans, Book 7)

Jake
(Immortals of New Orleans, Book 8)

Club Altura Romance

Solstice Burn
(A Club Altura Romance Novella, Prequel)

Carnal Risk
(A Club Altura Romance Novel, Book 1)

Wicked Rush
(A Club Altura Romance Novel, Book 2)

About the Author

Kym Grosso is the New York Times and USA Today bestselling author of the erotic paranormal series, *The Immortals of New Orleans*, and the contemporary erotic suspense series, *Club Altura*. In addition to romance novels, Kym has written and published several articles about autism, and is passionate about autism advocacy. She is also a contributing essay author in *Chicken Soup for the Soul: Raising Kids on the Spectrum*.

In 2012, Kym published her first novel and today, is a full time romance author. She lives in suburban Pennsylvania but has a not-so-secret desire to move to a beach in southern California where she can write while listening to the roar of the ocean.

• • • •

Social Media/Links:

Website: http://www.KymGrosso.com
Facebook: http://www.facebook.com/KymGrossoBooks
Twitter: https://twitter.com/KymGrosso
Instagram: https://www.instagram.com/kymgrosso/
Pinterest: http://www.pinterest.com/kymgrosso/

Sign up for Kym's Newsletter to get Updates and Information about New Releases:
http://www.kymgrosso.com/members-only